Deception on the Danube

by

Carolyn R. Bradley

This is a work of fiction. Names and characters are the product of the author's imagination and any resemblance to persons, living or dead or to any series of events, is entirely co-incidental.

ISBN: 978-0-244-53723-4

Chapters

For my parents,

Frederick and Helen Roll.

They were always there for me.

Main Characters

Holidaymakers

Pete & Polly Smith - *Gardeners*
Priscilla Pilkington & Lillian - *ladies*
Minnie & Lavinia - *very elderly ladies*
Bob & Diane - ex *reporter, ex PA*
David Forest - *barrister-at-law*
Elaine Forest - *UK Detective Inspector*
Felicity Fanshawe - *actor*
Sebastian - *her gentleman companion*
Susan Butler - *from USA and*
Christine, Mary & Jo - *her friends*

Staff and Crew

Paul Driver - *coach driver*
Captain Van Beeke - *of 'Danube Drifter'*
Antonio Ravielli - *Hotel Services Manager*
Melissa - *Senior Cruise Director*
Vicktor - *Assistant Cruise Director*
Anna - *Cabin attendant*

Others

Prince Dmitri Romanovsky - *Russian Prince*
Boris - *Assistant to the prince*
Gerhard Kaufer - *Kommisar of Landespolizei*
Angelo Bugatti - *Susan's boyfriend*
Ronaldo Marconi - *the elusive criminal*

In the Beginning

August 1944

The colonel ignored the ruts and bumps in the French road. The old army vehicle had seen better days but with luck, it would last a little longer - just long enough. His eager young driver, encouraged to put his foot down by his superior, navigated around the worst of the holes in the road but didn't reduce his speed. They needed to cover the distance as quickly as possible. The soldiers in the back of the beaten-up army lorry hung on for dear life as they were bounced and jolted along.

The 'Third Reich' was close to defeat in France, Paris would soon be liberated. The German army was still half-heartedly fighting but it was rumoured that the SS were leaving - leaving fast - and with them was going a lot of valuable stolen property. It was the colonel's task to get to as many of these treasure-troves as he could before they were spirited away.

The tip-off, he'd received, concerned a cache of valuables stored in an old château on the outskirts of Paris. The goods had been stolen from Jewish concentration camp victims. The unfortunate souls had been stripped of everything they owned before being exterminated; they'd even had the gold fillings prised from their teeth.

He ought to be hardened to it all by now. Throughout the war, he'd served in an intelligence capacity and had been parachuted into France on more than one occasion. A fluent French speaker and used to agriculture, he'd more than once, passed himself off as a cousin come to work on the local farm of some loyal patriot.

The resistance had benefitted from his visits. He'd brought vital information from England plus arms and ammunition for the local partisan groups. Once he'd accompanied a very young and incredibly brave English girl. Her French mother originated from the target area so she spoke the language fluently and importantly, with the local dialect.

She was a lovely girl, determined and unafraid; the colonel hated having to leave her in such a dangerous place. He'd met up with her on more than one mission and before he could help himself, he'd let personal feelings get in the way of work. It was the one thing you didn't do – get involved, and he'd nearly done it. Just in time, he'd brought to mind his wife and son. In any case, even if circumstances *had* been different, she was far too young for him. He'd resolved to *look out* for her though - just in case.

There were spies everywhere and not all ordinary French people were willing to aid the resistance; many were afraid or simply *out to save their skins*. No agent was ever safe and no-one could ever be completely trusted.

He was proved right when the resistance cell was informed on. It took a lot of his ingenuity and courage to save them and it made her adore him all the more. Her cover blown, he arranged for her to be returned to Blighty and assured her, despite everything, that they would meet up again after the war. She had bidden him farewell with tears in her eyes and a promise that if ever he needed her, she would be there.

His unit reached the address and soon he was able to locate the cache. The enemy had abandoned the stolen items and departed in an obvious hurry. He entered the store room alone and stood and stared. Incredible! The efficiency of the Germans! There were cases and boxes, all painstakingly sorted and catalogued, crammed with valuable items of all kinds. He noticed many small religious artefacts, some tiny works of art and jewellery galore.

Colonel Alfred Chivington was surprised to discover that in certain cases, the perpetrators of this mammoth theft, were even logging supposed ownership information. Was it so that the devious thieves could fabricate a sales receipt, in case ownership was ever challenged? Clearly, they were going to ensure that nothing would stop them from lining their pockets.

This was the problem with the aftermath of war, some people lost and others gained but no-one, including countries and politicians, wanted to restore things to their rightful owners. He had his doubts that this *treasure* would be returned to the victims' relations because so many families had been completely wiped out. No doubt a few as yet unknown victors, would claim most of the spoils.

He picked up a brass tube, it had a label with a Jewish name and a Dutch business address printed on it. He unscrewed the top and blinked rapidly. In a moment of madness, he made a decision. The tube went into his pocket. He really would try to trace the owners, he was not usually a thief, but if this was not possible – well better his good cause than others?

Chapter 1

The Holidaymakers

2010

Paul Driver's blissful dream was abruptly cut short by the alarm ringing in his ears. The bell was so shrill that as usual, it woke his wife who complained bitterly.

'That bloody thing always wakes me up and I can never get back to sleep afterwards.'

You should be so lucky, he thought, I can't think of going back to sleep, unlike you, I have to go to work.

Grumbling under his breath, he climbed out of his comfortable bed and stumbled into the bathroom. Half an hour later, having showered and dressed, he managed a hurried breakfast before he was off to collect the coach he had to drive that day. He was aptly named and was, therefore, the only member of the company, so employed, who could not take offence at being addressed as *Mr Driver.*

This particular journey in early July, was a very long one. Since two in the morning and from as far as the Midlands, the feeder coaches would have been collecting passengers. Paul would begin driving the main coach at eight a.m. and then it was his job to drive, via Dover, all the way to Boppard in Germany and then continue to Passau the next day. He must be insane, he told himself, why did he undertake these long-haul holiday trips? Oh yes, he remembered with a chuckle, it was for the money of course. No, not the wages, they were no more than average, it was for the *perks.* He wasn't alluding to the tips from the holidaymakers, though they added up and were not to be scoffed at, he meant the *other* perks that he kept very quiet about.

He probably would have left this type of work several years before but he was just prevented from doing so at the time, by a contact he'd made while on a similar long coach journey. He remembered it well. He'd been *fed up* with everything – not enough money, too much work and to top it all, his wife had been giving him a hard time; he wished he could have left her but he couldn't afford to do so. He had three children, teenagers, and all were expensive - too expensive, and he'd been at a loss to know how he could make ends meet. Then had come the contact followed by the *risk* that, surprisingly, had proved to be minimal, and then - relative affluence. Mind you he'd had a hard job explaining this to his wife, she thought he'd acquired a long-service pay rise; he couldn't say that he'd been promoted because his kind of work had a ceiling – if he was seen to be still driving, it was the one right above his head.

He didn't want her to know the truth for several reasons. She couldn't keep her mouth shut for one but also he was afraid that she might want a cut and he was saving for a sunshiny day; he'd had enough of the rainy ones. It seemed that there was a flaw in the security of Her Majesty's Customs and Excise and Paul had made good use of it.

He began to wonder about his passengers; what would this lot be like? The mixture of personalities and types who chose these holidays always surprised him. Was it more comfortable to spend so long in a coach rather than flying to a destination? Was it cheaper perhaps? Yet the river cruises were not an inexpensive holiday. Oh well, he'd soon find out whether this trip would be smooth or difficult and whether the passengers would be easy or troublesome. He couldn't complain about lack of variety, you never knew who you would get but he often wondered, when he met the passengers, what had prompted them to book this kind of trip.

....

10

The early months of the year had been a busy time for holiday reservations but some people were still booking their summer holidays late in May. Last-minute booking scenarios happened all over the country but one employee in a travel agency had a most unusual experience.

The busy travel agent glanced up from her computer. She'd heard the door chime and through habit, glanced up momentarily. She returned to the study of her screen before what she'd actually seen registered in her brain. She took a second look and felt acute surprise at seeing the two persons who'd entered. The couple in question, catching her eye, moved towards her and sat down on the chairs opposite her desk. There was a clear and obvious notice stating that this desk was for cruises only so irritated, and feeling sure that they'd made a mistake and would soon leave, she forgot her usual *polite enquiry* tone and asked them in a far more abrupt fashion than was customary, as to what it was they required of her. She blinked in surprise when the man answered in a strong West Country accent.

'We wants to go abroad for our 'oliday, on one of them riverboats.'

'River cruises are quite expensive,' she replied with a slightly condescending air, 'are you sure that is your requirement?' Her tone was slightly offensive and she realised with some consternation that she had allowed her professional standards to slip. Endeavouring to return to a more correct response, she affixed a smile to her face and pointed to a holiday camp brochure across the room. She was about to suggest this as being more suitable when the man replied,

'No worries about the money, me dear, we do fancy a river trip.'

Feeling sure that she was wasting her time, she rose from her seat and collected a range of brochures, thinking that they would now go away, read them, realise the prices and never return – but she was wrong. Firmly staying in place, the man began to turn the pages slowly while his female companion peered over his shoulder.

Sheila Patterson had been in the travel business for many years and mostly, she could sum up the *type* of holiday people wanted by looking at them. She knew the 'cruise' type, it was usual for them to have already made their choice and they merely came in to book a trip because they didn't trust the internet and liked the personal touch. Families liked the hotels by the sea with guaranteed sunshine, the younger set liked the 'fun' holidays, pensioners preferred the coach tours or guided holidays and the *riff-raff* liked the cheaper holiday camps. Occasionally she was wrong and today was one of those days.

'That do look nice,' the female enthused, 'look at them pretty pictures? I like that one.' They both studied the particular holiday details.

'Look, three meals every day,' the man pointed out in wonder. 'That be good value that.'

Sheila took stock of the couple and felt very confused. The man had long blonde hair which straggled out in greasy strands from underneath an off-white trilby style hat. His red-checked short-sleeved shirt was open to the waist showing a very tanned and hairy chest; his bottom half was clothed in denim shorts cut to the knee with his feet encased in woolly socks and lace-up boots. The man's weather-beaten face and hands suggested an outside worker. His companion was also tanned but wore her brown hair long with curls adorning the top of her head. Her brightly coloured floral blouse had puff sleeves and this was matched with a denim skirt trimmed with embroidered patterns at the hem and on her feet were bright orange trainers. Sheila took a deep breath.

Feeling sure that they could not have understood the costs and moreover, the type of holiday, she tried again.

'These holidays generally suit the slightly older clients; you know, er - those who enjoy dressing for dinner.'

'And quite proper too,' was Pete's immediate reply. 'I don't 'old with people wearing their swimming things or pyjamas and that when they're 'aving their dinner. It don't seem polite.'

Sheila gave up. The couple continued to browse the brochure and then made their choice.

'We'll 'ave this one, in July.'

'I'll need to check availability.' She began to press a few keys on the computer but they weren't finished yet.

'It says 'ere, we get a better window, one what opens an all, if we go up a floor,' the female interrupted. 'I don't fancy being down the bottom of the boat. It might let water come in.'

'Don't be daft, girl,' was the man's sarcastic reply, 'they 'ave windows in some boats what go under the water, don't they? *They* don't let water get in but if you fancy it, alright we'll go up a bit in the boat.'

'Oh dear,' Sheila interrupted, 'they have only one cabin free on the upper deck. I'm afraid that is one of the more expensive cabins.'

Here it comes, predicted Sheila, calculating the new price in her head, the deposit bit is usually a bit of a shock but a holiday taken that soon means I need full payment. That is if they still want to go ahead when I tell them the price. I'm not going to fill in forms of any kind yet as I have a distinct feeling that I'll be tearing them up soon after. The professional smile reappeared as she said,

'Very well Mr .....?'

'Pete Smith and this is Polly.'

'The trip includes drinks and excursions so for two persons in a luxury twin bed cabin, cruising the River Danube in July, travelling by coach to Passau in Germany with one overnight stop each way and returning one week later, the price will be three thousand and one hundred pounds. I have to have full payment as it is within six weeks of the holiday dates. Will it be a card or a cheque?'

'What's that? How do you mean?'

13

'How do you wish to pay?'

'In English money. I don't have no foreign money.'

Taking a deep breath, Sheila tried again.

'I have to have full payment now in *English pounds*. Do you have a cheque or a debit or credit card?'

I knew it, she thought as she saw his puzzled expression, here comes the excuse. But she would have been obliged to eat her words, had she said them, because from his back pocket, came the largest roll of banknotes she'd ever seen appear out of a pair of shorts and he proceeded to count out the money onto the counter in fifty-pound notes. Whatever his lack of education, clearly it did not include a misunderstanding of arithmetic.

Somewhat dazed, she counted the money, telling herself that his money was just as good as everyone else's. She wondered if the other passengers would think the same and what impact this unlikely couple would have on the sensitivities of the fine diners in their evening dress. She handed him a receipt, telling him that final details would be sent to his home address two weeks before the trip. She was snapped out of her stupefaction by realising that she had taken no contact details or other information. On enquiry, he chattily told her that he was a tree surgeon and a landscape gardener and that he often travelled all over the country. Not to worry, he told her, he would call into the office to collect the tickets.

Good grief, she thought, his name is Smith and he travels all over the place, how will we be able to contact him? Does he even *have* a home address? Her relief was profound when he was, at least, able to give her a mobile phone number. Fixing her most practised smile, she wished them a pleasant trip. His parting words were,

'It do seem good value, after all, we get three meals a day.'

Polly merely giggled.

The couple left the office and Sheila wiped her brow.

'Well, what do you make of that?' she called out to her colleague, 'we don't get that type every day.'

'A right pair of characters, by the look of them. Makes you want to be a bit nosey and find out some more, doesn't it?'

Pete Smith's background *was* a little unusual. Although he'd been brought up in a simple farm cottage and like his wife, he'd descended from *travelling* people, he *had* acquired an education of sorts. Pete could just about read and write plus he could use numbers very well. A large and fearless lad, he was never bullied as a child. He'd been a fairly convivial and friendly boy but there had been just enough menace about him to keep the would-be bullies at bay. His limited social experiences never allowed him to acquire any *polish* but he had a general understanding of most things together with the confidence to 'go forth and find out' when he didn't. Now a chatty, unconventional sort of chap, he liked to comment nonstop, on just about everything he saw and on the rare occasion when he knew more than someone else, he positively drooled with the enjoyment of superior knowledge. He was perfect for the uneducated Polly. It was a match made in heaven or more correctly, made down on the farm.

Pete had worked in various capacities on the land such as farm labourer, forester and gardener but he'd also managed to acquire some building skills. Putting all his knowledge together, he'd started to work independently as a landscape gardener and tree surgeon; soon he could undertake anything to do with plants, gardens or forestry.

In order to follow the work, he began to travel all over the country. There was, however, one inherited trait that Pete embraced; it was the 'cash' culture. Pete learned fast. Everything was for cash, no mention of annoying things like VAT or tax ever came to disturb his peace and certainly, no office address was needed. Eventually, Pete amassed a large amount of cash and was perplexed as to what he should do to keep it safe. Banks were not an option, people asked too many questions. He decided to invest in property. Luckily for him, it was a time before too many questions were asked as to the origin of funds but just in case, Pete had his answer ready. He invented a rich old aunt and uncle who'd left him a suitcase full of money in their will; no-one ever checked up on it.

For a much-reduced price, he bought a dilapidated house, one the owners were desperate to get rid of, and proceeded to work on it until it was habitable and then he and his wife, plus his parents (who'd left their old farmworkers' cottage), moved in. He still travelled, but now he had a base to come back to.

He became the father of two fine healthy sons and he made sure that they had good trades to keep them solvent. Both lads worked with their hands, did not relish school but were sensible enough to know that in order to earn a living they needed some kind of education. They had the splendid example of their father to emulate.

His wife Polly, was also very practical so she didn't confine herself to domestic duties. When her sons were grown up, she often helped Pete in his business and worked alongside him on the land. After all, he was her hero and he'd always been there to guide and help her in every way. She knew how lucky she was to have such an intelligent and clever husband.

Some years later, Pete was asked to do some landscaping on a country estate. His employer, the unmarried son of a peer of the realm, was of a similar age to Pete and much to the consternation of his mother, was apt to take a somewhat Bohemian approach to life. He took to Pete immediately. '*A man of the earth*', he called him and Pete found himself in the unusual and coveted position of having regular work ranging from hard landscaping to tree maintenance and - being treated as more of a friend than an employee. This was a strange state of affairs which a lesser man may have found difficult but Pete, with his happy-go-lucky attitude, was more than content to form what appeared to be, a most unequal friendship.

Lord Chivington's son, enjoyed the time spent with Pete. It was an escape from the stuffy world he'd been born into and he could often be seen working on the land himself. Anyone unfamiliar with the situation, seeing the two of them with their fair hair, could be pardoned for thinking that they were just two garden labourers who might well be closely related to each other.

Lady Chivington took her son to task when she arrived home one day and found him and Pete working side by side in a field.

'Really,' she told him, 'this has to stop; it is *not* dignified. Anyone who didn't know you would have great difficulty in believing that you are my son and a Chivington.'

Chapter 2

More Holidaymakers

On one balmy day in spring, Bob was feeling restless, he disliked inactivity, he preferred to be busy. It was exactly one year to the day since he'd finally halted his journalistic career and retired but still he couldn't entirely relax. Was he mad to have left a job he loved? He hadn't been forced to retire but he'd become a little weary, had less energy and he'd had a nagging suspicion that he'd only fool himself if he kept going. He surmised that one day, without realising it, he would become ineffective and an embarrassment; in the meantime, others would be looking at his position with acquisitive eyes - young, dynamic people, greedy with ambition. Was it best to go before you were pushed, or in his case, be swallowed up and overtaken by the younger generation? The decision had been made and he'd left at the top of his game, proud of his achievements and success – but now? He was bored.

He'd written a few articles since he'd retired, no writer could ever just stop, but the whole point of retirement was that you were supposed to enjoy it, do *special* things with the time; what could *he* do?

There was, of course, his wine-tasting group. Always a great connoisseur of wines, he did enjoy the tasting, discussion and the choosing of a fine wine. He had much more time to get involved now. Then there was his love of art and antiques. Yes, he'd managed quite a few trips to galleries and antique shops; his display cabinets bore witness to that, but still, he was bored. Why?

It came to him suddenly, it was time, sheer time. This had always been something in short supply; life was always a rush, a deadline, a race to get a story out in the next edition. Now he had so *much* time, leisure, time to do things at a gentler pace and how he hated it. He missed the cut and thrust of the newspaper world.

What was he going to *do* with his retirement? He and his wife had talked about it so often and yet now, he couldn't seem to remember what it was that they were so looking forward to doing. He began to think about his wife Diane and as if on cue, she walked into the room. She had simultaneously retired from the position of personal assistant to a high-flying civil servant but unlike Bob, she always managed to be busy; retirement had not slowed her down at all.

'Oh Bob, there you are. Did you look at those brochures I left for you?'

Bob guiltily eyed a pile of holiday brochures at his elbow.

'Yes of course,' he answered mechanically, hoping she wouldn't say any more until he really *had* looked at them.

'And?'

'Er – well - um.'

'You haven't looked at them, have you?' He crossed his fingers.

'Not true! Of course, I have.'

'Well, what do you think?'

'Think about what?'

'Which one?' She almost shouted.

Grabbing one off the top of the pile, he handed it to her, 'This one.'

Diane removed the brochure from his grasp, opened it to show a page that had already been folded at one corner and began to study it. Bob angled his head to try to see what he'd passed to her.

'OK,' she said slowly, 'I like your idea. It could be really good. Which particular one do you fancy?'

'The one you're reading,' he replied as convincingly as possible, still trying to see the page. Diane continued to read.

It wasn't that he was unhappy with his wife, he was just terrified of her. He was always going to do something and then he would forget all about it and Diane could be so fierce. When he was working, he could always blame the pressure of work, the latest deadline to meet, the hectic day he'd had but now he lacked the excuses and Diane was making up for lost time.

'Well Bob, at last, you've actually made a decision and I think it's a splendid choice. Go ahead and book it. My diary is in the kitchen so as long as you avoid any important dates I've booked, we can go any time.'

That was it! Bob remembered. They'd decided that retirement meant time to travel. He'd done quite a lot of travelling for his work but Diane hadn't and he remembered that they'd agreed, well Diane had agreed for him, that leisurely travel was the desired goal for all this spare time.

As she left the room, he really did look at the brochure and the page, which she'd helpfully left open for him. He saw that it was a European holiday, a river cruise on the Danube. That might be quite enjoyable, he told himself, what a relief. He read on, oh yes, fine dining with specially chosen wines to complement the meal, it was sounding better and better. Interesting places to visit, Vienna, Bratislava and Budapest with beautiful architecture, sculptures and paintings. It was improving all the time. He considered for a moment, early summer might be the best time, warm but before the school holidays and they would travel there by...... Diane's voice called out from the next room.

'So clever of you to find a trip with a coach journey. Obviously, you remembered how much I hate flying, thank you dear, and it will be interesting to see something of the countryside as we pass through, won't it? I noticed the stopover for dinner, plus bed and breakfast is in Boppard, Germany. That will be lovely; it's on the river Rhine I think.'

Diane could be heard humming 'The Blue Danube Waltz' from the kitchen as Bob's enthusiasm died. He hated being cooped up in a coach all day, he'd *dropped a clanger* alright but there was no going back. A river cruise on the Danube, plus a coach journey there and back; that was to be their holiday.

Diane hadn't been fooled at all. She knew her husband too well. It had been so easy to put the holiday she preferred on the top of the pile of brochures and then pounce when she was sure that he hadn't looked at any. She hated flying but she knew that Bob disliked being squashed up in a coach for hours and would have argued for a short aeroplane journey so this way was best; she was even thanking him for his consideration. It was really very funny

Several months later, with the final payment made and the holiday instructions spread out in front of them, they began to make some retail plans. Bob was thinking along the lines of a new camera and perhaps a guidebook or two.

'We'll go shopping and get some new summer clothes,' Diane began, 'there is no way you're wearing those old gardening shorts that you seem to live in when it's hot. I could do with a dress or two and some lightweight summer trousers and tops. Then I must buy a suitable dress for the formal evening. Is your dinner jacket still presentable?'

The voice droned on and Bob switched off. He hated shopping for clothes and thought that online stores and catalogues were wonderful. It was so hassle-free to order, pay and have everything delivered without the awful process of dragging around the shops. He knew his sizes, his preferred styles and colours. Why was it necessary to trail around shopping centres? He thought he would have a quick look online anyway. If he could see what he liked, he might be able to convince her that in his case, it was pointless to visit the departmental stores; she would find it much less stressful, and so would he, if she could shop alone. He was even prepared to buy a new pair of shorts.

He wandered over to his laptop and switched it on. On checking his emails, he spotted one from an old friend and colleague. Amongst the general news, his pal mentioned a character Bob was interested in, a man named Ronaldo Marconi. Bob remembered the name very well, a slippery customer who'd been on the international police wanted list for years. It seemed that there'd been a tip-off, a possible lead concerning his whereabouts and Budapest had been mentioned, however, it had all come to nothing. Bob read on, he was very familiar with this character, he'd once written an in-depth article concerning him. Information had been sparse, a mixture of folklore and half-truths; all anyone knew for certain was that he was a powerful figure in the underworld and he made his living by a multitude of illegal means. Marconi was a real mystery, no-one was even sure of his nationality, let alone his whereabouts or even his base of operations. The man was a modern-day Scarlet Pimpernel. Could he possibly be in Budapest? Just where Bob was off to. If only he could discover Marconi, that would be a major scoop. He felt the familiar excitement before crashing to earth – he was retired, remember?

Deflated he continued with his original task – men's shorts, how exciting! Did he fancy navy or beige? Oh, the excitement! He must watch his blood pressure. He became slightly morose at the thought of the boring years to come. Suddenly, he snapped out of his blues. He wasn't dead yet, a story was a story. He would keep an eye out for Marconi, you never knew your luck.

....

On a blustery day in March, four ladies were sitting in a cafe drinking coffee with a holiday brochure set out before them.

'So we're agreed, are we? We're all going on a river cruise again, right? And we all fancy trying this boat instead of the one we booked last year. This one will be on the Danube.'

22

'Yes,' came the chorus from the other three.

'So are we going to aim for roughly the same time as last year, early July?'

Again the chorus in the affirmative.

'Right then, I'll go ahead and book it. I'll pay the deposit and you can all reimburse me, just as we did last year. When the whole amount is due, I'll let you all know and then I'll collect your shares, pay it into my bank and send it off from my account.'

'Are you sure you don't mind doing all the work, Susan?'

'No, it's fine. I think this trip should be really good, don't you?' The other three agreed.

The group consisted of three who'd originally met at work plus Christine, an unmarried but retired friend and neighbour of Susan. Christine had willingly joined in all holiday ventures.

Mary was married but her husband was happy to send her off with his blessing because it gave him a chance to book a golfing holiday which his wife loathed. Jo was also married but her husband had severe mobility problems and could not manage a normal holiday and so he was pleased for her to accompany her friends. The last of the four was Susan Butler, an American divorcée living in London; neither Susan nor Christine had a male partner. The four women got on very well and had holidayed together for the past few years; Christine was the oldest at sixty-eight and Susan the youngest at thirty-nine.

Susan was the only one of the four who might have been susceptible to the idea of a new partner so her friends decided, that must be the reason why she tended to flirt dreadfully. Much to the amusement of them all, she seemed to be practising her *pulling* skills on anything in trousers. However, it appeared that she'd had no luck, despite being intelligent, slim and very attractive. Her friends failed to realise that the real problem for Susan was not the number of admirers but the quality; her flirting was merely superficial. Also, unbeknown to her friends, it was only a short while ago that she'd met a very desirable man who'd seemed very interested in her. Suddenly, something had gone wrong and a promising relationship had disintegrated. She was now putting on a brave face and trying to enjoy life.

Having agreed their holiday, the meeting turned to general gossip until suddenly Susan interrupted the flow of conversation with an exclamation.

'Oh, I forgot to mention! When I was researching this new boat, I had a look at the places offered as excursions and while I was searching, guess what came up?' Blank stares and shaken heads were the answer.

'There's a particular ancient castle ruin you can visit. It's in Austria, it's where Richard the Lionheart was held as a captive awaiting his ransom.'

Mary and Jo groaned but Christine's face lit up. A hobby and interest she shared with Susan was visiting castles, chateaus and any stately homes they could find; they just loved old buildings. Susan always said that they had nothing similar to these in the States so she couldn't get enough of them now she was in Europe. The other two didn't mind these visits but they were not too keen on old castles because invariably, they were situated at the top of a very steep hill.

'Never mind,' Susan told the other two, 'Christine and I will go on our own while you two lazy devils can lounge on the sun deck.'

At this suggestion, all four were in perfect agreement and they continued with their coffee and cake before the agreeable get-together came to an end.

....

During the same season, a bored and petulant Felicity Fanshawe was being difficult – again. The chair was not comfortable, she needed another cushion, where was her tea? Why was it being served in the ordinary china cups? She had made it quite clear that she liked the bone-china because the tea tasted better drunk from this tea-service. The room was too dark, now it was too bright, the room was chilly, good gracious she could not stand so much heat. Whatever were they thinking of?

Sebastian, her present male companion wearily fixed a very reluctant smile to his face and attempted to try to charm her out of her obvious bad mood. He was fond of her but he told himself that he must be mad, to put up with this. There was no doubt that she had once been very beautiful but time had taken its usual devastating toll; for all her creams and treatments, surgery and cosmetics, there was no disguising her advancing years. However, he wouldn't have dared tell her so.

A fading star of film and theatre, Felicity Fanshawe sighed and draped herself more comfortably across the chaise-lounge. She needed diversion, she told him; he must *try* to find something that would cheer her up.

'Would you like your old friend Mrs Beecham to visit?' He was rewarded with a catalogue of the failings of the said lady. Of course, she didn't want her around, fussing and fretting. She would go out, he must inform the chauffeur that she wished to take a drive. No, she wouldn't, was the decision fifteen minutes later when the car was waiting at the door, she'd detected a cooling of the air, she might take a chill.

Her long-suffering companion gave up. Was this really worth it? Ok, she was *loaded* but less and less seemed to be coming his way these days. He was good-looking and charming; he could still catch the ladies' eyes. Should he look for another billet? This one was losing its appeal.

The housekeeper entered the room and was admonished for not knocking. This did little to deter the astute lady. She too was quite fed up with it all but she had no intention of leaving; well not yet. She was *feathering her nest* nicely but had a way to go before she had enough of a nest-egg to clear off. She was a genius in handling the awkward lady and had never yet been rumbled.

'Oh dear! Did I forget to knock? I'm that sorry.' Her Irish blarney was at its best.

'Here's me, so intent on giving you this news that I clean forgot to knock on the door.' Holding a gossip magazine in her hand, she began to wave it about. Tetchy but curious, as Mrs O'Shea knew she would be, and interested because the conceited woman was always looking for news of celebrities or society figures whom she liked to discuss as if they were her dearest friends, Felicity paused and looked up. Mrs O'Shea was right, she knew exactly how to tempt her.

'I was just reading in me magazine, about these royal families from Europe and there's this here Prince Romanovsky, from Europe somewhere, he's going to be cruising on a *particular* river this year.' And with this comment, she pointed to a photograph of a handsome and debonair man shown in the magazine she was holding.

'Nonsense!' came the tart reply from Felicity, but she was interested in spite of herself. 'How would anyone know that? Give me the magazine. Oh,' she informed her housekeeper, 'it states - *He is frequently to be seen on European rivers, holidaying on his luxury cruiser. This year it is believed to be the River Danube.*' Felicity carefully studied the photograph of the handsome man; her mood had altered.

Mrs O'Shea winked at Sebastian as he thankfully stood up to leave the room.

'I was thinking, ma'am, t'would be a fine thing if you were to, you know, sort of *bump into* this peach of a man. I mean you being so high-class an all. I bet he'd take to you. Stands to reason, doesn't it, class sort of finds class, doesn't it ma'am?'

Gratified at the remark, Felicity began to smile but then she took hold of her herself and snapped icily,

'And how would we know for certain which river the prince will be cruising on and when? Stupid woman! These magazines often make up news, he could be anywhere.'

Undaunted, Mrs O'Shea continued in a conspiratorial tone. 'Well, it's like this, ma'am. My friend, who's the housekeeper to Lord Pembroke, told me last week that she'd heard his lordship mention that this prince was going to be on a cruiser calling into Vienna in early July when his Lordship would be there too. Well, it stands to reason, if the prince is going to be in Vienna, he *must* be on the Danube for his trip and the magazine is telling the truth.' She smiled in a very smug sort of way, 'and - I heard that he has no wife or even a fiancée so he'll likely be cruising alone. Now wouldn't a man like that, used to mixing with all the best people, be glad to accidentally bump into a lady of refinement like yourself? I'm hearing that it's the fashionable thing to do now, to cruise on the rivers in Europe. With all your connections ma'am, news would be sure to reach you to tell you exactly where he was. You could easily arrange for ....' Mrs O'Shea stopped, the bait had been dangled and swallowed. Felicity Fanshawe began to daydream. She saw herself being wined and dined by a prince who would, of course, prefer an interesting and famous celebrity as a dinner guest rather than perhaps a younger, but far less refined, individual that he might happen to meet. Pressing her advantage, Mrs O'Shea continued.

'You society ladies, you can always find out what's happening. Now if you were to arrange to take a little holiday on a luxury Danube cruiser in early July, around the time the Prince will be there, well I'm sure the rest would be easy to arrange. Don't you think?'

Felicity Fanshawe allowed herself to be deluded, she envisaged a tête-à-tête with the cream of society - a moonlight sojourn sipping champagne on the deck of a luxury river cruiser. The stupid woman believed it all to be possible. Sebastian returned to the room.

'Oh Sebastian, be a dear. I have a fancy to take a little holiday and I have quite decided that a luxury river cruise on the River Danube would suit me. Be a darling and arrange it for me, would you? Early July would be pleasant and don't forget to book the best suite.'

Surprised but not unwilling he replied,

'Any particular stretch of the Danube and for how long?'

'Don't be tedious dear, use your initiative. I can't work out all the details but somewhere near Vienna sounds pleasant.' And with that she floated out of the door, her mood enormously improved.

Mrs O'Shea followed her out of the room and then hurried to her own quarters. Laughing fit to bust she dialled a telephone number.

'Hello, Molly, yes that's all settled. I can come on holiday in early July. I told you it would be easy. I just hope this flippin' Prince really is there somewhere on that river.

....

In another part of town, two elderly and quite genteel sisters were glancing through some holiday literature. They sat in their comfortable upright chairs with a cushion supporting their backs. Their feet were encased in slippers and on detecting a little chill, they both had donned warm cardigans buttoned up over their blouses which were teamed with sensible worsted skirts. As Minnie, an ex-nurse, was often heard to say,

'You can't trust the English weather. Many a poor soul has passed on from a neglected cold or from sitting in a draught.' The ladies were actually as tough as it was possible to be and it would have taken more than a chill wind or the thought of germs to spoil anything that they wished to do. Ever resilient they were planning their annual trip abroad.

'Look Lavinia, they've printed such a nice brochure this year. Just look at these photographs of the Danube.'

Her elder sister glanced over her shoulder.

'The sample menu looks very appetising too and I always think how delightfully spacious the cabins are.'

'Yes, indeed. They have made it all look very pleasant. We *shall* look forward to the cruise, shan't we?'

'I have to admit, I found it all rather tiring last year. I did enjoy it so much but when we left the boat, those *rough streets* and *cobblestones* made it so difficult to walk.'

'I think, dear, our walking days are over. This year we'll just sit in the sunshine on deck and not worry about disembarking – unless we just pop into that particularly delightful village right by the dock, do you remember it? We could just have a cup of coffee in their beautiful little restaurant.'

'That would be very pleasant indeed. Let's do that,' Minnie replied'

'I think we have to face the facts now. We've always been dismissive of our ages but I think being in our late eighties means that soon we'll not have a choice about what we can and can't do.'

'Well, at least we do still get away. The coach does make it so easy for us. I don't think I could manage an airport or a train station these days and definitely not with a suitcase.'

'Oh, I'm sure we could manage if we had to. We never give up, do we?'

They both chuckled.

'Have we received the tickets yet?'

'No not yet,' Lavinia answered, 'but I'm sure we'll get all the instructions very soon.'

'Do you think we might need some new summer clothes? I haven't bought any for years.'

'Yes, perhaps we should. Tomorrow, we'll get the bus into town, stop for tea in the cafe on the high street and then invigorated, we should be able to have a look in the ladies outfitters for some holiday clothes.'

'At least we don't have to worry about our figures in swimming costumes anymore and I think my days of wearing shorts might just be over,' was the giggled reply.

'I think well and truly over.'

'By the way, we mustn't forget to take our walking sticks.'

'Oh I shan't forget that,' replied Lavinia, 'it's too important these days.'

With that, the two ladies put down the brochure and made ready for their afternoon ritual of tea.

Chapter 3

Priscilla and Lillian

Lillian was staring out of the window. The rain was coming down in sheets and the soggy garden was a mass of puddles and sorry-looking plants that had been battered by the wind. The weather was enough to make any person feel dispirited. Just a little sunshine would have helped but there was no hint of a break in the dull grey sky and the lady observing the dismal scene found herself in a sombre mood.

A voice was droning on behind her and at first, she tried to obliterate it from her consciousness but the same repetitive and grating tone continued. Lillian was so used to it now. It seemed an answer was required.

'Yes, Priscilla. Of course, Priscilla. I'm sure that you know best.'

'I'm glad you realise it. The trouble with you, Lillian, is that you are too easily led by the wrong advice. I'm always telling you that you should listen to people who are far more used to such things than yourself. I've had far more experience of the world than you, haven't I?'

'Oh yes, Priscilla.'

'Well, there you are then. Now let me see. What will be suitable?'

Lillian turned around and hopefully began a sentence.

'I wondered about......'

'One moment please, Lillian. I need a moment to digest this information.'

The slim and timid lady stopped in mid-sentence and sat down. She almost put her finger on her lips but just stopped herself. She looked down at the carpet like a naughty child.

Her companion, a much larger and formidable lady, held centre stage as she studied some of the holiday brochures laid out on the table in front of her.

'Whatever were you thinking of?' she uttered in a derisory tone as she sent a penetrating glance towards her companion, 'many of these are *most* unsuitable. I would *never* consider visiting a noisy hotel by a beach? I hope you have no intention of exposing me to ridicule by flaunting yourself in a swimming outfit and sitting on a common beach with all the undesirables?'

Visions of golden sands, ice-cool drinks and perhaps listening to some romantic moonlit music under the stars, vanished quickly from Lillian's thoughts.

'Oh no, Priscilla. Nothing could have been further from my mind.'

Lillian was cross with herself. She knew that she ought to stand up to her overbearing cousin but somehow, over the years, she'd got into the habit of just doing as she was told. To change the habit of a lifetime was somehow unthinkable, and yet – if only?'

'This looks better.' Priscilla held up a brochure showing a large cruise liner. 'This is more *our* sort of thing.'

Lillian sat in silence as her forceful cousin read the details aloud. She paused suddenly and began to read the print more closely before exclaiming,

'Oh dear, perhaps not. A little *too* large I feel. Such a shame, there is a definite lack of exclusivity in ocean cruising these days. Really! One would almost feel as if one was being *herded like cattle* with such large numbers. '

Lillian knew that unless she did something quickly, she would not get a decent holiday this year. This conundrum of *where to go* had happened last year and the year before and both times she'd ended up in the same hotel in Eastbourne, Sussex because Priscilla had decided that of all the options, it involved the least exertion. Lillian had hoped that this year, with a pile of brochures to look through, something might appeal to her cousin who would always have the last word about where they could visit. She'd hopefully slipped a particular brochure near the top of the pile.

Little did she know it but luck was about to play a part. Casting aside the open brochures, Priscilla demanded tea and while Lillian went off to make it, she picked up her favourite magazine, 'The Lady', which she'd not yet had time to read, and she glanced idly through the pages. An article caught her eye about the pleasures of cruising on rivers and how without effort, the river often provided an excellent viewing platform for various interesting sites and buildings of renown, but more importantly, the article hinted that it was the choice of the more *discerning* traveller because ocean cruising had become so popular now that it was almost *common*. Sitting near the top of the pile on the table, was a holiday brochure, showing a large photograph of a river cruiser and it immediately caught Priscilla's eye. On reading it, the text described the scenario of *fine dining* and sitting in splendid comfort, being waited on hand and foot, whilst the outside world drifted by. Photographs of elegantly dressed couples implied that this holiday was for a *certain class of person* and the numbers on board were small enough to make it *select*. Being an unremitting snob, Priscilla focussed on the words, *select - discerning - fine dining*. When Lillian returned, a brochure was waved under her nose and she was amazed to be told that Priscilla approved of *this* particular type of holiday. Priscilla didn't stop to think *how* they would be travelling to the destination; vulgar details seldom concerned her until the last minute when she would complain if all was not to her satisfaction.

The next morning, hardly able to believe her luck, Lillian went into town and visited the local travel agent. She was determined to waste no time in case Priscilla changed her mind. She spent some pleasant moments flitting through various

33

holiday brochures. There was a 'tall ships' holiday which sounded wonderful; she chuckled when she read that passengers were expected to assist the crew. She tried to imagine Priscilla climbing the mast. An irrepressible giggle broke out which made her turn a little pink as people turned to stare at her. She looked longingly at photographs of white sandy beaches, palm trees, ancient temples and wonderful antiquities; she sighed, Priscilla would never agree. She would condescend to travel somewhere warm but would expect them both to wear the almost regulation, *left over from the nineteen-thirties*, print summer dress, wide straw hat and white gloves. There would be no chance of sipping cocktails by a pool, having speed boat rides or wearing shorts and no chance at all of being allowed to don a swimming costume. Even an old fashioned *one-piece* would be frowned on – a *two-piece* would be considered positively decadent. She sighed again, there were so many other types of holiday but she was resigned, it had to be a river cruise because she had Priscilla's permission for this. However, on consideration, she did rather like the idea and anything was better than a week in Eastbourne - again.

There was a suitable river cruise holiday available on the River Danube so Lillian quickly booked two cabins and paid the deposit. She was informed that they would have to share a dining table with other holidaymakers and that there were no exclusive lounges to sit in; small cruisers meant people needed to mix. She wisely decided not to mention this when she returned with the confirmed booking. She also decided to keep quiet about the journey there. A choice between flying and travelling by coach had been offered; Lillian chose the coach, it seemed less stressful. Priscilla was a nightmare in an airport and if there was a flight delay.......! If asked, she would explain how easy it would be, they were to be collected from near to their home and taken all the way there in comfort. She would also fail to mention that it would take two whole days plus an overnight stop to reach the cruiser in Germany. When this came to light, she would *sell* the journey there and back as extra days sightseeing - value for money; she would not mention the fact that the motorways of Europe tended to pass through the less attractive scenery.

Lillian knew she needed to escape her domineering cousin's influence, she bitterly regretted the position she was now in, but she couldn't see how she could manage this. Sheltered and dominated all her life, she had no idea how she might break the chain that linked her to her forceful cousin. She had endured a lifetime of enforced gratitude and had been reminded so often of her good fortune in having a wise and superior cousin, together with having her hopelessness concerning her ability to manage her affairs constantly stressed, that she now believed this to be true. If only there were some other people to connect with, she mused, but she knew of none; Priscilla had long ago driven away any friends that Lillian might have had.

Priscilla Pilkington had no regrets about her own lack of close friends. She knew her worth and so declined to spend time and effort on undeserving inferior people who could not appreciate her superior status. She graciously made allowances for Lillian; she was well aware how feeble her cousin was.

'I despair of her,' she was often heard to remark to anyone who would listen. 'How Lillian would manage in life without me I cannot imagine. However, she is *family* so one *must* make sacrifices.'

Priscilla Pilkington was the only child of a vicar. It annoyed her that her late father had not risen further in the Church hierarchy so she often exaggerated his previous status. If she thought she was dealing with people who could not possibly know the truth, she became the daughter of a bishop but when meeting people who might have had some idea of his standing, he became a *church senior*. The poor man had actually been the

35

vicar of a tiny country parish but his wife, an ambitious woman, had expected him to rise higher and when he did not do so, felt obliged to invent as much promotion as she could. Her daughter caught the habit at an early age and became a mini version of her mother.

Amazingly Priscilla had once been married; in her youth, she'd managed to *catch* a chap with an impeccable bloodline. She'd been very proud of her success until she'd discovered, to her horror, that he was nothing more than a criminal homosexual and that he'd only married her to protect himself and his family name. Naturally, she'd never been in love with the man; foolish sentiments like that were not in her nature. He was quietly cast into oblivion.

There was no question of Priscilla showing tolerance or understanding. After the horrific revelation, she'd speedily moved out of the marital home, magnificently ignored any impertinent questions from others and reverted to her maiden name. Although the marriage was now repugnant to her, Priscilla could never bring herself to consider a divorce with all its embarrassing connotations and she had no intention of abandoning the leap upwards in status which she'd achieved by the marriage. Feeling she was owed something, she also had no difficulty in enjoying the generous allowance from her estranged husband; her price for silence. She now spent her time in bullying her cousin, holding her nose up to those she considered inferior and minding everybody else's business.

Listening to other people's conversations, was a favourite pastime of Priscilla; her hearing was excellent and she enjoyed relaying any such conversations that may have invited a topic for comment, to anyone else who would listen to her. Her nose for scandal was famous and wow betide anyone trying to keep a secret when she was around. She positively enjoyed criticising other people with never a thought that she might deserve any such character assassination herself.

Lillian, however, had experienced a very different life. Her parents had married in wartime and Lillian was born in 1945. Her mother had been the younger sister of that lowly vicar and her father had been a humble clerk in an office; his tendency to asthma had ensured that he remained in this work all through the war and beyond, until his untimely death at the age of forty. Lillian's parents had enjoyed a happy marriage and she'd enjoyed an idyllic childhood until losing her father to a chronic asthma attack at an early age, had meant straightened circumstances for Lillian and her gentle mother.

A kind and well-liked lady, Mrs Chalfont had managed very well on very little and Lillian had been happy until everything changed. The cottage they lived in was not their own and one day they were given notice to vacate the property; the owner wanted to refurbish the house and then would require a much higher rent. They had gone to live with her uncle and cousin and so Lillian had been dominated by her more forceful cousin from an early age. On the demise of Lillian's mother and after Priscilla's disastrous marriage, Lillian had found herself fulfilling the unofficial post of *companion and underdog* to her domineering cousin.

During the time Lillian was visiting the travel agents, Priscilla became aware that it was time for morning tea and she was most irritated that Lillian had not yet returned. Realising that she would have to make her own pot of tea, muttering and grumbling she entered the kitchen. Twenty minutes later, she wheeled out the elegant tea trolley, complete with teapot, milk jug, sugar bowl and a plate of biscuits, all balanced on a silver-plated salver. She might be on her own, she thought, but you never knew who might call and so standards must never be seen to be slipping.

She sat down in her favourite armchair in the primly old-fashioned drawing-room, straightened the lace table runner on the side table and prepared to pour her tea through a strainer, into a floral-decorated bone-china tea-cup. She added milk and then taking up the tongs and placing two cubes of sugar into her cup, she stirred briskly. She sat back in her comfortable armchair, collected her magazine from the nearby rack and prepared to indulge herself for half an hour.

There was an interesting story about a great aristocratic estate, it seemed that the new Lord Chivington was a little eccentric. She read on. He was seen to dress in a most unorthodox fashion and was well known for his gardening enthusiasm. He *actually dirtied his hands*! How quaint!

Something, which would have been seen as disgusting in a man of the *lower orders*, now became interesting and unusual. A man having a title made everything acceptable, didn't it?

There were some photographs of the estate and on the next page, she spotted a photograph with a distant view of the man; Priscilla studied it carefully. Really, from a distance, he did appear most unlike a peer of the realm. His hair was blonde and hung down to his shoulders, he wore a checked shirt with a dark leather waistcoat, his trousers were made of denim and he wore Wellington boots. Not shown in the picture was the most important fact of all, his wealth, lots and lots of it. He was of course highly respected; he had to be, he had a title! In an almost vulgar fashion, she started to eagerly assimilate the gossip.

Priscilla tweaked her double standards. A trifle odd, she conceded, but then a man of his social standing didn't need to worry about society's rules, did he? She read on and saw in print just how much he was worth; he suddenly became even more respectable, a leader of fashion, a man who could flout the usual rules. He was an *original* and besides, status and money excused everything that might be frowned upon in lesser mortals. Priscilla convinced herself that she had a very *modern* outlook and was not averse to keeping up with the times. Perhaps Lillian's holiday suggestions were not so outrageous after all, mind you, she couldn't tell Lillian this, oh no, the poor woman might start to get ideas that she could make her own decisions in the future. Priscilla would be gracious and indulge her.

When Lillian returned, Priscilla was quite pleasant about the fact that Lillian had made all the holiday arrangements without consulting her further and to Lillian's surprise, she declined to make any adverse comments. Later Lillian noticed the magazine open at the page of the article and realised that it had somehow put Priscilla in a good mood. She blessed Lord Chivington.

Chapter 4

David and Elaine

David collected together the sheaf of papers in front of him and passed them to his clerk. The judge had just called an adjournment to the proceedings and the court was still standing for his departure. David, barrister for the defence, left the courtroom with his clerk in tow and headed for the facilities set aside for members of his calling. He removed his wig and gown.

'We need to make this trial last for one more day,' he confided, 'and then we'll be home and dry.'

'Right Sir, shall I ask the remaining witnesses to stand by?'

'I'm hoping I might not need them but one must never be complacent. Yes, have them standing by.'

The case was not an easy one but David had spotted a flaw, a point of law, a time limit for submission, an omission on behalf of the police; if he could drag the case on beyond a certain time, he could call for the case to be dismissed because of this mistake. The judge had raised an eyebrow as witness after witness, had been called, most of them simply to testify to the good character of the accused.

Two days later there were red faces all round in the local constabulary when the point of law was referred to. Just when the police and the judge, were getting extremely irritated by the seemingly endless nonsensical trivia being put before them, the submission was made and the case was dismissed. David had done it again.

When Elaine, his wife, arrived home that night, it was to a candlelit champagne supper. David was celebrating but his wife, being a detective inspector in the police, was not exactly ecstatic on hearing the reason for his celebration. However they had an agreement, they never questioned each other about their work, in fact, they could not compromise the integrity of their careers by doing so, but it was enough to be told that David had won his latest case and, unfortunately, it was a defence against a prosecution brought by the police. Elaine sighed but *not* having had a good day herself, she gratefully sat down and sipped the champagne.

It was early summer, the weather had been surprisingly pleasant but neither David nor Elaine had found any chance to enjoy it; they were both workaholics. They did try to make time for each other though because their marriage was important to both of them.

Elaine ate mechanically but her thoughts drifted. She was fortunate, she knew that her house was beautiful, her furniture the best, she had a highly successful husband who adored her and had never strayed; he'd always seemed to be content with just the two of them.

She hadn't wanted children. She'd seen so many examples of the perfect marriage falling apart when babies came along. They were supposed to unite people but they often had the opposite effect. The men loved *wetting the baby's head* but weren't so keen to change a wet nappy. They liked boasting about their child's achievements but were reluctant to clean up after them. Worse still, after a baby was born, a man assumed that he carried on as before, his work, his recreational activities, meeting his friends - all of them continued but for a woman, it was so often an abrupt end to all those things, including their aspirations and career hopes. You could employ an *au pair* or a nanny but would you want a stranger living in your house? Elaine would not! Having a child could work but only if both of you had employment that could accommodate the flexibility of childcare; certainly not in their case. Then there was the damage to the woman's figure and more. How did you look sexy with baby sick all down you?

'A penny for them.' David's voice cut into her reverie.

'Oh I was miles away,' she forced a laugh and lied, 'still thinking of work I'm afraid.'

'We need a holiday,' he suddenly decided.' I could do with a break now before a new case comes along. I'd quite like to do something before winter sets in. A pleasant relaxing but interesting experience would do us both good. Are you due any leave?' Elaine thought for a moment, due? When had she taken *any*? She always covered for the *family* people, usually for the men who were either desperate to spend some time with their children before the boys grew a beard and the girls wore high heels or else they were under threat by their wives who wanted to take a family trip.

'A holiday? Maybe. It has to be my turn but it will upset a few others who were hoping I'd cover for them.' Doubts began to creep in.

'Right, that's settled then. I'd like to spend some time with my lovely wife for once. I fancy a romantic setting - say a white sandy beach and a very blue sea.'

Alarm bells rang. He was still very good looking, perhaps she'd better take some time off; she didn't want him straying. He never had but.........

'OK, why not. I'll put in for leave tomorrow. When and where do you want to go?'

'Get some dates booked at work first, I can hold off for a while but try to get time as soon as possible; say in about three weeks or so, a month at the most. If you make it much longer, we'll be surrounded by screaming children everywhere but there's also a danger that I might get a case that drags on and then any holidays will have to be cancelled.'

With leave arranged in three weeks' time, Elaine came home the next evening, opened her computer and proceeded to trawl late deals and last-minute holiday vacancies. As she searched, she realised to her dismay that most places that were still available were either in a family orientated holiday complex or else in a stuffy and very expensive child-free hotel that would bore them silly. There were sea cruises, which they'd tried before but found the 'at sea' days tedious. There were also drunken uninhibited holidays for *twenty-somethings*; definitely no, and it was not the season for ski-ing either so what other activities were there on offer? This trip was supposed to be restful and romantic so trekking was no good, nor camping or roughing it at all. It seemed that most of the things she liked were fully booked. Don't tell me, she thought, that I've booked this time off for nothing, there must be something, somewhere that we would like?

A notice caught her eye, a snippet of gossip in the travel news section. A large on-line agency, having gone into liquidation the previous year, had left many people trying to get their deposits back. Those prepared to find the deposit for the second time, had rebooked the trip with the new owners but many others had declined to do so. It was all up and running now and safely financed but because of the previous company failure, places were available and even more important, there were no children allowed. The company organised river cruises and she remembered that they'd tried one of these many years ago and had enjoyed it very much so she located the website and printed out the details. She took a liking to a particularly splendid cruise on the Danube with fine dining plus wines offered and the included excursions were to some of the places she had yet to visit. All she had to do now was convince David to forgo the beach and the blue sea.

The phone rang. She didn't recognise the number. On warily picking up the receiver, she was pleasantly surprised to hear the voice of an old friend.

'Margaret! How great to hear from you. What are you up to these days?'

There was a laugh on the end of the line,

'Oh, the same old things. I'm still getting into mischief.'

A cosy chat followed until Margaret suddenly announced that she had to leave or she would be late for an appointment. Could they, perhaps, meet up for lunch the next day? She was in Elaine's area and would only be there for a day or two. An arrangement was made and Elaine put a note in her diary to keep the lunchtime free. She would really look forward to that. Her friend had been with her in her early training days but Margaret's career had really taken off since and she was now in some *hush-hush* department.

The lunch, next day, went off well, they talked about old times but by tacit agreement, work was never mentioned though, from time-to-time, they did recall various people they both knew.

'And how is David?' Margaret enquired. 'Still working his socks off?'

Elaine chuckled and related the tale of the holiday they were going to book and how she'd had a fit when she saw what was still available but it looked as if this particular river trip she had found, would fit the bill.

'It will certainly fit this member of the Bill,' she joked. 'I'll give him a day or two so that he thinks I've spent endless time searching, then I'll suggest this trip to him.'

Margaret asked for more details of the proposed holiday and then seemed to look very thoughtful though she said nothing. Lunch over, they said their goodbyes and hoped to meet again soon.

Elaine was at her desk the following morning when she was called to attend a briefing by the District Commissioner.

This was quite an unusual occurrence so she hurried to comply. Leaving her sergeant to cope with the on-going investigation that she was trying to clear up before her holiday leave, she left the building and climbed into her car. Forty-five minutes later she was entering another building and fifteen minutes after that, she was curiously sitting in the exalted office and staring enquiringly at the senior man.

'DI Forest,' he began, 'my apologies for this meeting at short notice but I've just been contacted by one of the specialist branches of the force. A most unusual request has been made by them which concerns you.'

Elaine raised her eyebrows in surprise and listened intently.

'I understand that you are shortly going to be on leave and if I have this correctly, you will be on a river cruise on the Danube?'

My goodness, she thought, I have barely mentioned this to anyone and it will only happen if David agrees. I haven't even asked him yet.

'I will explain in a moment,' he continued, 'but may I just enquire as to which cruise line you are planning to travel with and what would be your itinerary?' Thoroughly bemused and slightly dazed, Elaine explained that she *had* found, what she hoped would be a suitable booking, but nothing was definite yet.

'Perfect! DI Forest, would you be willing to travel on a particular river cruiser of our choosing? Having you there with your husband would present you as merely an innocent traveller but you would be rendering a very useful service by keeping your eyes and ears open and should our suspicions be proved correct, we would need you to contact us on a special number. You would, of course, have most of the holiday paid for by the department.'

Elaine's curiosity was piqued,

'May I ask why *I* am selected? Surely this is a covert operation and there must be other personnel more used to this kind of work?'

'I asked the same question but it seems that there are difficulties in this particular case; the usual operatives may be recognised. No-one should suspect a normal couple on holiday and in addition, there would be no difficulties that might involve a Border Force. A *bona fide* married couple, sharing a cabin and with legal passports showing the same surname, would allay any suspicions.'

'Well I *could* swap holidays, I suppose, it shouldn't make a lot of difference to us but we are supposed to be on *holiday,* Sir? I don't know how my husband will take this.'

'I have been assured that you will be able to do all the normal holiday things but with your training and experience, you will be in a unique position to spot something that normal holidaymakers would disregard. The cruise has already been tentatively booked for a fictitious couple because the head of the operation was unsure who to send but now a change of names can be affected with little difficulty. So may I take it that you will agree? Before you say anything, I'd like to add that an undercover assignment like this will certainly advance your career prospects.'

'I should need more information.'

'All will be forthcoming when we have your agreement to undertake this assignment. Let me know your answer as quickly as possible, please. It's extremely important. Oh, and, I should add that this has to be kept confidential, even from your husband.'

Fifteen minutes later Elaine was out of the office. She'd agreed but had the feeling that she'd been railroaded into a situation that she didn't want. Furthermore, she didn't fully understand how or why she'd been selected - until the penny suddenly dropped. Margaret! Of course! That had to be where the idea had come from. It must be some planned operation from the department Margaret was working in.

She mulled over the proposition in her mind; there *were* some good things. Their holiday would be mainly paid for, there was no danger because she was only keeping ears and eyes open - and she would still be having a good time while helping her career. She was honest enough to admit that she would probably enjoy being somewhat of a nosey parker anyway. The one difficulty was David; he would be so angry if he found out. All she had to do was convince him that this holiday was going to be a wonderful and relaxing experience. She would tell him that she'd arranged to pay for the holiday as a treat for him, that way he wouldn't know that the trip was already paid for.

The situation was unusual and the Commissioner had been vague, though he'd impressed on her that it definitely would do her career a lot of good. She was unsure exactly who and what she would be monitoring and more importantly, why? He promised that the *gaps* would be filled in before she left. She was aware that she needed to know a lot more if she was to be of any use in this operation.

That evening, she ensured that she was home early; an unusual occurrence by itself. She cooked a lovely dinner and when David arrived and looked surprised, she informed him that she was working towards a holiday mood. After a delicious meal and a couple of glasses of wine, she told him that she'd booked a surprise for them; they were going on a cruise on the Danube, wasn't that wonderful? About to argue that he hadn't been consulted, Elaine kissed him and told him how wonderful it was going to be. This was followed up by a description of sun, fresh air, wonderful sights, cordon-bleu meals, superb wines and watching the world drift by as they lounged on deck. The argument died on his lips when she added that it was going to be her treat; he didn't have to pay for a thing. Phew, she thought, got away with it, as he smiled and agreed that yes indeed, it sounded lovely.

Chapter 5

Melissa

Melissa, the 'Senior Tour Director', was sitting in her cabin on the 'Danube Drifter' and working at her desk. All the cabins on this cruiser were of a generous size which made a pleasant change from the cramped accommodation usually allocated to staff. Melissa, being a large lady, was grateful for the extra space; it made her work easier.

She was checking the lists for the arrivals later that day; were there any special requirements and were there any physically challenged guests? She noted that she had two quite elderly ladies sharing a cabin, a Miss Minnie Scott and Miss Lavinia Cutler, they were both at a very advanced age. Oh dear! They've booked a cabin on the lower deck, she thought. There was a small lift but the stairs were a bit tricky, the older and more infirm guests usually booked the upper, more expensive cabins. Oh gosh, she surmised, I suppose they couldn't afford the more expensive ones. She decided to give them a complimentary up-grade as there was one vacant cabin due to a late cancellation; she would square it with the hotel services manager. Another lady seemed to have many dietary requirements plus mobility problems and there were a few diabetic guests; she made a note for herself and the other tour guide, to always have some emergency food with them, just in case there was an unforeseen delay anywhere.

Melissa took her work very seriously and was very conscientious in overseeing all aspects of the holiday. She was obliged to do this anyway because passenger satisfaction was essential for a tour director; it also helped with the receipt of *tips* at the end of the cruise. The general gratuities policy did not include tour guides, they were tipped separately at guests' discretion. These amounts added up and were not to be lightly dismissed. Melissa prided herself on getting good reports from the guests when they left but in any case, she *must* present as a model employee because she *needed to be on this cruiser.*

Her path to success had not been easy. One day, at the age of fifteen, Melissa had stared at her reflection in a full-length mirror and she didn't like what she saw. A lumpy flat-chested teenager who projected outwards where she should have curved in. Her mother had tried to boost her confidence with,

'It's just puppy fat dear, it will soon go,' and, 'your bust will develop as you get older, don't worry,' but she did. She felt like bursting into tears as she flopped down on the bed in despair. She was the joke of her class at school. There were other big girls, she wasn't the only one but the trouble was, she was the biggest. Her friend Mandy was quite large but Melissa had a sneaking suspicion that Mandy was only her friend because Melissa made Mandy seem thinner.

The problem facing her at the time was the *end of school* disco. She could blend into the background on most occasions but dances and social groups were difficult. It was a time when she didn't want to be near anyone else, fat or thin, because she stood out like a sore thumb and also, finding something to wear was a nightmare. In a dress, she looked like a walking campsite. Life was cruel. It was bad enough being this large but why did she have to have a mop of ginger hair on the top? She had one or two blessings, her eyesight was perfect so no spectacles and she had a clear and attractive speaking and singing voice. She was quite intelligent so perhaps when a career choice was needed, she could be a radio announcer, heard but not seen. This thought cheered her a little. She dipped into a box of chocolates by her bed; this always made her feel better.

Her mother didn't help at all, she was a large lady who preferred to blame it all on their family genes instead of reviewing the family diet. She moaned and complained and ignored what was obvious to everyone else. With a firm belief that teenagers needed feeding up for their growing bodies, she continued to serve her daughter a huge cooked breakfast every morning and an even larger meal plus a dessert in the evening. To help her daughter get through the morning, she sent her to school with a *tuck box* full of crisps, biscuits and chocolate - not forgetting her daily can of a sugary fizzy drink. Supper was usually biscuits, cheese and anything else that came to hand as a snack. The pizza delivery man knew the address very well.

'The brain needs feeding,' was her pet statement. 'You won't do well at school if your brain is not well-fed.'

Sure in her conviction that her daughter was not large, just growing, she continued with the most unsuitable diet ever and Melissa grew and grew. Sure enough her bust did grow but so did the rest of her.

By the time Melissa was in her final year at school, she was so large that it had become impossible for her to wear the standard school uniform, her mother was forced to have one specially made and she was furious.

'Do they think I'm made of money?' she complained. 'How outrageous not to have a suitable range of sizes to fit growing girls.'

Melissa's mother never attended the school for any reason and always ignored requests to meet a member of staff, so it wasn't until the end of Melissa's final year, when the headteacher made a special request to see her, that her mother complied. Mistakenly assuming it was to discuss her intelligent daughter's future career, she was shaken to hear the suggestion that her daughter should see a dietician because she was morbidly obese. It was only then that she began to wonder if perhaps Melissa was just a little overweight after all.

By then it was too late. Melissa had no will power. Pills were prescribed to suppress her appetite but she just ate through habit and the weight stayed there. By the time she left school, she waddled rather than walked, and she became out of breath very quickly. Drastic action was needed but in the meantime, she needed a job or a course of study.

Being a very bright pupil, the academic side of school had never been a problem. She left school with excellent examination results that should have easily gained her entrance to higher education. As Maths was a real strength, she was expected to make use of this but to everybody's surprise, she chose a degree course in *'Travel and Tourism'*.

Had she known it, when she attended an interview, the admissions administrator would normally have refused her on the grounds that she was unhealthy and unlikely to cope with the course in its entirety but at the time, he was at the mercy of the *politically correct brigade* and much was being made in the press about *big* being *beautiful* plus discrimination in any area was heavily frowned on. After all, if he could not refuse a man, dressed as a woman who would cause all sorts of problems with cloakroom use, he could hardly refuse a genuine lady just because she was *a little large*. He decided that it was not his problem. As long as she fulfilled the academic requirements, he was satisfied. Melissa joined the course and moved into student accommodation.

Of course, all the same problems she had suffered at school re-appeared and had it not been for one girl, who took pity on her, she would have quit the course. This girl confided to Melissa that she too had been hugely overweight but had managed to lose weight on a special diet. She offered to help.

With her friend's encouragement and supervision, she began to lose weight. She became very excited when she kept seeing the dial on the scales showing a reduction in number. Others joined in to help her; it became a sort of group project and some of the other girls, who had a little extra body-weight that they could do without, joined her in dieting. There were still some cruel and sarcastic people but her little support group did their best to protect her so slowly and surely the weight reduced.

She was ecstatic when the scales showed that she had lost three stone and nearly ruined everything by wanting to celebrate with a takeaway and a bottle of wine. It was often the alcohol that was the worst temptation. The other girls were happy enough to cut down on stodgy food but they were students after all and they did like to party at the weekends; there was only so much mineral water you could stand.

Melissa surprised her parent when she returned home for the summer. Her mother had not realised that her daughter had lost so much weight. After two visits when Melissa was bundled up in baggy winter clothes, the summer visit revealed all and her mother was shocked.

'Don't forget you need brain food,' was her worried comment. 'Aren't you losing too much weight too quickly?'

It didn't take long for the cooked breakfast to appear, huge dinners and in between, crisps and chocolate snacks; Melissa was persuaded that a little extra wouldn't hurt. She went back to university almost the same size that she had started.

Her friends were furious with her but she begged them to help her again so once more the diet started and this time she kept the weight off, lost more than before and was able to resist her mother's best efforts at sabotage during the next two summer breaks. Finally, flushed with academic success and having become a size sixteen, she felt she could face and conquer the world. She applied for and was awarded a position with a travel company and soon found herself on a train and heading for a London office.

This was probably the happiest period in Melissa's life because, for the very first time, she found a boyfriend. A man who worked in the next office started noticing her and began exchanging pleasantries. Melinda felt like a giggly schoolgirl and began to anticipate meeting him every day. He was rather overweight himself plus being quite tall so Melissa found herself looking up at him with a feeling of being feminine and petite; a sensation she had never encountered before. She was quickly besotted and he, not usually successful with women, became happily involved with her.

Her natural organisational ability and intelligence helped her to quickly receive promotion but loneliness would have been a big problem without her new romance because she seemed to have no real female friends here in the big city and there were no other boyfriends. She was often sent on assignments abroad and although she enjoyed them, she couldn't wait to get back to see James, her boyfriend. All was well until the day James asked to meet her after work because he had something important to say to her. She floated around all morning, spent her lunch hour looking in a jeweller's window and willed the clock to hurry up all afternoon. At last, she sat down on the park bench where they had arranged to meet and greeted him smilingly. She coyly lowered her eyes as he began to speak.

The coyness lasted thirty seconds before she realised that the words she was hearing were not the ones she'd imagined. She came down to earth with a bump at the part where he was very sorry but he didn't think it would work out between them and anyway he'd met someone else. He hoped they could remain friends.

Fighting to retain her dignity, she stuttered a reply then stood up, walked off and blindly headed for home where she cried her eyes out all night.

Knowing that she could not now continue to work in her old office, she asked for an interview with her superior and soon found herself working as a holiday representative and tour organiser for a subsidiary of the company, a river cruise line that operated in Europe.

She enjoyed her work but with no friends to keep her on the straight and narrow and no boyfriend to look good for and loads of buffet food on offer every day, she resorted to her old means of comfort, she began to nibble, then snack until she was back to her old habits. The cruise line she worked on provided wonderful meals and her resolve just faded away. Soon she was back to double eggs and bacon for breakfast with huge lunches and dinners. The weight piled on and she waddled around and was out of breath again. Blindly, she just continued taking the village tours while her colleagues watched uneasily and waited for her heart attack to happen. Fortunately for her, the travel company appointed an assistant, a junior tour director, so thankfully, she could delegate the most strenuous activities. Like a ticking time-bomb, she carried on.

There was a knock on the door.

'Come in,' Melissa called out and Anna, the Latvian cabin maid entered.

'Guest cabins all finished. You want your cabin cleaning now?'

It was a little perk of the job, not having to make your own bed or clean your room. However, on changeover day, the staff had to wait until the guest cabins were ready.

'Can you work around me? I need to finish this paperwork.'

If I *can* get around you in this cabin, thought Anna. How would this lady get on if she ever had to work in some of the tiny cabins in the smaller river cruisers?

Anna entered and swiftly began to clean the shower room, she changed the towels then edged past Melissa and made the bed; there were two though only one had been slept in. She gave the carpet a cursory clean and tidied everything but the desk.

'Is that all for you?' she asked.

Melissa felt a little humbled by the ability of so many ordinary and low-paid foreigners to speak understandable English. Just as well, she thought, as she replied in the affirmative, on a scale of 1-10, my Latvian is zero!'

Chapter 6

Paul Driver

Paul was on his way to collect the coach and passengers for the trip to Germany. As he drove, his thoughts wandered.

It had become obvious to Paul, that at busy times of the year, the border authorities were more selective with their searches. British passport holders, all of a *certain age*, leaving or entering the UK by way of a coach and ferry who were usually very unproductive with regard to contraband and people smuggling, tended to be waved through by the officials. These days, the focus was on the vehicle which would be checked by security personnel and *sniffer* dogs. Holiday travellers did not like to leave their jackets, handbags, cameras and other valuables on the seats, so when requested to leave the coach for passport control, they tended to take some belongings with them. The officials only ever scrutinised passports so small bags and pockets could, in theory, be full of contraband and nobody intercepted it. Paul had made good use of the knowledge. Mind you, he'd had one scary moment.

Drivers always had to present their paperwork first and then when the coach was given the *all-clear* they would be allowed to drive it to where the passengers would re-embark. It was usual, therefore, for Paul to be waiting by the coach door until the search had been finished. On one particular day, a dog stopped and sniffed at his jacket. Paul felt his nerves jangle as the operative immediately asked him to remove his jacket and then started checking the pockets. Laughter all round followed. It seemed it was a young dog, still under training, and he'd sniffed out the large sausage roll in Paul's pocket. Later that night, Paul dissected the sausage roll and removed the contents.

His illicit goods had no smell but that had been too close for comfort.

Paul couldn't afford to be late for the pick-up but still, he drove the company van at a steady unhurried early-morning pace, finally parking at the Hotel, next to where the coach should be, with ten minutes to spare. The coach driver and Paul were due to swap vehicles. However, the coach was late; it should have been there already when he arrived. The passengers should have been having a coffee and using the facilities and the driver should have been all packed up and ready to leave. Not today though. One of those days was it? Paul sighed. A delay meant a longer journey time, late arrival at the destination and usually irritable passengers. Thank goodness he had a toilet on board, it would save any emergency stops at service stations as sometimes, passengers in this age group needed hurried access to a means of relief.

Forty-five minutes and three phone calls later, the coach arrived. A series of disasters had delayed it. An hour later, the coach pulled away with Paul at the wheel plus a full contingent of passengers. Paul began his usual dialogue.

'Well good morning everyone. Are you all ready for a nice long drive? Let me introduce myself. My name is Paul. It's actually Paul Driver, yes really - so you can say, *'Hey Mr Driver,'* and you would be correct.' He ended his words with an artificial laugh. This was followed by a gentle titter from the coach occupants.

He went on to state the well-rehearsed information about points of interest they should see during the journey, when they would stop for a *comfort break* and roughly what time they would arrive at their destination that day. He knew it all by heart but the trick was to make it sound as if this was a new adventure for him as well as the passengers. You had to sound enthusiastic, even though it was just another day's work.

Paul noticed that most on board were of retirement age although there were a few who were obviously still in their forties but as usual, there was a large contingent who were well into their seventies, and if he wasn't mistaken, he could see his two die-hard ladies who had travelled with him before. They were an amazing pair, definitely in their eighties and one looked as if ninety had been reached or was not too far away. He chuckled as he saw them. There they were, getting on with everything, managing somehow - no complaints, all smiles and looking forward to their regular river trips which they loved. He thought of his wife and shuddered, *she* never stopped complaining. It would do his wife good to see these ladies. These two old girls were grand. That's what you should be like, he surmised, live life to the full and don't let old age make you give up.

Having negotiated the ferry crossing and after driving for an hour or two, Paul made the first *comfort break*. It gave him a chance to take a closer look at his passengers as they alighted from the coach and he scrutinised them again when they returned. It was a kind of game he liked to play - guessing who they were, what they'd done in life, what their employment was or had been, and so on. Many looked very ordinary, he had no doubt that they'd worked in offices as clerks or administrators, the odd nurse or teacher maybe and some of the men looked as if they were typical civil servants but there were always exceptions and this coach-load seemed to have quite a few.

After a few more stops, a variety of questions being put to him together with some annoying requests to access the boot of the coach when he'd just closed it, he began to have an understanding of his passengers.

If he placed them in order of *novelty* and *standing out from the crowd*, the couple near the back would easily come out top. They stood out like a sore thumb; their dress, their speech and their whole demeanour differed from everyone else. The man had shoulder-length blonde hair and his wife had long brown hair with the top permed into a frizz. He wore a bright checked shirt with a waistcoat and nondescript trousers over clumpy boots. On his head was a slightly battered cream coloured trilby-style hat. His wife wore a bright muslin blouse with a denim skirt decorated with multi-coloured embroidered designs; on her feet were flat leather sandals. The couple were sun-tanned and gave the impression that they lived much of their life in the outdoors. They spoke with something resembling a Somerset accent.

In second place, he wasn't sure whether he'd put the two grand old ladies or the snooty bitch who was always ordering her female companion around. The latter seemed to have mistaken the coach trip for a Royal procession. He'd call it a tie.

In fourth place he decided that it would be the group of four ladies; they ranged in age from about forty to maybe sixty? They certainly seemed to be up for a laugh. He'd overheard them saying that at the coach park, they'd forgotten that on the continent, you had to pay for *services* and, having only holiday money *banknotes*, they had no small change. They hadn't let this bother them as they'd just climbed over the barrier leading to the ladies' toilets.

Several other couples seemed pleasant and Paul was sure that they would cause little trouble, including the comedian with the phone that suddenly came to life with, 'Allo, 'allo. Night 'awk calling,' and caused nearly everyone to break into raucous laughter. The TV programme had obviously reached a wide audience and everyone recognised the voice of Gordon Kaye. Paul did hear someone muttering, 'How common,' and he was pretty sure it was the big sour-faced woman who fancied herself as '*Lady Muck*'.

Paul continued with his usual commentary, it was prudent to let the customers know something about the countryside they were passing through. It all helped towards getting a better tip at the end of the holiday. He braced himself for the usual stupid questions, there was always one and today would be no exception.

'What are those things by the roadside, Paul?'

'Trees, madam.' The reply was a giggle followed by,

'Oh, you are a one!'

He began to recite his repertoire of jolly quips and jokes and made a good job of sounding as if the whole thing was fresh and new. He heard the familiar chuckles and comments from the gullible passengers and relaxed. This lot would be easy.

However, seated towards the back of the coach were the couple Paul had voted number one - Pete and Polly. Unknowingly, they were in direct competition with Paul. They were unintentionally doing a splendid job of amusing most of the people who were seated near them. Their loud inane comments, coupled with a strong Somerset accent, was the stuff of comic sketches on TV and it kept the surrounding group entertained for some time.

'What country are we in now?' asked |Polly.

'We're in Germany of course,' came the reply as the coach passed a large sign indicating 'Brussels' and then later on from Pete,

'Oh look Nuremberg. That's where the Nazis did all their war crimes.' The intelligence level of the conversation deteriorated with each kilometre until it descended into farce.

Bob, seated in front of them, had a handkerchief stuffed into his mouth to stop him laughing out loud and others were holding their ribs and silently rocking with laughter. A whole group of people, using eye contact and gestures, made instant connections with each other through the shared experience. Friendships were being formed at the couple's expense but Pete and Polly were oblivious to everything.

As the journey progressed, the frivolity began to subside and the journey became a little tedious. The traffic was very bad in Belgium and again in Germany.

'So much for the famous German autobahns,' commented one passenger, 'they're worse than the M25.'

By this time Priscilla was getting annoyed. She hadn't bargained for any discomfort on this journey. At first, she'd raised an eyebrow in disdain, when she'd discovered that she would be travelling in such close confinement with others for so long but she had wrongly assumed that a *de-luxe* coach would be the order of the day and so fancied herself being carried forth in quite a degree of comfort; the reality was quite another thing. Although the coach was in reasonable condition, there was no doubt that backs and legs were going to be affected at the end of each day. About to make a fuss, she suddenly realised that should she complain of discomfort or voice any dissatisfaction, the two elderly ladies, who were travelling quite cheerfully and without a single complaint, would make her look ridiculous. Against her inclination, she stayed quiet but Lillian saw the look on her face and knew that she would be in for an unpleasant time later.

Though not on the coach, there was another unhappy traveller, it was Felicity Fanshawe. She would never forgive Sebastian for booking such a primitive form of transport. In vain did he try to explain that it was included with the holiday and he'd thought it would be less stressful for her than flying in an aeroplane. She'd refused point-blank to board a coach and had insisted that as she'd given her chauffeur holiday leave and her car was to be serviced in their absence, Sebastian must hire a private car and drive her there. Much to Paul's amusement, being unsure of his ability to cope and wanting the security of a group, Sebastian had undertaken the unenviable task of driving behind the coach for the whole journey. When they'd stopped for a short break, she'd marched into the restaurant and expected someone to come and *seat her at a table* and on being disabused of that notion, she was outraged to discover that she was supposed to queue for drinks and snacks. Sebastian was immediately instructed to obtain suitable refreshments for her but on looking for the superior lounge to sit in, she found only a noisy and rather full *common* seating area.

She then swept the room with her glance and waited for someone to leap up to offer their seat but after having been ignored for the best part of five minutes, she flounced into a corner when one tiny table became available. Sebastian groaned; wait until she realises that she'll have to join a *queue* for the ladies' toilets, he thought.

So far, events did not bode well for the next week. He took a surreptitious look at her, the wrinkles were creeping back, so much for the fortune spent on surgery. She was not looking good and her temper was getting worse every day. If only, he thought, God forgive me, but it would be wonderful if she just had a heart attack and *went* because if she doesn't *kick the bucket soon*, it could be me instead. He took another look at her; she had recently developed a somewhat grey pallor. Perhaps he would check up on the insurance policy. Had he insured her for enough?

Bob and Diane were also having regrets. Bob realised that he'd mentally floated past the details of the journey in order to relish the thought of the fine dining and wine tasting and Diane was wondering if she would ever be able to persuade him to go on holiday again.

David and Elaine were fine. Being two people who had their brains constantly bombarded with important detail, they were enjoying the comparative relaxation; someone else was doing all the thinking and all the work. All they had to do was remember the time to be back on the coach after the comfort breaks. It was just how David wanted things to be.

'I think this was a good idea,' David remarked, 'I need some de-stressing and this seems eminently suitable. I feel that, for once, I don't have to be formal and I don't need to worry about details. We're going to have a very relaxing time.'

Elaine smiled back at him but she was not quite so sure about the *relaxing* bit; she had a lot of work to do. Through her confidential sources, she'd managed to get a copy of the passenger list and some information about the personnel on board the river cruiser. She'd begun to realise that there would be a lot more to do than just simple observations. She hoped that she could still keep her intended surveillance from David. She smiled and agreed with him.

Sitting together and smiling at everybody, were the two elderly ladies, Minnie and Lavinia. They didn't seem to have a care in the world although both had difficulty walking and needed the assistance of a walking stick; the oldest lady relied very heavily on hers. However, when the coach stopped, even though it took them longer than everybody else and they found it hard to get out of their seats, they cheerfully followed the line of people. The sweet old ladies told everybody how much they were looking forward to their holiday and how they loved to be cruising on a river.

Eventually, Paul returned to his seat, counted the heads, checked the car travellers were ready and then began to drive again. He didn't need to say very much now as most of the coach passengers seemed to be sleeping or were at least closing their eyes. He began instead, to calculate roughly how much money he might make from this trip. He didn't anticipate any trouble, it all seemed so straightforward and after all, he'd followed this routine so many times before. He drove on through Germany, blissfully unaware that his optimism was about to be completely destroyed.

Chapter 7

The Arrival

Having spent the night in the town of Boppard, the next morning the passengers continued their journey until they reached their destination at Passau.

Paul skilfully guided the coach into the relatively small space by the riverside where the 'Danube Drifter' was stationed at the dock. A smiling Melissa, together with her young assistant Vicktor, was standing on the deck waiting to welcome the new passengers. Melissa was tired. It seemed only moments since she'd waved goodbye to the last group of visitors and she'd been able to allow her face to relax back into a natural droop and yet, here she was again with a stupid grin fixed in place.

She took her first look at the new crowd. As usual, they would all be English speaking. The staff and crew came from a variety of countries but with the exception of the deckhands, they were all able to speak at least moderate English; quite essential for this cruise line.

At first glance, the passengers seemed *much of a muchness* but then she did a double-take, she spotted Pete and Polly; these people were *definitely* not like her usual guests. Following behind them she could see another person and her heart sank because she knew the type. Priscilla had already started complaining. If that wasn't bad enough, a saloon car had pulled up and by the look of the lady who was being helped out of the vehicle by the silver-haired gentleman, this passenger too did not bode well for a trouble-free trip. The lady in question had glanced up at the vessel and then seemed to be less than pleased.

Gathering her mental armour and with that determined and assured smile that was all part of the professional image, Melissa stepped forward to welcome the guests. Paul had already moved around the outside of the coach and had opened the luggage compartments; the guests began to retrieve their suitcases. A trickle of people started to make their way towards the gangplank and Melissa readied herself to welcome them on board. She hurried forward to help when she spotted the two elderly ladies but with wheels on their cases, they were coping well. They'd done this many times before.

Two efficient crew members hovered inside the main doors, one with a *welcome drink* and one behind a counter, with a list of names, cabin numbers and keys. As the coach passengers passed by and the crowd thinned, Melissa looked back towards the coach and could see two ladies standing there and one had a very red face; it was the complaining lady.

'Shall we collect our cases ourselves, Priscilla? They do have wheels so I'm sure we could manage.'

'Lillian, have you taken leave of your senses once again? Ladies do not struggle with cases. Porters manage luggage.' She stood there glaring at Melissa with her arms folded.

There was a similar situation by the saloon car, the lady had absolutely no intention of lifting a finger but she had no objection to the silver-haired gentleman struggling with her three large suitcases plus his own. Leaving him to manage somehow, she sashayed forward, brushed past and majestically ignored the fuming Priscilla. As Felicity arrived on board, her theatrical entrance distracted Melissa's attention from the abandoned Priscilla and she watched, fascinated, as Felicity extended her hand to everyone in turn as if she expected it to be kissed. Seeing a man in uniform crossing the hall she immediately grasped his arm.

'Darling. Could you be a dear and help my poor Sebastian with the cases. I fear he may have a heart attack, poor lamb.' All this was said with many dramatic gestures and theatrical

66

posturing. A slightly dazed captain, found himself being demoted to luggage porter.

Priscilla did not have the same success. Finally realising that she could be left there, she grabbed at the handle of her over-large suitcase and puffing and blowing, headed towards the gangplank. At last a young seaman, seeing her exertion, hurried to help. Lillian was left to valiantly struggle behind her.

A few moments later Felicity Fanshawe was standing in the doorway of her cabin. She made another dramatic gesture, nearly poking poor Sebastian in the eye.

'Oh, darling. This is just too frustrating for words. Those silly people have given me the wrong stateroom. Ask them where the luxury suites are and demand one. I could not possibly manage in this tiny primitive accommodation.' This was said while looking at one of the superior rooms

Sebastian coughed and mentioned that in fact, he was fairly sure that this was *the correct* cabin and he'd booked it for the two of them to share as only one cabin had been available. Felicity was incredulous; this information did not go down at all well. When a member of staff informed her that not only was the cabin correct as booked, but it was one of the best on the boat, she was aghast.

Priscilla was having a similarly deflating experience. With economy in mind, Lillian had booked two cabins in the middle range, wisely remembering that to share accommodation with Priscilla was a non-starter despite the extra cost for single occupation. She hadn't mentioned to Priscilla that river cruisers, being much smaller than ocean-going liners, had of necessity, much smaller cabins. An imperious voice boomed along the corridor.

'There has been a mistake. Hey, you there, domestic person, kindly find us our correct cabins. It would be the luxury class. I am not used to economy-type accommodation.'

Priscilla's temper was not improved when the cabin attendant, Anna, came cheerfully along the corridor.

'Oh you are funny lady,' she smilingly uttered, 'this is a good room, no?'

'No!' was the unequivocal answer.

Realising that the lady was not joking, the confused attendant tried to placate Priscilla.

'This is very good room. You have nice view. The window, it opens, look, very nice view.' With this passing comment, the maid beat a hasty retreat thinking that her chances of a good end-of-cruise tip from this cabin, were very slim.

Lillian had been acutely aware that the next person to suffer would be herself, so she had hurried away, gratefully going to her own cabin which was conveniently situated much further along the passageway. She had been able to choose cabin numbers and had sensibly ensured that she was not within easy reach of her cousin. It would not be the first time the wall had been banged in the middle of the night because Priscilla demanded attention. Luckily Priscilla had no idea of this and later, Lillian sympathetically agreed how annoying it was to have her cabin so far away while all the time she was crossing her fingers. No Priscilla was definitely *not* happy.

However, the other disgruntled guest, Felicity, was now in much better spirits. She had been placated by a bottle of champagne being delivered to her cabin by a clever male attendant, who having being primed and bribed by Sebastian, had knocked to welcome her, kissed her hand and mentioned that he was a fan of hers. Luckily she did not ask for details of the plays or films he'd seen her in nor did she stop to think how unlikely it would be that such a young man would have seen her performances. Nothing could have improved her mood more and the cabin now became sweet, bijou and quaint and she *would* endure the miniscule space though, of course, she was disappointed with the lack of wardrobe provision and wondered how Sebastian would manage with nowhere to put his clothes.

The other guests were far less troublesome, particularly the two elderly ladies who were sisters. They took everything in their stride and won the hearts of all the staff with their smiling faces and their *not wanting to be a trouble* attitude. They were delighted with their up-graded cabin and pronounced it most comfortable.

The four ladies travelling together were all enthusiastic and immediately set about having a fun-time. They were sharing in pairs and had their two cabins next to each other. They pressed the service bell and began joking with the young male attendant who answered. Susan, the youngest, began flirting dreadfully with the poor young man who blushed but took it in good part, even though he was squirming. She then moved onto the seasoned male staff in the lobby, who laughed good-naturedly and took it all in their stride.

Bob and Diane were shown into their cabin in the *premier* section of the cruiser. Bob raised an eyebrow when he observed that Diane had upgraded them to one of the best cabins but he made no objection and was very pleased with the comfort and the lovely view. The cabin had large French windows and there was a small balcony outside. Immediately, he saw himself relaxing with a glass of excellent wine in the evenings. He beamed from ear to ear and couldn't wait to try it out. Diane relaxed. Knowing how hard it was to get Bob to do anything, she felt thankful that for once, she had got it right.

Polly and Pete had been shown into their cabin. To the surprise of the staff and later, the other guests, it seemed that they were in one of the best cabins. Polly exclaimed in delight when the door was first opened.

'This is alright, nice Pete. Look at them big windows! 'Ere Pete, we can lie in bed and look out and see the scenery and all that going by.'

'This be alright Pol, yea? Can't grumble at this, can we?'

Melissa was pleasantly surprised by their reaction. Having to show these odd people to their cabin had mistakenly been perceived by her as the *short straw*. They might be a bit odd but they were much easier to please than some of the snootier guests staying in similar rooms. As Polly opened the shower door and various cupboards, she exclaimed in wonder and when the convertible bunk beds were demonstrated, she was almost over-awed. Melissa left them to unpack with smiles on both their faces.

Elaine and David had been shown into a second class cabin. It was the same size as the more expensive accommodation but it didn't have French windows or a balcony.

'Tight sods,' she muttered under her breath and thought - so much for having it paid.

'Did you say something?' David enquired.

'A bit tight for two,' she improvised.

'No it's fine. Plenty of room - unless you've brought your usual overload of clothes?'

Diane smiled and began to unpack her case. Already she'd formed some opinions of the other holidaymakers, now she had to do a bit of snooping on the staff but David must not suspect. He would be livid if he thought she was working; all the way there he'd been stressing the importance of the two of them having time to relax.

Dinner was to be in about two hours' time but firstly Melissa had called a *'Welcome Meeting'* which meant that guests had only time to quickly unpack and freshen up before heading to the bar area where a watered-down concoction of orange juice and cheap wine with bits of fruit floating in it, was being offered to everyone on entry.

Bob took instant exception to the poor quality drink, he took one sip and grimaced.

'What on earth do you call this?' he spluttered at the Hungarian waiter holding the tray. Irony was wasted on the young man and he smilingly answered with a noticeably strong accent,

'This is called a *cocks-tail.*'

'More of a *cock-up*,' Bob replied scathingly before remembering his surroundings.

He was so incensed that he abruptly replaced the wine glass back on the tray and walked on. He would have something to say about this later. The wine at dinner had better be a darn sight classier than that or else. Diane also sipped the offered drink and pulled a face. A connoisseur she was not but anyone with half a palette could tell that this was poor quality.

Unfortunately for the waiter, it was Felicity who glided in next. With a majestic sweep of her hand, she removed a glass of the liquid, moved to a centre front seat and then sipped. All hell broke loose.

'What is this vile mixture?' This was said in an imperious stage voice, trained to carry across a room, and it did. The waiter's face reddened. Antonio, the hotel services manager, crossed the room and quickly guided the young man away. Out of sight, he sipped one of the drinks and was horrified.

'What is this supposed to be? Where is the sparkling wine you were supposed to serve?'

The young man paled.

'It did not come so we mix up a drink like a cocks-tail.'

Antonio raised his eyes to heaven.

'If there is a problem like this, you speak to me; do *not* use your own ideas. The guests are upset. We shall have to serve them some free expensive wine now and the cost can come out of your wages.'

71

Antonio was not usually so unkind but he'd had a very bad day. He was struggling with problems of his own and did not need further upsets of any kind. He was, at that moment, finding life very stressful.

Bob, however, was delighted when it was announced a few moments later, that there had been an error and Antonio was coming round to all the guests to personally serve them with the sort of quality wine they could expect on this cruise. It saved the day but it made a very sulky waiter.

Priscilla sailed into the bar area several minutes later. She was annoyed to discover that the meeting had already started. She marched into the room with a grim expression on her face, looking for a seat in a place of prominence. Lillian trailed behind; she'd failed miserably in her attempt to persuade Priscilla to hurry to be in time for the start of the proceedings. People politely ignored their lateness but the ever-helpful waiter tried to usher Priscilla to a seat at the back; Priscilla *never* sat at the back. Ignoring the waiter, she caused a disturbance by marching forward towards an empty seat at the side of the front row before catching sight of the defunct tray of drinks which had been placed out of the way. She made another deliberate disturbance by walking between Melissa and the first row of chairs; she was incensed that she had not been offered a drink. In full view of everyone, she helped herself to one of the rejected cocktails. The poor waiter tried again to intercept her but was met with such a glare that he backed away. Lillian, who had tip-toed along the side aisle to an adjacent seat, had noticed that everyone else was drinking a different drink and she wondered if all was in order but when she tried to whisper to Priscilla, she was hushed up with another impatient glare.

Melissa began to tell everyone about the trip. There were several excursions, she told them, and each one would be amazing and interesting. She went through the usual *tried and tested* lecture to tempt the audience. Then she mentioned the entertainment for the next evening, a cabaret, and soon she was in full flow about the delights to come but unbeknown to her, not many people were listening because Priscilla had now become the object of everyone's attention. It had not gone unnoticed that she'd collected the wrong drink and all around the room, everyone waited for her reaction – they were disappointed. Priscilla took a sip of her drink, avoided gagging and pretended to like it. This was not because she wanted to avoid a fuss but because she thought it was a sophisticated cocktail and she wasn't going to admit to anyone that she was not used to such drinks which, of course, must be an acquired taste. With her nose in the air and a condescending look on her face, to the fascination of the whole room, she continued to sip the drink.

If she noticed any extra stares, she assumed it must be because of her attention to detail. She had arrived with an immaculate coiffure and wearing a new outfit. Her smart appearance was the reason for her lateness. She'd heard that there was another person on board, from the theatre or somewhere, who fancied herself as a fashion leader or something ridiculous like that. Priscilla would *not* be eclipsed, oh no, *she* was a leader in everything and everyone would soon comprehend this. She began to bask in the attention she was receiving while Lillian, having been offered the correct drink and a whispered explanation, squirmed but said nothing.

Priscilla sipped and preened and the whole room, fascinated, watched in disbelief as she emptied her glass.

I'll show these peasants, she thought, smugly congratulating herself, they can observe how a lady behaves in public.

Felicity Fanshawe, now clearly her rival for attention, was watching interestedly and was hard put to not burst out laughing but she knew that would never do - her expensive face-lift made such actions difficult and inadvisable. She draped herself over her chair in her best seductive pose and set out to reclaim all the attention for herself. As for Melissa, she might as well have saved her breath, she was talking about a cabaret that night but the majority of her guests were already enjoying the cabaret set out before them. Only Polly and Pete seemed not to get the joke; they sat gawping around the room.

Although Elaine had been sitting quietly throughout the meeting, she was observing everyone. Melissa intrigued her, there was something strange there - her enormous size for one thing. It was most unusual to find a person with such a non-athletic figure, working as a holiday rep. Then there was Antonio, the 'Hotel Services Manager', he frequently looked *uncomfortable* in an unguarded moment, as if something was on his mind. Some of the guests were *odd* too. Her intuition told her that there was definitely going to be scope here for her detecting skills.

David, however, was completely oblivious to her racing thoughts. He sat in the chair next to her, mostly looking out of the window at the scenery. It's great to have a carefree holiday, he thought.

Elaine had guessed correctly. On duty at the meeting, Antonio's, demeanour was that of a professional; he smiled ingratiatingly at all the guests but his mind was in turmoil. Gripped by personal problems, he racked his brains for the umpteenth time for a way out of the mess he'd got himself into. It seemed that he just *had* to do what was asked - there was no other way. He thought back over the events that had brought him into this sorry situation and shuddered. So far he'd got away with it all but the thought of exposure terrified him; he would never cope with that! Now here he was, having to take a huge risk. He calmed down a little and reflected. Was it such a risk? No-one should suspect him. The worry was, how long would he have to continue and would his luck hold? In a few days, the cruiser would be back in Budapest and the horrible memories would come flooding back to him. He'd run out of excuses as to why he didn't go ashore there anymore; he hated the sight of the place. He remembered all the events with a shudder; if only he hadn't…. He'd been so carefree before, so pleased with life.

Chapter 8

Antonio

It had been a typical evening on the Danube Drifter when the slightly wobbly and off-key tones of 'Nessun Dorma' had rung out from the shower room of cabin 5. Antonio Ravielli, had been singing at the top of his voice. Though a typical Italian, his heritage did not include a singing voice. The occupants of the next cabin had put their fingers in their ears.

On that evening, Antonio had rubbed himself dry, donned his clothes and splashed cologne about his person. He'd stared in the mirror and then smiled. Looking at his reflection was one of his favourite pastimes; he liked to remind himself how lucky he was to be so handsome. Antonio was a pleasant person, full of smiles and cheer but he possessed a huge ego with a vanity to match. There was no doubt that he was very handsome. The older ladies often informed him that he resembled Rossano Brazzi in his heyday.

Being the 'Hotel Services Manager', his position was exalted enough for him not to have to share a cabin; he was grateful for the indulgence and so were the other more musically attuned staff. Ablutions completed, he'd preened as he'd fixed his white cap on his head at a jaunty angle. As the guests were out on an evening excursion, Antonio was permitted to leave the cruiser and head into the town for some free time; he meant to do just that.

With this kind of outward appearance, it would have been easy for him to have been a *ladies' man*; he certainly had no difficulty in gaining female attention. However, the simple truth was that he was not that interested in women as sexual conquests, he just liked to be admired by them. On occasion, this caused a difficult situation when an all too eager lady tried to develop a more intimate relationship with him.

In many ways, he was a man of simple pleasures; happily married to an Italian lady, he was the proud father of four children, all of whom he adored nearly as much as himself. It should have been an idyllic existence. His background and slightly unusual history all pointed towards a happy ending.

He was born in Lombardy, in a small town near Milan. His maternal grandparents owned an advantageously positioned hostelry. Tourists travelling to Milan would often stay there to avoid the exorbitant charges of a city hotel. His grandfather, Signor Angelinetti, had prospered because his *pensione,* being rather above average, had been upgraded to an *albergo* - a hotel. With business doing well, his grandfather's sole concern in life had been his only child.

Mathilde was twenty-five, plain and had no marriage prospects on the horizon. Signor Angelinetti wanted grandchildren.

Salvation came in the person of Silvio Ravielli. The dashing young man arrived at the *albergo* and booked a room for several weeks. Mathilde was immediately interested. This man was different; he was not just incredibly handsome, he was talented, an opera star no less. Mathilde fell in love.

However, when the hotel bill was consistently unpaid, Signor Angelinetti did a little checking up and discovered that the man was indeed an opera singer but in the chorus, he was not the big star he pretended to be. He also discovered that the man had quite a few debts and if he continued down his present path, he would find himself in a lot of trouble *and* his career with the opera would end ignominiously. He decided to have a quiet word with this opera singer; he would offer him a proposition.

Several weeks later, Signor Angelinetti announced the engagement of his only daughter Mathilde to Silvio Ravielli. Mathilde, totally unaware of events behind the scenes, having been swept off her feet, became a self-delusional blushing fiancée and was convinced that she had *hooked* her man. After making it clear that he had to continue with his career which, unfortunately, would take him away from home for a lot of the time, Silvio, on considering the advantages of a rich wife who would eventually inherit a profitable business, became resigned to his fate. He did promise himself though, that he would try to avoid the Milan opera as much as possible.

However, there would be no escaping the honeymoon. Pulling himself together, he decided that things were not *so* bad, her body was passable and he didn't need to look at her face more than was necessary. If he had to have a wife, he might as well have a rich one and anyway, like all good Catholic men, he would like to have a son to follow in his footsteps and - the marriage would provide a ready-made bolt hole in times of difficulty.

The marriage went ahead and everybody was pleased when in due course, Mathilde announced her pregnancy. In 1970 a son, Antonio, was born.

It was immediately obvious that Antonio took after his father with his charm and looks. His large brown eyes melted hearts from the cradle and his mother and grandfather doted on him. There was a problem though. In her sheltered life, Mathilde had no idea how to bring up a boy; there was no concept of rough games or muddy clothes and when the time came for her darling to go to school, Mathilde was not at all happy. She had guarded him and kept him at home for as long as she could; she was worried about him mixing with unsuitable and rough boys. She began to wonder if she could acquire a permanent tutor for him. However, both her father and Silvio protested and for once she was overridden. Her father knew that if Antonio was to become a grandson to be proud of, he needed a good all-round education and he needed to find his place in the world. Silvio was delighted to side with his father-in-law.

Despite his mother's best attempts at sabotage, Antonio did well at school. Mathilde was alarmed to hear that he was playing dangerous team games and fearing that he might suffer an injury, wanted to put a stop to it but her father was adamant. Antonio was a *boy* and in a few years would become a man, he *must* take part in everything that came his way and furthermore, he must *excel* but there did turn out to be one exception. On hearing that Antonio's father was an opera singer, the school was delighted and immediately put him forward for music classes and the school choir but they quickly regretted this when they discovered that music notation on the page was nothing but a range of squiggles to him and as for singing, he was tone-deaf. Musically, he did not follow in his father's footsteps at all. He had acquired his father's looks but his mother's musical ability.

The young Antonio grew up into a likable young man. He was teased for one particular habit but in a good-natured sort of way which he accepted without rancour. He just couldn't stop admiring himself in the mirror and all his friends knew it.

As his family had a history of working in the hospitality industry, it seemed an obvious choice for him to follow suit and so after a blameless school career, he trained in hotel management.

A few years later he surprised himself by falling in love with a beautiful local girl who even managed to placate his mother who would normally have taken exception to any girl who might have eclipsed her in her son's eyes. A sensible girl, who cared about him, was just what he needed. Claudia understood him, laughed at his conceit but made very sure that *her* position in his life was unassailable. With a mother like his, this could have been a formidable task but Claudia was clever; his mother was praised for her wonderful son and on her ability as a parent and soon the silly Mathilde was *putty in her hands.*

Claudia's parents were quite happy with the match; a decent young man with a future inheritance was most acceptable to the strict Catholic and moral parents. Indeed, it was Antonio's spotless reputation that made him acceptable to Claudia; one hint of immoral behaviour and that would have been the end. She didn't mind the silly girls who made sheep's eyes at him, she was secure in her relationship but just in case, she made it very clear to Antonio, that the one thing she would never forgive, was infidelity and scandal. Antonio assured her that would never happen and he meant it. They were married in the local church.

Claudia gradually weaned her husband away from her mother-in-law and somehow, Mathilde was not quite sure how it had happened, her son no longer sought her advice or consulted her before any decisions were made. He relied more and more on his astute wife and went from success to success including the production of a beautiful family of four children. Life was perfect.

The ambitious young man worked for some years in the hotel industry; he was popular and steadily gained promotion. With his wife's encouragement, he was working towards obtaining one of the top situations with a hotel chain but when he applied to be considered for the position, he *hit a brick wall.*

'To gain respect from your workforce and to impress the Board, you need to have had a much wider *all-round* experience,' he was told. 'We need evidence of organisational and leadership skills in a variety of other, perhaps more challenging, circumstances.'

The interviewer could see the slight perplexity showing on Antonio's face.

'Look here, you are positively top management material but you do need to gain at least *some* other kind of experience. Have you ever thought of applying to work on a cruise liner? Even a river cruise line would help.'

Disappointed, Antonio went home to discuss the problem with his wife. She was very decisive.

'You will have to look for such a position, Antonio. It will mean some separation from us but we will cope. You must succeed in your work for all of us.'

In truth, Antonio was not a good sailor and he didn't like the idea of being at sea but a river cruiser? He decided that would be acceptable and it would be easier to get home fairly frequently. He saw an advertisement for a 'Hotel Manager' on a river cruise line, applied and was appointed. The wages were not an improvement but the experience would add to his career prospects; he decided it was worth it.

The company operated two fairly large river cruisers and employed a team of men including two senior managers who usually worked on a three-week shift without a break and then went home on leave. Employed as one of the senior managers he could fly home every three weeks to see his wife and family.

Antonio found the work easy but every time he went home on leave, he found it increasingly difficult to return; he missed his family so much. In addition, Antonio knew the dangers of being attractive to women, his wife was his stability, but now he was on his own, he found it more and more of a problem to rebuff the *ever so keen* ladies on holiday. There were not many places on board that he could go in his free time without being pursued by someone so when he had some leisure time in port, he began to make his escape by visiting a local bar or restaurant.

On one of his visits to Budapest, he'd found a little local bar situated quite near to where the boat was docked and he'd been

81

sitting on a stool and day-dreaming when a voice nearby, ordering a drink, caught his attention. Was that an Italian accent? Catching the man's eye, he smiled and passed an idle comment to the fellow drinker who was delighted to meet a compatriot; they soon indulged in a cosy conversation.

The man in question was smartly dressed, clean-shaven with dark hair and brown eyes and from his clothes and demeanour, appeared to be some kind of a travelling salesman. After twenty minutes, he looked at his watch, announced that he must be off and thanked Antonio for the conversation. He was often here, perhaps they could meet again? It was so comfortable, wasn't it? Talking in one's own language was relaxing. A *bit of home* for a weary traveller. Antonio agreed with him. Yes, he'd certainly look out for him in the future.

It was four weeks later when Antonio was at the same destination and had wandered into the same bar. He was delighted to bump into his Italian compatriot again. This time they went to sit at a table and they swopped stories of Italy and home in a spirit of great camaraderie. It was hard to leave the family at home, wasn't it? His new friend agreed with him, Would Antonio like to see a photo of *his* wife and children? He loved his family and missed them so much when away. Antonio was sure that he'd met a kindred spirit and immediately produced his family photograph.

'You know what I miss the most?' the man confided. 'It's when I'm away for their birthdays or even when I have a birthday of my own away from home. This is going to happen soon. I think,' he paused and looked at the diary on his phone, 'Yes, in fact, it will be the next occasion I'm here. In four weeks it will be my birthday. Hey, *amico*, will you be here then? You could help me celebrate. That will make a change not to have to toast my advancing years completely alone.' He laughed at his own joke.

Antonio could only commiserate with him.

'I will be here if I can, my friend.'

Four weeks later saw Antonio in the usual bar at the usual time but of his new friend, there was no sign. Antonio waited an hour and then, somewhat dispirited, prepared to leave but was halted in his tracks because his friend, hot and sweating, hurried in the door.

'So sorry! I had an awkward customer today. Thank you for waiting.' Clearly flustered and perspiring uncomfortably the man perched on a bar stool for a few moments.

'It's no use,' he declared, 'I need to go back to shower and change my clothes. I can't sit here like this.' As he rose to leave he had an idea.

'Why don't you come back with me? My hotel is only around the corner and I'll order some champagne there to celebrate my birthday.' Antonio hesitated.

'Please allow me to do this by way of an apology for keeping you waiting?'

They wandered down the street and sure enough, the hotel was nearby. Antonio waited in a pleasant room while his new friend went into the bathroom. Room service promptly appeared with the champagne and glasses. On being encouraged to not wait for his friend, the cork soon popped, the liquid bubbled and Antonio expertly caught the champagne in a glass and began to drink. His friend appeared a few moments later and taking the now empty glass from Antonio, poured his guest another drink. Glass in hand, Antonio relaxed on the settee and sipped his drink.

Many hours later he opened his eyes. Where was he? It was not his cabin, it was unfamiliar as was the bed he was lying on; he felt cold. In shock he looked down, he was stark naked. In pure disbelief, the events of the evening came back to him. Now he was quite alone, his clothes were on a chair in the corner of the room and his shoes were next to them. Had he been robbed? His expensive watch was still on his wrist. He staggered over to his clothes; his wallet was still there and untouched. His glass of champagne was gone and so was the bottle and the other glass. He glanced back at his watch and reality kicked in. It was four 0'clock in the morning and the boat sailed at five. Forgetting all else, he threw his clothes on as fast as his fuddled brain would allow and hurtled out of the hotel, much to the consternation of the night porter who tried to speak to him. Racing through the streets, he arrived at the ship with ten minutes to spare. He had no idea what it all meant but soon he was to find out.

Chapter 9

All Aboard

After his disastrous hotel visit, Antonio had raced back to the cruiser without pausing for breath. On arrival, he'd found himself shaking. For a supposed man of the world, Antonio was still a little naive and he'd immediately concluded that it must have been a practical joke?

As days passed and nothing else happened, he began to completely relax. It *was* a joke, he reasoned, and in *extremely* poor taste. I shall certainly avoid that bar in the future. In a fool's paradise, he brushed the event from his mind and continued with his normal duties in a detached manner – until the new group of guests arrived - followed by the brown envelope.

The smiling girl behind the reception desk called out to him, 'Antonio, there is a big letter for you.'

As there were people of many nationalities working on the river cruiser and most of the guests tended to be English speaking, this was the universal language spoken on the boat but often the translations were not immediately understood. Antonio perceived *big letter* as a parcel. He assumed it was just stationery for his office so he was surprised to be handed a large brown envelope. Some sixth sense made him pause and take it to his cabin to open. He slit the envelope open and shook the contents onto his bed; the photographs tumbled out, one after the other - Antonio in the nude, Antonio with a girl on top of him, more and more appeared and then, worst of all in his eyes, photographs of him with a man *and* a woman and what they were doing made him turn beetroot coloured and then break out in a sweat. There was a typewritten note.

'Wait for instructions and tell no-one. You will do exactly as you are told or copies of these photographs will be sent to your wife, your employer and the newspapers.'

Antonio almost collapsed onto the bed. He remembered none of this. He studied the photographs – so clever! The man and the woman had their faces obscured at all times but his face was so clear. They had arranged his body so that it looked like he was willingly taking part. Even his closed eyes gave the impression of enjoyment not sleep. He was trapped and the knowledge hit him like a cold shower. He could do nothing but wait for instructions. He had too much to lose, he would have to comply; perhaps whatever might be asked of him would not be too difficult? Deluding himself, Antonio relaxed a little. He would just have to make the best of it, wouldn't he? He tried not to think of what he might be asked to do because refusal was not an option and judging by their methods, they were utterly ruthless.

Another member of staff also had concerns. Melissa knew how important it was to protect herself, consequently, she had to be extremely careful. Her official position was 'Senior Cruise Director' which gave her no real authority to delve into other areas but there was so much more that she needed to discover. A lot depended on it. She would start with the captain then the reception staff, the hotel services manager and the catering staff. She had to consider all of them and she knew that it wouldn't be easy, plus there was also her Hungarian assistant. She had no complaints about Vicktor, he was a sweet boy who worked very hard but he was still new to the work and not always confident; she needed to keep an eye on him in case he made any mistakes. Then, while she was checking all this, she mustn't forget to look after the passengers. Good grief, what a task I have she sighed.

Vicktor was aware of her intense scrutiny. He'd noticed that she seemed to check on him a lot and he nervously wondered why. Did she think that he didn't work hard enough? He resolved to double his efforts. He mustn't lose this job under any circumstances because his widowed mother and younger sister were dependant on him. His old grandad had somehow used a *contact* and begged a favour, to get him this position and had told him that he mustn't waste this chance because good employment was hard to come by. Vicktor must do everything in his power to give satisfaction. He should be careful and industrious but not be afraid of using his initiative. He must follow his old granddad's fine example of loyalty and dedication. He'd promised grandad that he would never let him down.

Melissa would have been alarmed to know that *she* was included in the group of people Elaine was looking into. Elaine had drawn up a list but found, to her dismay, that almost anyone could be the link she was looking for. She decided to analyse each one; her list would show the pros and cons of the likelihood of each one being involved. Compiling it required her to know something about each person's background so she would just have to become one of those nosey people you meet on holiday. People usually opened up, thinking they wouldn't see the person again so it wouldn't matter what was said. Anyone very reticent would go to the top of her list of suspects.

Priscilla was indulging in a similar activity, she was assessing the guests. There was no real reason for her interest other than snobbery. She gave herself the excuse that she liked to know who she was mixing with but really, she was just a nosy busybody.

Anna, the cabin attendant, was the fourth person who was *people watching*. She originated from Latvia and although she

87

felt content with her employment, which enabled her to regularly send money home to her family, she'd been very lonely in the past. However, the situation had changed when she'd met and became besotted with Boris, her Russian boyfriend. He was handsome and fun and told her that he cared about her *so* much. He had a very good job, he worked on a luxury yacht as a sort of personal assistant come bodyguard to the owner. After telling her how beautiful she was, he'd added, in a caressing voice, that he needed her help. Did she care about him enough? Would she help him? Of course she would, she'd told him, as her gaze melted into his dark brown eyes.

He'd mentioned that sometimes it was important to know what was happening on these river cruisers, she should keep her eyes and ears open for anything or anyone who seemed suspicious.

'What sort of thing would be suspicious?' she'd asked him?

'Anything at all that seems strange or out of place or anyone asking too many questions or acting in a peculiar manner. Just inform me.'

Blinded by her romantic vision, Anna didn't question further and instantly agreed to be his informant; she would tell him about anything out of the ordinary. Boris was satisfied, his boss would be pleased. He needed all the extra eyes he could get if the disquieting rumours bore any substance.

Dinner was at seven and on the first evening, the guests arrived in the dining room to find that they'd been allocated seating on a particular table which they would retain for the whole cruise. As there were eight ladies without a male escort, these guests had been grouped next to each other on two tables of four. The four women, who were on holiday together, had all been seated on one table, which pleased them immensely but it left the two sweet old ladies to sit with Priscilla and Lillian. Priscilla was annoyed. She'd hoped to *lord it* over dinner and somehow two decrepit old ladies and Lillian, who didn't count, were not a satisfactory audience. Lillian was unhappy, her outfit for dinner had been severely criticised by Priscilla and she'd found herself returning to her cabin to change into something, that in Priscilla's eyes, was more dignified and suitable for sitting down to dine. The two elderly ladies were sweetly dressed in lace blouses and full skirts which suited them admirably but it did not conform to Priscilla's idea of an outfit for dinner; she gave a sniff of disdain. She was elaborately over-dressed in a full-length chiffon gown with a row of pearls around her neck. Her new perm had glued her curls into tight rolls and her inexpert attempt at evening make-up did nothing to improve her image. Unaware that she might be a target for ridicule, she looked around the room in distaste at the lack of breeding shown by the other more casually attired diners.

The other guests were distributed around the room sitting in groups of four or eight. Bob and Diane were seated on a table for eight and when Bob was offered the *included* wine, he took one look at the label and asked for the wine list. He chose a very expensive wine, he'd been promising himself a treat all day. The waiter hurried to the wine store to produce the required bottle. Bob leaned back in his chair as the waiter poured a sample for him to taste and a moment later Bob was rolling it around his tongue - it was superb. The waiter filled Diane's glass and then Bob's while the others on the table just drank the free *table* wine. There were two places opposite them still unoccupied but to Bob's disgust, the latecomers turned out to be Pete and Polly.

'Good this, yea?' was Pete's opening remark as he clumsily plonked himself down on the opposite chair; Bob smiled a grimace and grunted an agreement before turning to talk to a pleasant man and his wife, who were seated across the table to his right. Diane had begun the conversation and he'd looked across to join in. Bob was relieved to find an articulate and educated man in the group; what a joy to have a decent dinner companion, he thought, and promptly gave the man his full attention. He would do his best to avoid the two in front of him who were still making inane comments. The soup arrived and Bob found himself hugely irritated by Pete constantly remarking,

'This be good, yea? Three meals a day, every day! S'good yea?'

He was, however, not just irritated but incandescent with rage when he went to pour himself another glass of wine. Bob stared in disbelief at the empty bottle having discovered that while he was engaged in conversation with the man on his right, Pete had helped himself to Bob's wine. Assuming it was the table wine, he'd filled two large water tumblers for himself and Polly. Both were in the act of sipping their drinks.

Bob could hardly contain himself when he picked up and stared at the empty bottle and Pete cheerfully said,

'Did you want a drop more mate? There's some in the bottle down the end,' and then called out, 'Pass the bottle mate, there's a thirsty geezer up 'ere.' Bob knew that if he said anything there would be an unpleasant and embarrassing scene so, with enormous difficulty and iron self-control, he remained silent. Later he would speak to the waiter about clearly marking his bottle.

Felicity Fanshawe was in her element holding court. She had two quite personable men either side of her and poor Sebastian, sitting opposite, was being completely ignored. Then the captain strolled through the dining room and Felicity instantly called out to him in theatrical tones that no-one could avoid hearing. The captain, surprised but ever polite, turned around and walked over with a sinking heart, he recognised the lady who thought he was a porter.

'Oh Captain,' she cooed, 'I wanted to apologise to you. Silly me, how could I not have noticed who you are, with all that lovely gold braid? Silly, silly little me. You know my eyes were quite misted up with fatigue (she would never admit that she needed spectacles) so I didn't realise. Can you forgive little me?'

The Dutch captain, gallant and polite as ever, assured her that he had not taken offence and that it was his pleasure to assist such a lovely lady. Felicity drooled at such an answer, nothing could have pleased her more.

Sebastian was becoming bored and just a little irritated. For all the notice being taken of him, he might as well not have been there; this was happening far too often. He looked around the room and at once spotted and heard, Priscilla spouting all kinds of nonsense to her captive audience. The two elderly ladies sitting at her table were both smiling, it seemed to wash over them. Priscilla had also noticed this and had written them off as cretins, probably suffering from dementia, who were unable to understand an intelligent conversation, or in her case not a conversation but an ill-informed lecture. Lillian, however, was looking miserable and from time to time, glanced wistfully at the table where the four friends were laughing, joking and flirting shamelessly with the young male waiter. Sebastian felt so sorry for her, her case was worse than his own. He caught her eye and smiled and she smiled back before hurriedly averting her eyes in case Priscilla saw her.

Elaine, seated at another table, used the opportunity to look around the room. Her superiors had given her a little more information but it was still very sparse. It seemed that there was a very successful international crime syndicate operating in the area with a definite link to the UK. A tip-off had advised that there might be a connection with touristic river journeys on the rivers Rhine and Danube. Suspicion had fallen on the 'Danube Drifter'; it was suspected of smuggling goods of high value, probably diamonds. The boat was well placed to be involved in something like this because she crossed the border of several countries regularly. The probable source of the diamonds would be 'The Hague' but that was as much as anyone could conjecture. This syndicate was extremely sophisticated and left no clues. One name kept coming up though - Ronaldo Marconi, a wanted man that no-one could find. Marconi could well be at the head of such an organisation. Elaine was instructed to carefully observe as many people on board as she possibly could. Anyone could be involved.

She noticed the captain passing through the dining room, he was Dutch; could she read anything into that? The waiter was Hungarian, the chef was Austrian and other staff came from a variety of countries. No, she was clutching at straws.

She was annoyed to find that guests had been asked to retain the same seats for all meals. She'd planned to circulate by changing seats each mealtime, as wine usually loosened tongues and snippets of gossip could easily be gleaned without suspicion. Should David have commented on the frequent change of place, she had her reason prepared, she would simply have said that they were going to be sociable and talk to lots of other guests; it was good manners to do so, wasn't it? Well now, she would just have to manage by observing from a distance and trying to socialise at other times. She glanced at Felicity but discounted her immediately, she was too high-profile and that awful woman Priscilla was another to dismiss; people who engaged in criminal activities did not draw attention to themselves as she did.

Elaine mentally reviewed all the passengers she'd met but none of them seemed likely. She hadn't encountered all the staff yet; the fact that they were here all the time made them more likely to be involved but then, they were tied to the restrictions of their work. To be involved in crime, you needed a certain amount of flexible time. Then suddenly an idea struck her – the coach driver! What a perfect cover! He travelled back and forth all the time. If anyone was up to anything, it could be him. He became number one on her list of suspects.

David had enjoyed his meal and was now feeling replete. He swapped stories with a few people sitting at his table and at last, felt himself entering the relaxed state that a holiday engenders. He glanced at Elaine, she was *not* relaxed and, if he didn't know that it was impossible, he would have said by her facial expression, that she was *working*. A modicum of suspicion entered his brain but just in time Elaine realised and retrieved the situation by telling him how tired she felt and how a good night's sleep would set her to rights. David was satisfied. Elaine was relieved and resolved to be more circumspect in the future.

Back at Priscilla's table, Lillian was also feeling tired, sick and tired, of the sound of Priscilla's voice droning on and on.
'I am so sorry Priscilla,' she interjected suddenly, 'but I'm afraid that I have a headache, it must be the tiring journey. Would you please excuse me?'
'You really are very feeble, Lillian. Very well, we will excuse your bad manners, won't we ladies?'
The two elderly ladies, Minnie and Lavinia, realising that they were being addressed, smiled and nodded vaguely. Priscilla almost screamed. She was surrounded by idiots. Lillian rose from the table and left the room. She didn't want to sit in her cabin by herself so she went up onto the deck where, at the stern of the boat, she found a small secluded area with seating. She sat down and closed her eyes but five minutes later she was awakened by a male voice saying,
'Do you mind if I sit here?' It was another escapee, Sebastian. Felicity was having such an entertaining time that she hadn't even noticed that he'd left.
'N – not at all,' stuttered Lillian and found herself blushing. Luckily the darkness hid her confusion.

Back in the dining room, Priscilla rose noisily from the table and then, in an attempt to draw attention to herself, proceeded to walk in a stately fashion towards the door where she paused and looked fixedly at the nearby waiter who, missing his cue, politely smiled at her and said, 'Good evening'. Priscilla glared at him and looked pointedly back at the door then back at the waiter. Flushing he hurried to open the door for her. She swept through without a backward glance or a *thank you*. Fortunately, there were no other Hungarian nationals nearby who could translate the words muttered under his breath.

The two elderly ladies also prepared to leave.

'OK, I think it's safe now dear, we can switch our hearing aids back on.'

Chapter 10

Susan

Later that evening, the group of four ladies were sitting in the lounge and swapping stories. It was Susan's turn to speak.

'Why did I come to England? Didn't I ever tell you? Well, my mother is English and I wanted to see something of her country. I liked it here so I decided to remain.'

There was a lot more to it, Susan reminded herself, but all ancient history now so it's best not to discuss it. With that, Susan changed the subject but the question had stirred up memories and she couldn't help reflecting on the past.

Susan had been born in New York in 1970. Her English mother was very beautiful but rather empty-headed and was totally under the dominance of Roberto, her American husband. A complete autocrat, he ran the household with a rod of iron and his word was law. There was plenty of money in the family and Susan and her older sister Gina, never went without anything, in fact to all intents and purposes, they lived in the lap of luxury. Susan grew up being in awe of her father but unlike her mother and sister, she was not afraid of him.

He'd met her mother in Hastings in 1965. Being of Italian descent, he'd first decided to visit 'The Old Country' and while he was touring, he widened his travel experience to see something of the place in England where his father had been stationed as a GI during the war. He'd wandered into a dance hall and spotted the most beautiful girl he'd ever seen. This was typical of Roberto, he saw something, he wanted something, he *got* something. Unfortunately, he saw this lovely girl as more of an object than a person; her intellect or personality didn't come into the equation. On her part, this dashing Italian American, the stuff dreams were made of, came into her life, flashing oodles of cash and making it plain that he wanted her. For a girl from a very ordinary family with extremely modest means, this man was hard to resist. The fact that he had honourable intentions swayed her similarly overawed parents and almost before she knew it, she was married and on her way to the USA.

Life settled quickly into a predictable pattern and Carol found that she had plenty of money but little freedom of choice. After a few initial sulks, she decided that perhaps she was not so badly done by after all. Although her husband dominated her, he never offered her violence and there was no doubt that the family seemed very important and rich and she would never have to worry about money. All the women in the extended family, including her mother-in-law, seemed to have a similar existence. Not being particularly bright or having any intellectual leanings, she accepted her lot and ceased to question anything. Gina was born a year later and Roberto named her after his mother but when a second daughter followed five years later, Carol was allowed to choose her name; she decided to use her own middle name of 'Susan'. To Roberto's disappointment, no sons appeared and after Susan, no more children. As a good Catholic, he had to accept that it was God's will but his wife, a reluctant Catholic, had a more scientific approach and used the contraceptive pill. She had slipped up once and produced Susan but she didn't mean to lose her perfect figure by having lots of children. It was the only time she disobeyed her husband; her vanity was more important than her fear so she found a discreet source and kept pregnancy at bay.

Gina, being the older daughter, was the first to marry. To the fourteen-year-old Susan, this came as a big surprise. One minute there was this Italian man called Mario visiting, he was a distant cousin or something, then the next minute her nineteen-year-old sister was engaged to him. To the feisty Susan, he seemed a bit of a disappointment and she thought her sister could have done a lot better. The wedding following so quickly seemed even stranger but she soon began to get an inkling of what the whole thing was about. Her father had arranged it and Gina had meekly acquiesced to her father's choice.

Then, on one particular occasion when Susan had been suffering from a bad cold and she'd been kept indoors for a few days, something happened. Full of cold virus and the unpleasant side effects of runny nose and cough, her mother had dosed her with strong medicine and tucked her up on the settee in the spare day room. She had slept and then been woken by the sound of a voice in the next room. The door was slightly open and the voice carried. It was her father.

Talking on the telephone in his study, he'd not been aware that anyone was in the next room and could hear him. Drifting in and out of sleep, Susan was not particularly interested in the conversation until she heard her name mentioned and then she listened intently as she registered surprise and disbelief.

'Yes, one married and one to go but my other little gal, Susan, is far too young yet. ...... Yea, I do have someone in mind for her but there's plenty of time. ..... In the meantime, Mario will join the firm; yea, family is real important........ Who for Susan? Oh probably Giovani, you know my second cousin's boy.'

Susan was dumbfounded, did that conversation mean what she thought it meant? No, it couldn't, could it? Surely she'd misunderstood. However, as nothing was ever said and she never heard any more, she gradually forgot all about it.

A couple of years later, therefore, it came as an unwelcome shock when Susan, the 'A' student, full of excitement at having been predicted really good school grades and with details of colleges to apply for, came home from school excitedly and found that her father seemed surprised at her enthusiasm and further informed her that a college education would be a waste of time. What would a good Catholic wife need a college education for? Susan suddenly understood that she had to fight for the outcome of the rest of her life. Unlike her sister, she *was* intelligent, her father's daughter no less, and she knew that downright disobedience would get her nowhere, she had to be cunning.

Using every ounce of her wits, she went to work on her father, hinting that *her* success in education, would be attributed to *his* skill as a parent. She buttered his ego, telling him that she was sure that her brains came from him and she would prefer, if possible, to explore a little more in life before she settled down to make some man a good wife. Even though he'd never mentioned his plan to marry her to an Italian relative she'd recalled that past phone call and had been further alarmed when he'd casually mentioned that a relative from Italy, might be coming to stay with them soon. By not defying him but by using every bit of guile she had, she seemed to be successful. She was relieved to once again overhear him on the phone telling someone that there was plenty of time and as a *modern parent*, he was inclined to indulge his daughter a little first.

The second part of her plan was the hardest and she wasn't sure if she could pull it off but by now she was adamant that she was having no arranged marriage. She understood that her father was important and influential and it wasn't just the women who were afraid of him because armed guards now featured in all their lives. She knew for certain that this scheme was her only chance to have a life, a life of her own. It had to work.

Little by little she talked him into letting her go to England to college. She told him how she longed to be a wonderful mother to fine sons and as mothers had so much to do with bringing up sons, wouldn't a well-educated mother be a good idea for fine sons? Her dear father had visited England, she would love to do what her wonderful father had done. It was so safe in England, she would be fine. She was so subtle that gradually Roberto began to think that it was his own suggestion; having been surrounded all his life by empty-headed women, he had no idea he was being played like an old violin. It was beyond his understanding and tradition that a female could be so clever, so he assumed that the idea must have been his own; vanity was something he had plenty of.

It was decided; Roberto would start a new tradition and allow his intelligent daughter, who obviously took after her father, to finish her education in England. Once the idea took hold he was very involved in the planning and happily agreed to pay the considerable fees. In quite a short time it was all arranged and Susan was relieved to hear her father talking openly to family members and saying that Susan could easily wait a year or two to get married and a British University education would raise the profile and standing of his family. Any dissenters knew better to argue so now it was thought a great idea by everyone.

What her father didn't know was that Susan had no intention of returning to the USA. He'd provided her with considerable funds but she meant to be very economical with these, living as frugally as she could. She went to England on a study visa but she had a *card up her sleeve*, she had dual nationality, a fact her father had overlooked, and she meant to apply for a British passport so that she had a legal right to stay there - indefinitely. She would worry about the rest much later - after she'd gained her degree.

While at university, she thought it wise to distance herself as much as possible from her American family so although she wrote regularly, she was very vague with information and always found excuses, such as work experience, to prevent her from going home in the holidays. At the course completion, she could make no more excuses so she simply disappeared but now with a legal British identity. It didn't mean that no-one would search for her but at least she knew that her father couldn't come to England.

Before she'd left the USA, Carol had imparted a piece of useful information to her daughter. Her mother had sulked that she would have liked to have visited Susan while she was in England but Roberto would not let her go alone. Fighting rising panic at the prospect of her parents calling to visit her while she was there and discovering her plan, relief followed when her mother informed her that Roberto was unable to visit England. It was some petty thing or other from years ago, she was told. There was still an arrest warrant out for him in the British Isles but her father had pulled some strings and stopped any ideas of extradition. Her mother hadn't a clue why he was wanted. Susan was puzzled by this but could only be grateful.

Sometime later, Susan was happily living in an apartment and holding down a responsible job in an office. She'd braved the towering rage of her father by writing to him, she felt she owed him that. She'd told him that she was aware of his plans for her and that she had no intention of complying with them. She thanked him for his care of her and also for her education and told him that she was very like him, independent, and she wished to make her own way in the world. She was not ready to be merely a wife and mother; she needed to use her brains and she needed to be able to choose her partner in life.

She'd hoped that if she explained things in detail, he might understand but she should have known better. Roberto was unused to being crossed and never by a female. She'd been ordered home immediately and told that Giovani was waiting for his bride.

Just in case someone had been sent to find her, after graduation, Susan had taken the precaution of moving addresses quickly. She moved right away from the university town and headed for London. She'd already changed her name by deed poll. She now felt fairly safe. She hoped that maybe, in a few years, her father might calm down and then she could try to make contact with her family again.

With a good education behind her, she'd had little difficulty in finding work and was soon happily employed. When the handsome and charming Nigel became her boyfriend and then her fiancé, she was still nervous about her family so she told him that there was a family estrangement and her parents were in the USA but would not come to their wedding. She pretended that she had invited them but they had refused to come.

Her *parents-in-law-to-be* were slightly offended by the lack of relations on her side of the church but she made up for it by inviting lots of the many friends she had made at university and work. Susan married and settled down to what she thought was an equal partnership.

However, it soon became apparent to Susan that she had swapped one kind of pressure for another, Nigel wanted children but Susan wanted a career. The timing of having a family was put on hold, reluctantly by Nigel and his upper-class mother who, seeing no competition from her daughter-in-law's mother, had re-assumed a dominant role in her son's life and thought she had the right to dictate how the young couple should manage their affairs. Susan, who was used to strife in a family and fighting her corner, took most of it in her stride but wished she could detach her husband from his parents as easily as she had separated herself from her own.

She battled on until she was thirty-three when both her husband and mother-in-law began a concerted effort to force her to attempt to become a mother. Her husband continuously carried on about body clocks and wanting heirs and her mother-in-law tried to tell her that it was her duty.

Gradually Susan came to the conclusion that her reluctance to have children was not just because she'd fallen out of love with her husband, it was because she'd never truly been in love with him in the first place. Perhaps he'd just been a handsome face who'd arrived at an opportune moment? She still felt young and vibrant and a voice inside cried - romance, fun, moonlit dinners and beaches with golden sands; there were no maternal longings at all. Nigel, on the other hand, spent his days reading financial pages and talking stocks and shares and dynasties; he was becoming old before his time and very boring and she had no intention of becoming the same.

Decisive as ever, Susan made her plans. She had never been financially dependent on her husband. Much to her mother-in-law's interfering disapproval, she had always kept her finances separate and would not entertain a joint bank account. She also had savings of her own - a secret nest egg.

Matters came to a head one day when after another bout of pressure tactics, Susan informed her husband that she did not want children - ever. A furious row followed but somehow he would not end the marriage. He seemed to think that if he kept on nagging at her she would eventually give in. Susan played her trump card and told him a lot more about her father and that he was wanted by the British police; she was quite happy to spread the information around to some of his influential friends. Nigel and his parents were horrified. They had no desire to be linked to a criminal. Nigel left the marital home, returned to live with his parents and Susan sued for divorce on the grounds of desertion. Susan was delighted to be free and gain her half of the family finances. She didn't mention the secret nest egg.

After that, she avoided permanent relationships with men and remained single for several years. A group of ladies at her work became close friends and gradually her desire for a hedonistic lifestyle reduced as well. She didn't need a hectic social life anymore but she still relished company and friends, though somewhere, hidden inside, was the tiny voice that called for *just a little romance* before it was too late. Oh, what the heck, she thought, I'll flirt a bit and have a laugh but nothing serious. Look where men have got me in the past. So when she'd met the handsome Angelo she'd been on her guard but the sneaky little voice inside her kept announcing its presence and a wistful thought or two for some romance just wouldn't go away and after all, he *was* gorgeous!.

On an assignment for work, to meet and greet a client, she'd found herself sitting in a hotel bar next to a very handsome man. At first, she'd thought it might be her client so, with a very business-like but polite inquiry, she'd asked him if he might be the person she was sent to meet. Grinning, he'd admitted that he was not but said that he would be happy to meet her if she so wished; she could not be sure of the accent but it sounded Italian. Smiling, in spite of her attempt to keep everything on a correctly impersonal footing, she'd thanked him and just in case he'd received the wrong idea, she'd explained who she was waiting for. Her client, a slightly older man, had arrived a few moments later and Susan whisked him off in a taxi to the office.

A couple of days later, when collecting another client from the same hotel, Susan saw the handsome young man she'd spoken to before. This time he approached her and asked her if she would meet him for a drink. He was polite and charming and assured her that he was trustworthy. Something about the man appealed and before she'd realised what she was doing, she found herself hurriedly giving him her mobile number.

Susan met Angelo Bugatti the next day and after that, they were inseparable; it seemed to be love at first sight. Susan was convinced that she had, at last, found her soul-mate. They shared the same humour, they were not easily shocked and both of them came from wealthy backgrounds but had no snobbish pretentions; neither of them wished to discuss their families. They laughed, they had fun and they wined and dined and visited all sorts of places. Was it only three weeks ago they'd met? Susan, usually so wary, found it harder and harder to keep her normally *under control* heart from straying but somehow as no commitment was asked of her, it didn't matter. She began to count the minutes each day until they could meet.

Angelo had told her he was unmarried; he'd had girlfriends, of course, but he'd never, until he'd met her, found such a kindred spirit. She'd discreetly inspected his left hand, she could usually tell if a man had just quickly removed a ring, no - there was no tell-tale lighter band of skin. Susan's defences were down and her heart was so light that it could have flown away. She was madly in love.

However, Angelo was very worried, he knew he was getting involved too deeply and in such a short time. Was he mad? Yes, he was - but he couldn't help himself. He knew it would all end in tears but maybe, just maybe, there would be this lovely interlude. He was going to be strong, he would not seduce this woman, it was harder to end things after an affair; he would force himself to keep things light.

Susan was puzzled, a woman of the world she had half expected it at the start and certainly had expected a sexual encounter by now. She decided that he was waiting for a special moment. OK, that was fine by her, a bit of romance would be wonderful. She could wait. She waited - until one day he didn't arrive for their meeting and she never saw him or heard from him again. Her heart was broken but not her spirit. 'Oh well,' she sighed, 'it's the story of my life. I'm better off without men.' Soon her feisty spirit reasserted itself and she continued to flirt with any personable man she came across but from then on, she had no intention of getting involved in anything serious - ever.

Chapter 11

During the Holiday

The first full day on board promised to be enjoyable. Ambient temperatures with a gentle breeze made the day perfect for exploring. From the cruiser, the guests had all been taking in the first glimpses of the magical scenery in the Wachau valley; now it was time to get involved, to get their feet on the ground. A feeling of pleasant anticipation filled most of the passengers.

Arriving at the quaint little town of Melk, guests were invited to take part in an excursion to visit the Benedictine Abbey that could be seen majestically towering above the rooftops. For those who were not enthused by the idea of viewing abbeys, the little village below was charming and interesting with its display of fascinating buildings, wooden beams and whitewashed exteriors. A pleasant hour or two could be spent wandering along the cobbled streets and browsing into the little shops and cafes. Later, in the afternoon, they would all be cruising along the river to view the rest of the valley scenery in all its glory.

Minnie and Lavinia had wisely decided that the outings were not for them, they were going to rest quietly on the deck and enjoy the sunshine. When Susan spoke to them, saying that it was a shame that the local terrain was a bit tricky, otherwise, they might have enjoyed an outing, they replied that it didn't matter because they'd been on this holiday before - when they were *younger*. It was kind of her to worry but they'd be fine. The two ladies called for a cup of tea and they settled down in comfortable chairs with their books while the others went off with Melissa and Vicktor.

It was times like these when Melissa was really glad to have Vicktor's assistance; she really couldn't cope with the amount of exercise required. It was shocking really, most of the guests were about thirty years older than her but were much fitter. She usually managed to separate the guests into two groups, those who wanted the more energetic version of an outing and those who preferred a gentle stroll. She made sure that she was always with the latter group.

She knew this side of the work was too much for her and in normal circumstances, she wouldn't have undertaken anything that required so much physical effort but if she refused, she couldn't remain in this employment and then her *other* activity would be impossible. She wished that she'd been able to regain those brief years of self-control when she'd lost so much weight. It was hopeless, one look at the fabulous food offered and she was filling her plate. That morning she'd meant to have a small bowl of cereal for breakfast but somehow she'd found herself consuming egg, bacon, sausage and bread rolls.

Vicktor, young and very fit, was happily striding ahead; he always looked forward to the outdoor part of his work. He enjoyed the informality and interaction with the guests. He glanced over at Melissa. It was not lost on him that she always ensured that she was taking the *slower* group. He couldn't understand her at all. Why would such an unfit woman undertake this kind of work? She must be very well paid - that must be the reason. Well, if that was true, he wouldn't mind taking over her job. If she did much more of this, her position might be vacant a bit sooner than anyone thought. She was looking hot and bothered and the perspiration was running down her neck. She'll have a heart attack, he thought, she surely can't go on like this much longer. Melissa was thinking the same.

Felicity, wearing delicate silver sandals, a canary yellow flimsy sundress complete with a wispy shawl and topped with a large white sunhat, having taken one look at the hill plus the rough ground that she might have had to negotiate, decided that it was all too much; if she was not careful, she might start looking hot and *glowing* like that poor overweight lady. She insisted that Sebastian call her a taxi to take her to visit the Abbey. On discovering that there were none and even when assured that the coach would take them quite near to the building, she declined to go further. Felicity draped herself on a chair under a parasol in a nearby restaurant. She would prefer, she decided, to while away the time people-watching whilst sipping a cool drink.

In the meantime, Priscilla had startled everyone by appearing in what could only be described as an outfit from the 1930's or before. She wouldn't be seen dead in shorts or jeans but she knew that her ordinary day clothes and court shoes wouldn't do for energetic outings. Not wishing to be classed as *too old* for any strenuous activities and taking her tone from some very outdated photographs of royal shooting parties, she'd acquired, what she considered to be, a smart but practical country tweed outfit. She looked ridiculous. Once again Priscilla had provided the entertainment but assumed it was her superb dress sense and *class* that had drawn people's attention. Had she been told the truth, she would have dismissed the notion as nonsense and never even entertained the idea that it was ridicule and not admiration that fuelled the glances she received. Lillian in blue linen trousers with a simple white blouse, topped with a saucy sun hat, totally eclipsed her.

The rest of the guests, who didn't wish to visit the Abbey, wandered about the delightful village below. Pete and Polly were in flamboyant evidence; you could see them coming a mile away. Never one to dress quietly Pete's checked shirt was

107

so loud that it could have played a fanfare and Polly's orange trainers appeared to be luminous. Villagers, well used to visitors, usually took little notice but today they found entertainment they'd not had for years.

David told himself that he *was* having a good time but already he'd found himself fidgeting because he was so unused to lazy days. No that wasn't strictly true, he'd always enjoyed his leisure, it was like medicine you took to get better and then, happily medicated, you went back to real life. His normal life would soon resume, there would be another case waiting so why did he feel so unsettled? It was Elaine, wasn't it? She didn't seem relaxed at all. She was probably missing the cut and thrust of working too. What a pair of fools they were? He made a firm resolution - there would be a concerted effort to completely forget about work and he would make sure that Elaine followed the rule as well. He hoped that she'd told no-one of their professions - it was a bit like being a doctor, people seemed to think that you were always available for advice, even on holiday. He'd had people ask for free legal advice so many times and in all sorts of social situations and as for Elaine! In her case, it was even worse because her bosses expected her to always be on duty, no matter where she was and whatever she was doing. Well, this was going to be an exception – absolutely no work.

Wandering through the village, Bob and Diane stumbled across a small wine cellar and wandered inside. The room was full of barrels and they were invited to sample them. Reluctant but curious Bob tried one or two, they were ghastly. About to leave he shook his head and informed the proprietor, in his proficient German, that he preferred quality, he was a connoisseur. The proprietor asked him to wait, disappeared into the back and returned with a cobweb-covered bottle. Bob glanced at it and then looked intently at the label; if that was genuine, that was a very superior wine. There was some spirited bargaining and Bob decided to take a chance, money changed hands. This would have to travel back home with him, it was going nowhere near the dining table on the boat.

The groups arrived back on the cruiser in good time and were asked to please wait in the wood-panelled saloon for a short while because Melissa had some information for them. Some of the guests had already become acquainted with other holidaymakers and had formed little coteries; most were avoiding Polly, Pete, and Priscilla and by association, Lillian was also excluded. She was very upset, she could see that the rest of her holiday would be like this, then she lifted her eyes and met the twinkling orbs of Sebastian. He smiled, then gave a little sigh as he was being ignored again; Lillian felt that she'd found a kindred spirit and felt better.

Bob had encountered his previously met and preferred, dinner companion and the two men, together with their wives, sat down to chat. One of the wives had already spoken to Elaine, so when she and David entered the room, they were invited to join the group. As soon as Bob heard David's cultured tones, he relaxed. Thank goodness, he thought, there do seem to be a few intelligent people on this boat.

Melissa interrupted the proceedings to inform everybody of the next day's enormous treat – for those who had paid for it of course. There was a Vienna city tour in the morning and then in the afternoon a tour of the Schonbrunn Palace. After a short pause, she imparted some further information which produced a multitude of reactions. Fixing a huge smile to her face, she told everybody that the following evening was going to be a 'black-tie event' - wasn't that great?

'Right girls,' she cheerfully stressed, 'it's going to be *dressing-up time*! Get your sparklers ready, your silver and gold shoes and your fabulous evening gowns. Oh OK, we'll let you wear cocktail dresses if you prefer, but remember it's *Hollywood* night so glitz, glamour and sparkle for everyone.'

'I forgot my tiara,' one male *would-be* comedian called out. 'Now, now, gents. You know I'm talking to the ladies. You gentlemen will all arrive in your devastating evening jackets, black or white, and you'll all look like leading men in a Hollywood blockbuster.' Oh God, she thought, I must think up a better line, this is getting so tired and boring. With the smile still fixed firmly in position, she left the room.

Returning to her cabin, she sighed. More work to do, she thought as she sat down with her laptop. From her bag, she withdrew a memory stick, plugged it into the computer and began to study the lists of figures.

Antonio was also preparing to work. The guests were settled in now so it was time to do a little stock-taking. He walked into the office to collect the files and froze. Sitting on the top of a pile of mail was a plain brown envelope addressed to him.

As nobody was about, he grabbed the envelope and then work forgotten, he hurried back to his cabin, the only place where he could ensure privacy. It was the familiar writing. His heart plummeted, he'd received no previous instructions and had started to hope that it would all come to nothing; clearly, it had not.

Sitting in his cabin he read the worst possible news.

Caricon Hotel Budapest, 21, Budapest, 1012, Hungary, (near Buda Castle)
In Budapest, you will visit the hotel named above and ask for a delivered item addressed to yourself. Take your passport or identity card with you; without either document, you will not be able to collect this. Failure would bring immediate repercussions. You will hide this item in your belongings and pass it on at the end of this present cruise. You will be contacted later with further instructions.

Antonio sat on the bed with his head in his hands. When would this torment end? He would have been even more worried if he'd known that busy-body Priscilla, in the act of returning to her cabin, had seen him come out of the office with the envelope in his hand and worst of all, she'd seen the look on his face. She had, however, completely misunderstood the situation. She'd assumed that he was in trouble, well that assumption was correct, but she thought it was because he was not doing his job properly. If he *was* the Hotel Manager, as she had told them in reception yesterday, he really ought to be more meticulous in monitoring the work of the cabin staff; her cabin had not been cleaned when she'd wished.

'I really cannot be expected to fit in with *your* timetable. If I require my room attended to in the afternoon I expect to be able to call for attention and have immediate results,' she'd told them in no uncertain terms. Clearly, his superior was taking him to task by way of a written warning. Mind you he *is* a foreigner, she conceded, and may not understand the requirements of an English lady. It would be an act of charity to explain this to him, she magnanimously decided, I should not wish to be the reason for the man losing his position.

Deciding that it would be her Christian duty to inform the man herself, she walked down the lower stairs and past the sign stating *'Staff Only'* until she saw a cabin with the sign 'Hotel Manager' on the door. About to knock, she noticed that the door was slightly ajar; in his agitation, Antonio hadn't shut the door properly. She peered in, the shower room door was closed, the shower was running and there on the table was the note. Looking around and seeing no-one, nosy Priscilla nipped inside quickly and read the note; it was not at all what she had expected to read. Hearing the water stop, she hurried out of the room on tip-toes and returned to her cabin - but not before her prying had been observed.

Priscilla's thoughts raced, what could be the meaning of this? The man is clearly up to no good. I should report him but to whom? They are all foreigners here and probably all in league with each other. For once she used her brains. I'll say nothing for the present but I will report this to the British police on my return; someone there will know what to do.

Melissa's announcement had started several conversations. The two, elderly ladies, Lavinia and Minnie, were a little perturbed,

'This is something new. We've never had to do this before,' Minnie declared. 'I don't have an evening dress, do you dear?'

'No, of course not. No-one is going to mind us. We'll just dress as usual.'

Diane was looking pleased, she had packed a rather lovely gown in the hope of dressing up at least once and Bob grumblingly conceded that she was right to have made him bring a dinner suit.

Some guests looked concerned and others stated that they would just dress smartly and that would have to do. Felicity was delighted and so was Priscilla, both had brought suitable dresses, or so they thought. Lillian was worried, she didn't own an evening dress but she did have a pretty georgette dress, she thought that would be acceptable if she wore a gold necklace and earrings.

Pete and Polly appeared to have no idea as to what *'black tie'* meant. Pete commented out loud that he thought it was a strange idea and wasn't that for funerals? He then exclaimed that actually, he didn't have a tie of any kind but if it was that important, he should be able to buy one in a town the next day. Polly agreed and said it was lucky that she had her Pearly queen outfit with her; if they wanted her to glitter, that had loads of shiny beads.

The next day passed without incident. Arriving in the world heritage site of Vienna, with the weather bright and sunny, the travellers were keen to explore and all seemed to enthuse about the coming treats. Some looked for the famous riding school only to find that the wonderful Lipizzaner horses were not there but had moved to their summer quarters. Others wandered around the fascinating city, visiting little cafes and generally taking in the general ambiance. In the afternoon, they visited the Schonbrunn Palace with its stunning gardens. An air of pleasure and contentment pervaded the whole group.

It had been a delightful day but all too soon it was over and tired explorers returned to the boat to prepare for the evening activities. Anticipating a good evening, flagging bodies were restored after a reviving drink. Without exception, the guests left the various parts of the boat in good time to ensure that they wouldn't need to rush to get ready. Priscilla started very early. Having washed her hair, she planned to *set* her tight curls so that her hairstyle would be faultless. However, having overestimated her ability, she became aware that she could not arrange the back of her hair as she wished. Lillian had absented herself some half-hour before so hurriedly donning a headscarf, in case anyone should see her in her curlers, Priscilla marched down to Lillian's cabin to instruct Lillian to assist with the back of her permed hair. There was no answer to the imperious knock. Priscilla was furious.

'How thoughtless of her to be off somewhere when I require her services,' she muttered aloud and stormed back to her cabin to manage as best as she could.

In fact, Lillian had suddenly decided that she would enquire as to whether it might be possible to get her hair washed and styled and had been lucky to find that just one appointment in the cruiser's tiny salon was vacant. The stylist was very accomplished and she managed to talk Lillian into changing her look altogether; the severe pulled-back style, which did not suit her at all, was replaced with a soft shorter style which almost transformed her. She left the salon feeling more confident than she had in years.

Priscilla worked out her campaign. *Never be first if you want to make an entrance,* she recalled. I will arrive at the venue about five or ten minutes late and ensure that I walk right through the centre of the room so that everyone will notice me. I'll show that theatrical floozie that breeding always wins. She and everyone else will soon see who the *real* star is.

As good as her word she entered the room late and absolutely no-one even turned around; they were all drinking and chatting and couldn't have cared less that she had entered; they couldn't even be bothered to laugh at her dress sense.

Lillian crept in behind her looking delightful with her new hairstyle and soft georgette dress in direct contrast to the grey, old fashioned empire-line gown that Priscilla was wearing. The grey dress failed to conceal an over large bottom and protruding stomach despite the severe corsets Priscilla was wearing underneath. However, if anyone *was* noticed, it was Polly and Pete who'd both dressed in an amazing fashion. Pete had a cowboy-style black string tie around the collar of a billowing shirt, worn over shiny trousers with turn-ups. Polly had a jacket, skirt and cap covered in pearl buttons. They had entered totally unconcerned and as most people had already written them off as weird or eccentric, after a quick chuckle, they too were ignored.

Being ignored was annoying but would not rankle as much as what was to come. Priscilla was soon to learn a bitter lesson – never try to outperform a professional; never play a drama queen at her own game

About fifteen minutes into the pre-dinner meeting, Melissa picked up the microphone and asked for quiet – the timing was perfect. Everyone became silent and looked towards the stage

114

situated next to the double doors. It was then that Felicity made her dramatic entrance; the door *accidentally* slipped from her grasp and banged. All eyes looked in her direction and many gasped. An older woman she may have been but her figure was superb; *she* needed no corsets.

The silver lamé dress hung in graceful folds to the floor where spidery silver sandals adorned her feet, her hair was in a soft bobbed style and an elegant diamond tiara framed her face. She looked wonderful and she'd made the perfect entrance for a Hollywood evening.

Resting one hand on the door frame and with the other on her hip, while her gauze stole, carelessly arranged around one shoulder, trailed on the floor, she held a typically photographic pose till, dramatic as ever, the hand was removed from the door frame and extended towards the bemused Captain Van Beeke who was smiling at the performance. Ever gallant he walked across, took her hand and led her to a seat while the other guests burst into spontaneous applause at the impromptu drama played out before them.

Priscilla was so angry she was almost sick. There was nothing she could do to retrieve the situation so she took it out on Lillian all evening, starting by telling her that her new hairstyle made her look ridiculous. Lillian bore as much as she was able and then, pleading the familiar headache, she left the room. Once again she went up on deck and in the gentle darkness, she began to sob. A comforting voice spoke softly in her ear.

'Don't let her upset you like this.'

Hurriedly drying her eyes in confusion, Lillian could just make out the kind face of Sebastian in the gloom.

'You know you look pretty amazing tonight. I love your new hair-do. That old harridan is just jealous. Why do you let her bully you like that?'

115

'I don't know. Well, she's just always been there and I suppose I'm so used to doing what she says.'

'I bet she doesn't know you're up here talking to me. Let's go to the end of the deck, to the little outside bar area. I'm hiding too and it would be nice to think I'm not the only one who is playing truant.'

They went quietly to the end of the deck; Lillian was feeling mischievous and daring and suddenly knew that she was also having fun.

Chapter 12

Secrets

Priscilla was determined that by fair means or foul, she was going to get the better of that dreadful actress woman. She looked around for Lillian. Drat, the woman, she thought, where is she? She absentmindedly looked out of a window but could see little in the darkening gloom. There were some low lights outside for the convenience of guests who enjoyed the deck on the warm summer evenings. She opened her eyes very wide. Was that? Could that possibly be Lillian – with a *man*?

'What nonsense is this?' was her opening remark as Lillian re-entered the room. 'What were you thinking of? Fancy venturing outside on your own with a *man*!' Lillian's brief spell of cheer vanished immediately.

'I did *not* venture outside with anyone,' Lillian timidly replied. 'I just returned at the same time as he did.' Priscilla sniffed.

'You will be thought of as a *loose woman* if you behave like that.' Lillian found herself feeling angry rather than cowed but said nothing more.

A similar conversation was taking place across the other side of the lounge.

'Oh darling, where *have* you been?'

'Oh did you notice I was missing?'

'Naughty boy,' Felicity teased, 'I needed you and you weren't there.'

The rest of the evening passed in a buzz of conversation and music. The lone pianist did a wonderful job of singing and playing and most people, having imbibed freely, joined in the dancing; those who couldn't dance attempted to shuffle their feet in time to the music. Pete and Polly stole the show by asking for Rock'n Roll and then demonstrating how it should be danced. They gained a new following and this time for a positive reason.

It was traditional that the senior staff should be present for this special evening and Antonio, resplendent in a crisp white shirt and pressed uniform was no exception. He smiled and joked with the ladies, performed his duties as one of the hosts and appeared to be enjoying himself. Elaine, used to making judgments by people's expression and demeanour, was not so sure. She'd been watching him closely. She was jerked out of her observations by a voice in her ear,

'He's mine! You've got one. Don't be greedy.'

Susan, to whom she'd been chatting earlier, was standing behind her and laughing. Elaine laughed too but with wine dulling her senses a little, she was caught off guard and blurted out without thinking,

'It's my line of work you know. You often find yourself studying people for no good reason.'

'So what do you do?' asked Susan, now interested.

'Er ... Police.'

'Wow!' was the reply. 'Is that CID?'

Elaine was now cursing her thoughtlessness but nodded her head in reply.

'I'd better make sure I behave myself.'

She wandered off as David returned to Elaine's side.

'Did I hear you tell that woman that you were in the police?' he demanded, in a slightly louder voice than he should have used. He was about to remind her that they were on holiday and that they'd agreed that they wanted no reference to either of their professions.

Priscilla appeared as if from nowhere and sat herself down opposite them. In a similarly incautious tone, she immediately demanded to know if she had heard correctly because, if Elaine *was* a member of the British Police, she Priscilla, had some important information that would no doubt, be of interest to her. She was positive that criminal activities were being undertaken on this boat - it was serious enough to close down this holiday company. She'd discovered ....

Elaine, in eager anticipation of, at last, getting a glimmer of information, leaned forward in her seat and was about to reply when David cut in angrily.

'We are on *holiday*. My wife has no interest in any nefarious activities that may or may not be happening on this boat. If you have a complaint, take it to the proper authorities.'

Elaine could have screamed in frustration but she could say nothing because David believed that work had been left behind. He looked very angry and Priscilla, offended, stood up and walked away with her nose in the air.

'The cheek of the woman,' David began, 'how hard can it be to take a break from work?' Elaine smiled guiltily and agreed with him, deciding that she would have to find a moment the next day when she could speak to Priscilla privately. She knew she would now have to grovel a little to acquire the information which just might be the clue she was looking for.

Several other people heard the exchange between Priscilla and David and were curious enough to listen intently to the raised voices and the topic of conversation. Some people chatted about it to others so that within a short space of time, a lot of people were aware of the fact that Elaine was in the police and Priscilla had information concerning serious criminal activities happening on board. Some dismissed it as silly unfounded gossip which should be ignored but others were far more concerned. One was so interested that a decision was quickly made.

They were due to spend the next day in the town of Budapest. Paul appeared on the dock with the coach, ready to take the holidaymakers for a tour of the area. The tour guide told them that they were going to visit one of the world's most beautiful cities and explore both sides of Hungary's capital – traditional 'Buda' and cosmopolitan 'Pest'. All agreed that it sounded very impressive and everyone looked forward to a pleasant day. Lillian, still harangued by Priscilla but somehow not too bothered by it, was later to be seen wandering around taking photographs and feeling a degree of independence for the first time in years.

While the holidaymakers were enjoying the city, the staff on board were very busy. Melissa was studying her computer. She had a spreadsheet on the screen and she was frowning in concentration. The clue had to be here somewhere. She was glad she hadn't needed to accompany the tourists, Vicktor was on duty and he knew Budapest well; he would be fine on his own.

Antonio was also deep in contemplation. This evening he had to go to *that* hotel; he was very worried about collecting the parcel.

Anna the cabin cleaner, was trying to gather information about any guests who might be of interest; she had her own reasons for checking cabins far more carefully than was needed for a spotless finish.

There was a lot to see in Budapest so many people stayed after the official tour had finished, in order to see the rest of the city at their leisure. They were also told that Budapest by night was a wonderful sight so all were encouraged to join in an optional excursion that evening. Lillian mentioned to Priscilla that she would like to take part as she thought it would be interesting but to her astonishment, Priscilla told her that she must go alone; Priscilla had a date!

That morning, Priscilla had been approached by the receptionist on duty in the cruiser, to inform her that she was wanted on the telephone.

Assuming it was about her complaint to the management, she strode down to the desk where she was waved into a small office with a telephone.

'Priscilla Pilkington speaking. Who is this?'

'Ah madam,' the heavily accented voice began,' I am from the *Nemzetbiztonsági Szakszolgálat.'*

'The what?' Priscilla forgot her ladylike accent.

'From the 'Hungarian National Security Service' - our work is to uncover organised crime and I understand that you may have some valuable information that could help us in connection with, shall we say, some illegalities happening on the 'Danube Drifter' cruiser. You were overheard mentioning this. We would be most grateful if you could assist us by telling us all you know. We are sure that we are very close to arresting a most unpleasant group of people and it is the help of such upright and principled people, such as yourself, that makes our work possible.'

Upright and principled? Yes, that was her; it was gratifying to have someone be aware of this.

'I will be most happy to assist the authorities; I would consider it my duty,' she responded.

'Thank You. We would *really* appreciate your help but the utmost secrecy is vital. Please let me offer you dinner tonight, at one of our most prestigious restaurants. You will be able to tell me all you know in confidence and without other ears listening.' Priscilla mentally preened. At last! Someone who recognises my superiority.

'That will most satisfactory but how will I get there?'

'I will send a taxi for you. The table will be booked in your name then if I am slightly delayed by work, as sometimes happens, there will no difficulty in seating you. I should not want you to be inconvenienced.'

How agreeable that someone should be so considerate, Priscilla mused, I shall enjoy strolling out in full view of everyone and I might just let slip that I am dining with a gentleman.

'Shall we say at eight?'

'That would be convenient. I shall look forward to dinner.' Priscilla strolled away from the office in an ambient mood.

'Wow!' commented the receptionist to her colleague, 'something *has* pleased her. The sour-faced old harridan is actually smiling.'

To Priscilla's annoyance, her majestic exit later in the evening was hardly noticed by anyone because the 'Budapest by Night' excursion had left half an hour before and Lillian, all set to enjoy herself, had not taken the proper notice that Priscilla was dining in an exclusive restaurant. On returning to the cruiser after the day trip, Sebastian had mentioned that Felicity felt too fatigued to join the group in the evening and so he might be going on his own. Lillian daringly wondered if perhaps they might sit together.

Antonio waited until the group had left and then casually announced that he was going into the town. Captain Van Beeke, walking through the foyer, heard him and offered to accompany him. For a moment that seemed like an hour Antonio struggled to answer then luck saved him, someone called for the captain, there was a problem.

'Some other time,' the captain ruefully told him and Antonio, adopting a suitably disappointed expression, agreed that duty always called at the wrong moment before beating a hasty retreat in case anyone else offered to join him.

The disinterested man behind the hotel reception desk listened to the request for a parcel collection. He looked at the proffered identity card and after a cursory look at it, hauled a small suitcase across the counter and passed it to Antonio. This was a shock. Antonio was expecting a very small package, something he could conceal under his jacket or place in a pocket. Now, what could he say if anyone saw him with this? How could he explain?

Having no choice, he walked out with the suitcase but decided to check the contents before taking it back to the boat. He wanted to know what he was dealing with. There were even worse things than losing his family and job; he didn't want to be blown to bits or suffer the death penalty. A small restaurant nearby would be ideal, he entered, ordered a coffee and liqueur to steady his nerves, then lifting the case, strolled into the toilet. He headed for the door marked 'disabled' went inside and locked the door. The case was locked but it looked normal enough. Nervously he took a chance and used a penknife to prise open the lock; wads of American dollars met his gaze. Now even more confused, he closed the case and headed back to the boat.

The girl on duty was bending down as he entered, he managed to quickly get in front of the desk and place the case out of her eye line. Then he asked her to get something out of the office for him and when she turned left to comply, he whisked the case into the stair entrance calling,

'It's alright, I remember now. I don't need it after all.'

Perspiration dripping, he made it to his cabin unobserved. There was nowhere to hide the case so he put a strap around it and padlocked it in place then put the case in his tiny wardrobe. However, he wasn't quite as secretive as he thought he was, someone *had* seen him.

Elaine was frustrated. Where was the blasted woman? Normally, you couldn't move on this boat without hearing Priscilla's booming voice or tripping over her portly form. Elaine fumed inwardly. Just when it's so important and when I have evaded David, the silly woman does a disappearing act.

123

David was playing bridge. He'd found some other like-minded people and was hugely enjoying himself, Elaine had this free time and now she couldn't use it.

They had all come back from the night city tour and the woman had not been on it so Elaine had assumed that she would be on the boat but she had not been there for dinner. Where was she?

Priscilla's travelling companion was sitting with a group of people which included Felicity Fanshawe. Felicity had been a little peeved to find Sebastian straying from her side but then she'd realised that he had a kind heart and was obviously sorry for that woman, little mouse that she was. She was no rival, Felicity could afford to be magnanimous. So to Lillian's surprise, she was invited to join the group of sycophants grouped around Felicity; she was delighted to be included.

Elaine walked over and greeted Felicity, then a few others and finally Lillian. Too skilful to make her quest obvious, she asked casually,

'And where is your travelling companion tonight? Not unwell I hope? Lillian whispered that Priscilla was dining in town with a *friend.* Elaine was genuinely shocked; the woman had *friends!*

Elaine was very irritated, she was getting nowhere with this investigation; it was so difficult having to keep it a secret from David, it hampered her ability to respond to a situation. On impulse, she decided to go to her cabin and phone her boss.

Persuading her boss was not easy but finally, she managed to get permission to allow her husband to know she was working. It would be difficult but she would have to pretend that her superior had only just contacted *her* after a *lead.* David was no fool, would he swallow it? Then she had a brainwave; it was naughty but it might work. She remembered that he'd become a little bored with the mundane court cases he was usually involved with and he'd always hoped to be involved in a truly sensational case. He'd been talking to Bob who'd mentioned 'Ronaldo Marconi' - the master international criminal who was believed to be in this area.

David and Bob had enthused about the apprehension of this star criminal and the story and court case that would come out of it. Well, she would let slip that it was possible that this particular felon could be involved. Pure enthusiasm should override any wish for a peaceful holiday; old Bob would love it and if David was hesitant, he wouldn't spoil things for his new friend. It was risky but it might work. Should she include Bob in her secret, could she trust him? Heavens no! What was she thinking of? He was an ex-journalist, nothing would be secret. She needed to think and think fast. Got it! I'll just casually mention that this chap has been seen in the area, like a piece of gossip, then later I'll tell David that my boss mentioned the idea of my looking out for this wanted man. I could say that I prevaricated and did not commit myself as we were on holiday. Would it work? It might. I'll just introduce the conversation and play it by ear.

....

Priscilla arrived at the venue and was delighted with its obvious quality. She had overdressed as usual but for once she didn't look completely out of place; the restaurant boasted many distinguished clients and many ladies were very expensively dressed.

On giving her name she was ushered to a table and informed that wine had already been ordered for her, unless, of course, her choice of a meal made another more suitable. Would she like to study the wine list? Priscilla wavered, she knew nothing of quality wines. The waiter continued, perhaps she would prefer to have an aperitif while she waited for her host? Yes, she would prefer that, she ordered a dry Martini hoping it was considered a suitable drink. She didn't really like it, she preferred a sweet sherry but somehow she thought that might not be considered sophisticated enough.

Priscilla sipped her Martini and tried not to grimace at the bitterness. The Maître D came to her table.

'A message for madam. Your host has been delayed. He insists that you begin your meal, he does not wish you to be waiting without nourishment. He sends apologies and will be here as soon as possible.'

'How tiresome,' she muttered, 'very well, I will consult the menu. Bring me one at once.'

She had momentarily forgotten that she was in a foreign country and when the waiter delivered the menu, she looked in confusion at the list of dishes she could not decipher.

'Well really! Where is the English menu my man? This is not good enough.'

'Perhaps madam forgets that we are not in England and regrettably, do not have English menus.'

'How dare you be so impertinent?'

'My apologies madam, I meant no offence but your host has already ordered for you, one of our national specialities.'

'Well, why didn't you say so? I might need a word with your superior about your attitude,' she added.

He walked off grinning, he had already been paid to serve her a particular dish; she would be served a very, very hot goulash.

Priscilla looked around; it was a beautifully appointed building with views over a large pleasing and verdant garden that had been tastefully illuminated with a profusion of coloured low-lights. With her nose suitably in the air, Priscilla preened and prepared to partake of her meal in the exclusive surroundings.

The first course arrived, the soup was superb, the wine pleasant and Priscilla began to enjoy herself, although it was a pity, she thought, that her host was so late. A waiter cleared away her soup bowl, a waitress laid her new cutlery, another waiter arrived with the main meal and immediately afterwards, a second waiter arrived with a small jug of cream sauce to pour on the top. Priscilla was impressed with the service and attention to detail. There was even a separate member of staff to bring water for her. Priscilla approved; this was how things ought to be done. It was her host's responsibility to leave a gratuity but she made a mental note to leave a complimentary comment at the end of the meal.

The food looked delicious; she allowed the waiter to pour sauce on the goulash and then she took a forkful, placed it in her mouth and swallowed. Her throat was immediately on fire, she began to cough. She grasped at the tumbler of water and frantically tried to cool her throat. It would be so embarrassing, she concluded, to give up on the national dish, people were looking at her. Pouring a lot more sauce on top of the meal, she sought to drown the hot spices and tried again. This time the effect was even more dramatic so she gulped more water. Her head swam, her eyes bulged. She choked, coughed and fought for breath. A member of staff rushed over and appeared to offer her more water. In the throes of coughing and spluttering, she and everybody else failed to notice the needle being inserted into her neck. She continued to cough, fight for breath and then – *oblivion*. She slumped backwards in her seat and slithered downwards till she landed in an untidy heap on the floor.

The waiter who'd served the goulash, turned at the commotion and gasped in horror; would he be blamed? He'd had people cough and splutter before but never pass out. It was a joke! It had been suggested as a joke! The person who paid him to make it *extra hot* assured him it was for a joke - but it was supposed to be funny.

A few moments later he was even more worried. A doctor, dining in the restaurant, having rushed over to help, announced that there was nothing he could do. It looked as if she'd had a heart attack. She was dead.

A group of shocked employees congregated around the table, a mixture of curiosity and concern. One, however, was very concerned, but not for Priscilla's good health; this one needed to ensure that Priscilla definitely was dead. Mission accomplished the bogus member of staff quickly slipped away out of sight.

Chapter 13

Happenings

Now back on the cruiser and safely in his cabin, Antonio was looking at another envelope. It had been taped to the underside of the suitcase he'd collected and somehow he hadn't noticed it before. He removed the envelope and read the contents. He sighed - more instructions.

When the guests were ready to leave at the end of the week, he usually gave a hand with sorting the baggage. He was instructed to help as usual but while doing so, to add this suitcase to the assortment of luggage waiting to be loaded. He was to attach the supplied label which displayed a fictitious name and address in the UK. The case would then be loaded with all the others. All he had to do was walk to the coach loading area, carrying the case as if he'd helped a passenger. Paul would do the rest; he would be expecting it.

Antonio had wondered who else might be implicated in the schemes, so it was Paul. He'd expected to deliver one or more small packages somewhere but a suitcase was a surprise. However, it was clever, he conceded, a suitcase on its own could look suspicious but in the middle of a holiday party with loads of others, no-one would bother to even glance at it. Until then it would reside safely in his cabin.

The beautiful city of Budapest shone by night with over a thousand bright lights; a sight not to be missed. Antonio was quite happy to miss it; the city held nothing but bad memories for him. The boat would remain in Budapest overnight and would wait there during the next morning to allow many of the guests to visit the Puszta Horse Show. The cruiser was due to set off at midday for Bratislava, so tomorrow, Antonio would have a most welcome free morning. He was just trying to decide what to do with the time when the sound of loud voices could be heard coming from the reception area. Intrigued, he went out to investigate, he froze, there were several members of the Rendőrség (Hungarian Police) standing there. The captain, having called for his second-in-command, who spoke fluent Hungarian, was protesting on being told by the police, that he may not be able to move the boat the next day as there'd been a sudden death of one of his passengers. The woman had died in town last night. A look in the deceased's handbag had shown that she was named 'Priscilla Pilkington' and that she'd been a passenger on this cruiser. The captain was informed that her cabin would need to be checked and her travelling companions, if she had any, interviewed. In fact, everyone on the boat would need to be spoken to and possibly their cabins searched because the death at the moment, was unexplained. It was just routine procedure, they insisted but in the meantime, the police wished to cordon off Priscilla's cabin. There would be a police guard outside and no-one must leave the cruiser. They would return in the morning

Antonio paled, if they searched his cabin, they would find the suitcase and the dollars and they would correctly conclude that this was something connected to organised crime. He would immediately be arrested. Panic was not the word, he was petrified. He rushed back, picked up the case and hurried out of his cabin. If he could just find a hiding place, he thought wildly, they might not find it but at least if it *was* found, the suitcase might not be associated with him. He hurried out onto the deck and then darted towards the prow; there were some rope lockers there, he might be lucky.

He passed Minnie and Lavinia in the corridor and barely noticed them but they observed his distracted and almost hunted look. Curiosity got the better of them and they slowly followed him. By looking through the dining room windows then quietly opening the back door, they were just in time to see him place something inside a rope locker on the deck, before disappearing around the outside walkway. Antonio's thinking was too addled for sensible and practical deductions, all he wanted to do was to get away from the incriminating evidence.

Lavinia peered into the gloom; the deck lights were just bright enough to show silhouettes.

'I think our friend has got himself into a pickle, don't you dear?'

'It would certainly seem to be the case. What do you think he's hiding? Shall we look?'

The next morning passengers were startled to hear an announcement informing them that, due to unforeseen circumstances, plans for that day were going to be delayed and would everybody please assemble in the dining room. Just before that, a knock on Lillian's door had startled her. She'd not seen Priscilla the previous evening and had assumed that because the boat was docking overnight, Priscilla must have stayed out late with her friend. It was very unlike her but then, she *was* on holiday and even Priscilla must enjoy herself sometimes. Lillian was completely unprepared to see a white-faced Melissa and even less prepared to receive the shocking news.

Priscilla – dead? A hundred thoughts flashed through her brain; some were not very charitable and feeling ashamed, she quickly brushed them aside. The others rose to a prominent position – how- what – why? Before she could gather her wits the second news followed; the Hungarian Police were here and wished to speak to her. She felt her knees begin to knock, she'd heard such dreadful things about foreign police and their methods, what if…? She reprimanded herself. Stupid woman, why should I worry? I have nothing to be afraid of, I have done nothing wrong, I am a British citizen and - *I* was with others all evening.

The police had brought an interpreter and they spoke to Lillian for some half an hour but it became obvious to them that she knew very little. She gave details of Priscilla's name, address and circumstances then told them that she thought Priscilla had been in good health but she knew nothing of Priscilla's arrangement for the previous evening, only that she had been told Priscilla was dining with *'a friend'*.

The meeting in the dining room caused dismay and concern and another emotion - curiosity. Elaine listened with heightened awareness; in her considerable experience, any unusual circumstance was never a coincidence. Bob listened with the enquiring mind of a journalist; retired or not, it sounded like a good story. David listened with professional interest and wondered how the law differed in Hungary from England.

Apart from the obvious shock, no-one felt the normal emotion of sorrow at a loss of life. Some more charitable people offered condolences to Lillian when it was made clear that they had been cousins but as Priscilla had made herself obnoxious to all, there was no genuine sorrow at her demise. Felicity, never one to miss the dramatic action, managed to utilise the moment by delivering a tragic theatrical performance, the part came from one of her vintage stage roles and did not quite fit the requirements as it was the part of a bereft daughter for her adored mother – but at short notice, she decided, it would do.

On being told that all cabins might have to be searched, there was outrage and annoyance but as all were in a foreign country and they were slightly nervous with unfamiliar police, the proceedings began without too many protests.

The search took all morning and then it moved to the outside deck areas. The two elderly ladies, who sat on a covered box seat and smiled at the police as they searched, were treated with unusual indulgence. The older officer was impressed that ladies of such a grand old age were travelling this far; he took care not to upset them.

The police found nothing suspicious and left the boat. Permission was granted for the cruise to continue later in the day but the police warned that by the time the cruiser reached Boppard, some of the passengers and crew might need to be contacted again. As they would be in Germany by then, two police forces would be investigating the death; the *Rendőrség* of Hungary would be working in co-operation with the *Bundeskriminalamt* (known as the BKA) of Germany.

Almost swooning with relief, Antonio went to recover his case. It was still in the rope locker but he was surprised because he was sure that he'd put it in the other way up and what was a table cloth doing in there? No time to wonder, he quickly decided; he hurried back to his cabin with the suitcase before he could be seen by anyone who might be curious. He *was* seen but the reaction this caused was just a smile.

Elaine was puzzled. This whole thing was running away from her. A bit of gossip was one thing but what could a rather obnoxious and stupid woman have to do with international crime? What information could she possibly have had that might bring about her death? Who would want to silence her in such a drastic way? Was it possible that her death *could* be just an unfortunate and unrelated coincidence? Her demise was going to complicate matters because it meant that the people Elaine was trying to find, would halt or delay operations because of the police presence. She bit a nail in frustration, would she ever get a clue? It would make little difference now whether she told her husband or not but she decided that she'd better tell him quickly because the police asking questions, might possibly bring on another response – panic. Criminals who succumbed to panic made mistakes and she wanted to be free to follow up any leads without David putting a spoke in the wheels. She made another decision. I'll have to give them something to justify the cost of this trip. The one thing I'm fairly sure of is that Paul the driver is somehow implicated. His coach must be used to take whatever is being smuggled into England. I must alert the authorities to search the coach when it reaches the UK border.

Pete and Polly had listened open-mouthed to the police but had raised no objection to their cabin being searched. The officer delegated to search their accommodation blinked at the colours of the assorted clothing in the wardrobe but found nothing to concern him. Their room safe was locked but they were not asked to open it, this was going to happen at the end of the search before anyone would be allowed back into their cabins. The staff member who had key access, together with another member of staff from the cruiser, acting as witness, would be asked to open all the safes in the presence of the police; the police wanted no accusations of theft which might cause an international incident.

Pete didn't worry, he'd heard about robberies abroad and he was taking no chances; his cash was hidden in his underpants and the passports were in a belt around his waist. He didn't like safes; he could never seem to work out how to use them or he'd forget the number or lose the key, then someone had to come and open the safe for him. So, he reasoned, if a staff member could come and easily open the safe, it wasn't safe, was it?

Search over and with nothing suspicious found, guests were free to leave the cruiser. Pete set off with Polly into the town without a care in the world. That was soon to change.

Having made several decisions that morning, Elaine was on her way to her cabin to phone her boss, when passing through the foyer and glancing through the office window, she noticed Melissa who appeared to be acting suspiciously.

134

Melissa was going frantic. How could she complete her task with Police all over the place disrupting everything? She'd managed to get into the office, had papers spread all over the surfaces and was in the act of getting out some more files when a head popped around the door. After biting her lip in vexation, she managed to alter her expression into her professional smile as she turned around.

'Can I help you?'

Elaine answered with a similar artificial smile. What was this woman up to? She improvised as she walked further into the office, surreptitiously trying to look at the files on the desk.

'I just wondered if and when our normal programme was likely to resume?'

'I think we should soon be able to continue as planned. Possibly just a delay, that's all. Er - I hope you don't mind me mentioning it but guests shouldn't really be in here you know.'

Elaine thanked her and walked off with her brain furiously working. The files were all accounts and not those connected with excursions which surely was Melissa's *only* area of financial responsibility. The woman had to be *on the fiddle*. Why else would she need to access those sort of files?

Safe in her cabin she put through the call. She reported her findings so far. The information included her suspicions of Paul the driver and her recommendation that the coach should be searched at the border, she informed them of the suspicious death and the presence of the Hungarian police and finally that Melissa was probably involved as she'd been behaving strangely.

On completing the call, another problem surfaced. Elaine had still not found an opportunity to tactfully let her husband know that she was working and, therefore, needed to report information to the UK police.

Back in the UK, various departments were alerted and arrangements were made concerning the Calais border.

However, it was decided that the death of a British subject in Hungary was a matter for the Embassy and the travel insurance company; there was not an obvious connection. Despite Elaine saying that it seemed too coincidental and therefore, suspicious and maybe, *should* be investigated, nothing much was done. A junior who was despatched to check on the identity of the deceased, came back with the information that Priscilla had been a pillar of the community, the daughter of a vicar and the epitome of respectability. The death was disregarded.

Chapter 14

Prince Romanovsky

The magnificent silver and white cruiser glided along the River Danube. It made an enviable statement of wealth and class. Dripping with luxury and glamour and boasting every modern convenience, the vessel was superb.

The cream leather seating on the deck, tastefully arranged and covered with a set of matching soft deep-filled cushions, supported the body of a handsome, tanned and expensively dressed man who could be seen lounging at his ease. Near at hand was an open cocktail cabinet and a large ice bucket. A white-coated attendant hovered discreetly in the background. A flick of the wrist immediately brought this individual forward to fill the crystal glass with an ice-cold concoction.

Discreetly out of sight but very much in evidence, were two armed guards. Having convinced the various European countries of his status, Prince Romanovsky was allowed firearm permits for his two personal bodyguards; he'd pleaded that wealthy foreigners were often a target for abduction and worse. Legal permission made his protection arrangements much simpler. However, he would still have had armed guards had permission *not* been forthcoming, he knew that he couldn't be too careful; nearly *all* of his staff were armed.

The Prince found it very easy to get his way in nearly all things; money opened doors. Everybody he came into contact with knew he was extremely wealthy and powerful. Those who took the time to wonder at it, assumed that as a Romanovsky, he must have inherited an enormous fortune which no doubt, had been deposited in a safe country before the Russian revolution. There was talk of fabulous jewels kept in deposit boxes – icons and works of art studded with precious gems.

There must have been an awful lot to support the style the Prince lived in. However, there *were* those who doubted. How could a man who didn't seem to work or own more than a modest business empire, have so much cash to spend?

Prince Romanovsky was not oblivious to the curiosity of others but he *kept his cards close to his chest* and did not share information concerning the origins of his wealth or indeed, the total sum of it. Various tax authorities, in particular, would have liked to have been better informed but the team of brilliant accountants the Prince employed, with the devious methods they used, always managed to just hold them in check. It was for this reason, he told friends that he travelled a great deal; he had no intention of any bureaucrats dipping their greedy fingers into his pie - not if he could help it. His advisors selected the most tax-efficient country for him to be domiciled in and his small donation to the country's coffers was dutifully paid each year together with the large bribes to their tax inspectors. He retained a house in the said haven and though he owned other properties, he was careful to stay in them only for short holidays. Most of the time he either cruised on the rivers or perhaps the sea when he would swap his river cruiser for an ocean-going vessel.

A select few were let into his confidence. To these people, he mentioned the name of his father, the late Prince Nicholas, and informed them that he, Dmitri, was in fact, the only child of a second marriage. He told them that his correct name was Prince Dmitri Nikolaevich-Romanovsky - Russian traditions for naming sons being very particular and royal bloodlines very complicated. To ensure that his status was instantly understood, however, he tended to announce himself as Prince Dmitri *Romanov*sky - that surname seemed recognisable everywhere.

Today the Prince was a little bored, he considered visiting a casino. Where was the nearest one? He sighed, he needed diversion.

A lissom blonde, scantily clad in a bikini, caught his eye as she strolled across the deck. That would do as a diversion. He grabbed her and pulled her down on to the couch. He snapped his fingers at the waiting servant who instantly removed himself and at the same time operated the mechanism that rolled down the exterior curtains. Giggles could be heard as Dmitri prepared to be entertained in one of his favourite ways.

Contrary to popular belief, the Prince had not been born to a life of luxury. His lineage, of course, was true blue-blood and his connection to the house of Romanov was indisputable; he should have been born with the proverbial silver spoon in his mouth, not a wooden one as was the case.

Although the dramatic and bloody events of 1917 and 1918 had not taken the lives of his great grandparents, who forewarned, had just managed to escape to England with their children, these events had seriously affected his family's wealth. However, with arrogant indifference to their state of near penury, his relations had gone into exile and lived their life in regal poverty, scrounging from richer relations and acquiring money wherever they could. Consequently, Dmitri's formidable but stunningly beautiful mother, a Russian Duchess, had also never allowed a little thing like the Russian Revolution to diminish her status. She sailed through life, accepting, not charity, but those donations from inferior persons, she felt were her due.

She'd eventually married another exiled Russian aristocrat, a handsome man with an exalted title but being a younger son, had no wealth to speak of. On his unexpected demise, she and her son were left in a most precarious financial situation. To her initial dismay, his over-stretched and slightly disapproving family began to tighten the purse strings. She was told to economise and be grateful that Dmitri was fortunate enough to still have his education paid for.

Dimitri attended a prestigious public school in England and then later, completed his studies abroad where he perfected his knowledge of the arts. A natural linguist, he became fluent in some European languages as well as continuing to follow his family's tradition of speaking Russian.

Ever adaptable, and with a complete disregard for conventions that might inconvenience her, in return for discreet financial support, Dimitri's mother used her name and title to introduce various wealthy persons into social circles that would normally have excluded them. She taught her son the values of class, status and family name but mentioned little of the real world. The vulgar topic of *money* was never mentioned.

Dmitri grew up believing that he was still a class above everyone else and although he'd been supported by various relations and acquaintances, the true state of affairs had not occurred to him.

A typically misguided and arrogant boy developed. He happily accepted financial gifts from anyone and everyone and had no concept of questioning anything providential that came his way. He was *entitled* - he was a *prince*. With no career in mind, he failed to recognise the fact that he was close to being a pauper.

As all delusions must end, so did Dmitri's - with a bang. Over a period of time, having casually accepted a lot of cash from a certain wealthy Italian man he'd met socially, and having dismissed any qualms with his usual sangfroid, he'd had a terrible shock when this person explained that of course, as a gentleman, he abhorred discussing money but he'd had to force his sensibilities to one side because *business was business,* and could the Prince inform him when the *loan* would be repaid.

140

The word *loan* had assailed his ears with the same intensity of shock as having a bucket of cold water thrown in his face. He was just coming to terms with the fact that he'd heard such a word when far worse followed – *'fifty thousand American dollars,'* reverberated around his brain.

Feeling faint and looking genuinely confused, Dmitri had stood rooted to the spot as his now, *not so friendly friend*, explained the consequences of non-repayment. However, before Dmitri was able to bring his now enfeebled brain into some sort of working order, it had seemed that things were not so bad after all. His new friend would continue to finance him and furthermore, Dmitri could still live in the lap of luxury; all he had to do was to follow quite simple orders and from time-to-time, introduce one person or another into various *select* groups of society. As his mother had been doing that for years, Dmitri hadn't seen anything wrong with the proposal. Then it was all smiles and back to the happy carefree life – for the time being.

Slowly and with sickening inevitability, as Dmitri matured, he'd been confronted with the fact that he was now being controlled by some very sinister and powerful people. Somehow, he'd been *sold* and he was now being used as a *front* for a host of illegal activities. His brain, which had been in hibernation mode, had gradually come to life and he'd realised that he'd been lazy and ill-informed and all that needed to change. There was nothing he could have done at the time so he'd watched and waited and continued to play the part of the empty-headed and wealthy playboy prince.

However, despite the continuing charade, he'd begun to find out all he could about the people he was dealing with. He understood that it was a kind of *Mafia* organisation and he easily identified the man-in-charge, he was known as 'Capo'.

It seemed that the sycophants surrounding 'Capo' were mainly *muscle* so it was just the one man who controlled everything.

He also discovered that there were other factions, deadly rivals, who wouldn't hesitate to try to take over any of the money-making schemes. Dmitri also learned something about himself; he was *not* stupid, he had brains and given the chance he could become something - but, for the present, how secure was his future? Could he end up in prison? The man who ordered him about was a criminal; if that man made one slip, Dmitri would go down with him - or worse. They were all armed. What could he do?

He also knew with certainty that he could never hope to continue his affluent lifestyle if he parted company with this group - that's if he was ever allowed to do so. He began to plot. Royal he might be, that was always acceptable, but living in poverty was not. He would do anything to secure his future and if it involved a bit of cheating and swindling, well he was used to that, and if it involved murder, well with a name like Romanovsky, his family was used to that too.

His plans were carefully made. Contact was contrived with a rival and a scheme to carve up the territories and divide up the profit-making ventures was drawn up. To ensure agreement, Dmitri conceded the most lucrative parts to the other group. The rival appreciated him; he could see that Dmitri was just as morally deficient as most lowly-born crooks but he had a lot more to lose if he reneged on the deal.

Dmitri put his plan into action. Looking bored and uninterested, he casually informed Capo that a child had handed him a note, telling Dmitri that he'd been paid to deliver it. The message contained a request for a meeting with the said rival, together with an offered truce and *a too good to miss* deal. Of course, the message implied that the sender believed Dmitri to be the *main man*; just the subterfuge that Capo, the boss, had strived to arrange. Ever keen to consider anything that might be to his advantage, Capo agreed that he would accompany Dmitri to this meeting at a neutral spot in a disused warehouse. The note stipulated that, as a show of good faith, *only one other person* should accompany the boss inside and they would do the same. The rest of the men would wait outside

The fine details were ironed out and Dmitri, accompanied by his boss, walked them into a trap. Capo was speedily dealt with and before the rest of the team waiting outside, could react, they were surrounded. Dmitri took over, telling them that they had a choice, they could go down with their boss or follow a new leader as he'd made a deal with the rival to share out the territory and business. There was enough for all, he told them, and no point in both factions killing each other off unnecessarily.

Staring down the business end of several gun barrels and shocked at the turn of events, most of the men decided to comply and throw in their lot with Dmitri. One old retainer tried to avenge his boss and went down in a hail of gunfire; this decided the waverers.

Thus the available and lucrative big-time crime schemes were carved up and peace reigned for quite a while. Prince Dmitri Romanovsky carried on with the public illusion that he was a fabulously wealthy and respectable Royal Prince while running a successful crime syndicate. His mother, magnificently ignoring the reasons for the change in their fortunes, continued to thrive.

The prince had soon come to understand that it was vital to be one step ahead of the game; how you did this was to always know what your rivals were thinking and doing. Dmitri moved away from the standard model of just one gang and all members being known and united in a kind of grand club, no he used a far older model – a spy system.

A great reader of history, Dmitri knew that the resourceful and long-lived monarchs were those who'd had a successful spymaster and had informants always in the enemy camp. In the line of work he'd moved into, lives were often very short. Also, like the lions of the jungle, the younger and strong males, though not necessarily the brightest, were always looking to challenge the leader. Dmitri was cunning, he used and rewarded the physically weaker but brainy men, for doing his bidding. These men would never openly dare to challenge a strong leader but they would be loyal if they were paid well and brains won over brawn every time. These types of men were often ridiculed by the brainless muscle men but they were far more superior aides and could be considerably more deadly. Dmitri kept men like that on his side.

With this model of operation in mind, he'd gradually infiltrated the very gang with whom he'd agreed a truce. An accountant, appearing to be working for the rivals, kept Dmitri informed of deals made and allowed him to build up a picture of his rival's methods and operations. Nothing was allowed to be traced back to the said accountant, secrecy was absolute, and no-one, other than Dmitri, knew of this man's co-operation. The raid on the rival's premises, just as they were taking delivery of a rather nasty drug haul, could not be attributed to any leak from the said organisation. It was assumed to have been a lucky guess by the authorities.

Dmitri became the 'King' but he was not interested in smuggling drugs. Lucrative they might be but they were also the most obnoxious of cargo and carried the greater punishment if anyone was caught; some countries still used the death penalty. No there were plenty of other illegal but profitable activities. Dmitri still had a vestige of aristocratic pride and drug-running seemed distasteful and vulgar. When he'd learned that the other entity was drug-running on a large scale, he'd felt no remorse at breaking the truce they'd all subscribed to. He salved his conscience by telling himself that he'd wiped out a trade only suitable for guttersnipes.

He had no scruples at all about anything else. Cigarettes, expensive wines, scotch, saffron, designer goods, counterfeit money, gold bars, art theft, people escaping justice - all had helped to make him very rich. However, the most lucrative trading of all was in precious stones; these had brought vast rewards. It had taken a while to get into the trade but it had worked out well; his river cruiser was frequently in Amsterdam. Mostly it was diamonds but also black opals and other precious stones were smuggled; they were small, easy to conceal and *so* valuable - they were an ideal trade.

However, a problem had developed. Dmitri had always known there were other players in the gem smuggling game, who might provide some competition, but it had never really inconvenienced him before. Suddenly he was not able to acquire his usual quantities because whenever the product was available, he often found himself being outbid. This confirmed a *serious* rival - who was it? Dmitri needed information. Of even more concern, was the niggling suspicion that someone may have used his own methods? Could someone have played him at his own game? He must be on the look-out for a spy.

Dmitri was determined. He *must* find out who the rival was, then be ruthless and arrange to get rid of him or her. He'd done it once, he was sure he could do it again. He was still preserving the image of a clueless aristocrat so his right-hand man Boris was nominated as the figurehead. Dmitri knew that mobility on the river helped in *his* business, so he thought it not unreasonable to suspect other river operators. He arranged for Boris to recruit someone to be his *eyes and ears* on as many riverboats as possible and Boris, using his charm with the ladies, had dutifully managed to recruit a few young women who, if they found anything of interest, would report directly to him.

The mobile phone was quick and efficient but the communication was dangerous and traceable, therefore, in case the authorities should ever monitor calls, all the spies contacted Boris by sending a coded text message, worded as if they were his girlfriend (which they all believed they were). Dmitri needed all the information he could get, he must ensure that he was the only viable game in town.

Chapter 15

The Spy

The office of the theatrical agency was busy as usual. Two phones began to ring at the same time. Grabbing one, Mo Bartholemew indicated with an impatient gesture, that the lady seated at the computer keyboard, should answer the other one. Slightly irritated, as she was in the middle of typing a complex contract, she leaned forward, flipped the switch to transfer the call to her desk and spoke into the receiver.

'Bartholemew Theatrical Agency. Can I help you?'

She listened intently for a few moments. 'Of course! Mr Batholemew is engaged at the moment but if you would like to give me the details, we'll search our database for you and ring you back. I'm sure we'll be able to help.'

Mo finished his call and looked over at his assistant.

'What was that all about?'

'Realtime Production Company is casting for a film but they're having difficulty in finding someone for one of the parts. They want to know if we have anyone suitable on our books.'

'Well, that's a turnaround. It's usually me asking for parts and sending my clients to auditions. What the hell *is* this part?'

'An ageing female film star. They want someone who hasn't put on weight, who has some sort of a *name* but would play an old has-been who thinks she is still as good-looking as she was at twenty; they need someone who would genuinely look the part.'

'There must be tons of actresses who would take the role, *make-up* would do the trick. I don't get it. What are they playing at? I'll give them a ring.'

A long telephone call followed and finally, Mo put down the phone.

'It's the cash! The film is low budget so not enough to tempt a quality actress plus anyone who took this part, who still had some vestige of presence in the industry, would probably lose it after this. The film calls for a lot of intense close-ups which will be cruel and invasive and the studio thinks that it just wouldn't work with a younger woman being made-up to that degree. Even if they could do it, extensive make-up for each *take* costs a lot of time and money; they need the real *McCoy*. Now, who do we have who would be stupid enough to take the part?'

The two looked at each other and chorused – 'Fanny Fanshawe.'

....

Felicity was languishing in her cabin feeling a little peeved; this holiday had not worked out quite as she'd intended. She hadn't been tempted by the excursion to a traditional stud farm, which included a tour of the grounds in a horse-drawn carriage plus a live Puszta horse show. She'd decided to take a little rest. It was all too fatiguing. Her mobile phone rang in her handbag and she fumbled to answer it.

'Hel-lo,' began the artificial theatrical voice, 'Felicity Fanshawe speaking.'

'Fanny! Darling! It's Mo. How are you dear?'

A little sniff answered the question. Felicity was rather peeved with Mo Bartholomew, he was her agent but she hadn't heard from him for a very long time.

'I'm taking a vacation and am at present sojourning on a cruiser on the river Danube,' came the slightly acid reply.

'Wonderful darling. That will set you up nicely for work when you return. I have a part in a film for you. It's just made for you; you would be perfect for it.'

All the peevishness vanished.

'A part? Oh darling, how wonderful! Do I play the heroine?'

'Well yes, in a way, though of course you have to accept that a character with a *slightly* older age may be called for,' and before she could object or ask for more details, he continued with, 'but I told the production company that I had the perfect actress for the part, so experienced and talented that she could rise to any occasion. They were thrilled when I told them your name.' Mo crossed his fingers. 'I believe the producer is quite a fan of yours.'

By this time Felicity was glowing.

'Oh, you are a dear. Do you know how nice it is to hear my old stage name again? *Fanny* Fanshawe - at one time that name used to be known everywhere. When do I start? I do hope I don't have to cut short my little holiday, Sebastian would be so disappointed. .... Oh, splendid. .... Sign a contract as soon as we return? Should I not read the script first? ...... Oh, I see, no time. ...... No, I most certainly do not want the part offered to someone else. That will be quite agreeable.'

Mo put down the receiver. He was grinning from ear to ear.

'Well, that solves two problems and gains me one favour,' he told his assistant. 'Not bad for one deal. I get the commission, gain a useful friend for helping them out and no doubt lose a useless client afterwards.' He couldn't stop laughing all afternoon.

....

An altogether different Felicity breezed along the corridor, she had to find Sebastian immediately. He was most surprised to be told that they were going to be dining in town *somewhere,* for a special celebratory dinner. The boat was due to dock next at Bratislava so he must find a lovely restaurant there and book a table for that evening because Felicity had something to celebrate. No, she wouldn't tell him now but she would give him a clue, she might want champagne.

In her usual careless fashion, Felicity had failed to take note of the correct itinerary for the holiday; the cruiser *was* sailing that afternoon but it was not due to reach Bratislava until the following day and was only remaining there for a few hours. When this was pointed out to her, her good humour started to vanish and her habitual pout began to form on her face. Luckily for Sebastian, events beyond their control changed the plans. It seemed that they were to stay in Budapest for one more evening. Felicity was all smiles. Budapest is a far more sophisticated destination for my celebration, she decided.

Later that evening, Felicity was to be seen, gorgeously attired, sitting at a restaurant table, eagerly awaiting the opening of a champagne bottle. She was delighted with everything. The tasteful decor, the low and elegant lighting and the quiet and efficient service of the staff had instantly won her approval. Relaxing back into her maroon velvet padded chair, she prepared to enjoy herself. She told Sebastian that she refused to say a word about the reason for the celebration until they had a glass of bubbly in their hands and they were ready for a suitable toast. Sebastian, puzzled but just pleased that she seemed in such a good mood, happily went along with the mystery.

The restaurant he'd chosen was, in fact, a very up-market and expensive concern, catering only for *exclusive* clients. Persons taking a holiday on a commercial riverboat, would normally not have been able to get in the door but an exception had been made. Sebastian, well used to conniving and bribing to keep Felicity happy, had asked a member of the reception staff, to recommend a very select venue where English was understood, then on telephoning, had asked them to book a table for a visiting English *Film Star*, who was travelling incognito. It had all worked out well and not only had he been able to reserve a table, he'd also managed to secure one in the most sought after part of the restaurant.

To cater for the privacy of their most prestigious clientele, the tables in one section were arranged in separate booths; groups next to each other could not see their neighbours. However, in rare quiet moments, it was sometimes possible to hear a little of the conversation coming from the adjoining booth. Thus it was that Prince Dmitri Romanovsky overheard part of the conversation between Felicity and Sebastian.

Having given Sebastian her good news, Felicity was enthusiastically inventing the part she was to play. She'd had no time to get details but she did manage to elicit the title - 'Shot at Dawn.' The title really referred to a *photoshoot* but Felicity had convinced herself that it was a spy story and that she was to take the part of a brave heroine.

'You? A spy?' Sebastian registered surprise at the role and spoke a little more loudly than usual. 'Could you maintain that?' Sebastian was thinking of her age.

'Of course, I could!' There was a slight pout. 'Well, I've already agreed so it's all arranged.'

There was a lull in the conversation in the next booth which contained Prince Romanovsky, who was dining with friends. In a brief moment of quiet, while they were all eating, he just caught the phrase - *'You a spy?'* He immediately pricked up his ears. Being constantly aware, had saved his life in the past. He decided to listen a little more closely. A spy for what and for whom? Who was in the adjoining booth? He concentrated on listening.

Felicity blithely carried on. She was into her artistic stride now and began to make up a storyline.

'I have to keep my wits about me and be resourceful. There's a great deal of intrigue and crime and I'm going to be the one to expose the people concerned.'

Knowing that she couldn't possibly have read the script yet. Sebastian replied,

'Aren't you taking a little too much for granted, my dear? You don't know about any particular crimes.'

However, by now Felicity was in dramatic mode and so with a theatrical sweep of her hand, she announced, a little too loudly, that she would be the single-handed cause of the downfall of such villains as were involved. Extemporising skilfully, she continued with a fanciful story of international espionage and smuggling, little realising that her words were not only being overheard but were also being believed. Prince Romanovsky had taken her words at face value and when she mentioned that she would inveigle her way into the presence of the main titled and handsome villain, he'd assumed that *he* must be under suspicion and therefore, the target. He concluded that Felicity must be a *plant* by the authorities.

Felicity had enjoyed her evening and, though a little tipsy, when she and Sebastian stood up to depart, she was in an excellent mood. Their leaving the restaurant coincided with the departure of the Prince's party and Felicity, never too inebriated to mistake a celebrity and well primed by pictures from her gossip magazine, spotted and recognised the Prince immediately.

With the invigorating effect of too much alcohol egging her on, she made sure that she was clearly in his sight. Before he could leave she exclaimed,

'Well, I declare! I do believe it is Prince Romanovsky.' She held out her hand to him in a limp wrist gesture and continued with, 'Let me see, where was it we met? Perhaps it was at Cannes last year? Oh, my poor memory. You must forgive me.'

Sebastian and all the other men from the Prince's table refrained from comment; they were too astonished. The Prince's companions looked at each other in bewilderment while Sebastian flushed pink with embarrassment. Prince

Romanovsky, recognising the voice and guessing correctly that this was the lady he'd overheard, used his wits. She was so unlikely a person that, had he not heard the conversation, he would never have believed it of her. By God, he thought, the police are getting so clever and devious that they send dressed-up old ladies to spy. He would have been suspicious of a young and sexy woman but not an old *past her sell-by-date* one. He must beware. What a scheme! He couldn't afford any mistakes.

He deduced that this little performance must be the ploy to meet him. He resolved to play the game of being the empty-headed aristocrat and pretend that he thought he *did* know her. The old story rang true, keep your friends close but your enemies closer. He wasn't a fool, even if others thought he was. Here was his chance to find out more, he needed to be duplicitous. Lifting her hand he kissed it and said,

'My sweet. How lovely to see you again.' Sebastian was stunned and then, suspecting sarcasm and embarrassment, began to mutter,

'Er Felicity, I think we'd better be returning.'

So that was her name.

'Felicity, of course! A charming name for a charming lady. How could I forget?' He ran out of ideas but Felicity was well into her stride and had no intention of letting this opportunity slip by.

'You must have seen my most celebrated film – 'The Heroine was Gold' where I played a...........'

'Indeed, a stunning performance.'

By now the other men of the party were looking rather bored and one whispered in the Prince's ear.

'Alas, I am reminded that we have an appointment. We shall renew our acquaintance soon. You are staying......?'

Sebastian, in an embarrassed tone, interjected.

'Miss Fanshawe is cruising on the 'Danube Drifter. She is travelling somewhat incognito - er - having a *low-key* holiday, away from the glare of publicity, you understand. It is to allow her to rest, er.., away from the stresses of the stage and screen,' he hopefully suggested. The Prince smiled, shook his hand, blew a kiss to Felicity and left with his companions.

Sebastian wiped his brow, he was very confused. Had the Prince mistaken her for someone else? That had to be it. He couldn't possibly know her. Felicity, on the other hand, was euphoric; she virtually danced back to the cruiser having convinced herself that the Prince was interested in her. A teeny bit of sense tried to surface. She knew she was no longer the young beauty she once had been but, there had to be something - *class* - that was it! The Prince would recognise class. She had plenty of that. *Class* was more important than youth and, she gulped, beauty, then quickly pushed that thought away. The prince could see past the common view; he recognised that she was still alluring because she had that certain special something that attracted men to her. Delusion firmly fixed, she readied herself for bed in the best mood she'd been in for years.

Dmitri did not enjoy the same euphoria; he was quite perturbed. What did it mean? This old affected woman a spy? Who were her paymasters? Had she been some kind of a movie star? Maybe she was in silent movies because he'd certainly never seen her.

When practising his aristocratic empty-headed role, Dmitri was often thought to be clueless and not only did he enjoy playing up to the notion, he saw it as a necessary deception. If anyone suspected him, they would surely assume that he was the dupe of some character behind the scenes, as originally had been the case. However, there was always a danger that the authorities or a new rival, could be onto him so he was cautious in any unusual situation but - using someone like her was a very new *modus operandi*. He couldn't afford to let anything jeopardise his operations. His income, not to mention his liberty, depended on secrecy; there must be no lapse in security.

He made a decision - he would befriend the woman, play up to her fantasies and see what he could find out but if there was any danger, she would have to be dealt with. Boris would see to that; he was most efficient.

Reluctantly he resigned himself to the awful realisation that he would have to invite the hag to his yacht. He would invite the companion too, it would be safer. He could bear flirting with the old has-been but the old man would prevent anything more. He shuddered; the things one had to do for the sake of money but there was a limit!

Dmitri had been away from the cruiser all that day. He had no idea that in his absence, another scheme would raise its head and that his ever-faithful, but not always wise sidekick, would decide to use his initiative and follow up this latest development. Boris had decided, that in the absence of his boss, he was in charge and this scheme was too good to miss.

While guests had been at breakfast, Anna, one of Boris' recruited *girlfriends*, employed as a cabin maid on the Danube Drifter, had spotted a magazine in the bin in Felicity's cabin. Felicity had not bothered to read past the first couple of pages, she'd become bored and discarded it prematurely. Anna had been about to throw the society journal into the black plastic bag when she'd idly flicked through it. She came to an abrupt halt when she spotted an article, complete with a photograph, which made her look intently. She began to scrutinise the writing but her reading of English was not of a high standard. However, there was nothing wrong with her eyes, she recognised the person in the photograph - that man was now on board the cruiser. She had a feeling that this information might be useful so she took her phone out of her pocket and photographed the picture and article. She would send this to Boris. Was this person someone of importance? Boris would

155

be pleased with her and, reporting this person on board might be to her pecuniary advantage?

Moments later, sitting in the large saloon on the prince's cruiser, Boris looked closely at his phone. Anna had sent a cleverly worded message with the article attached. He understood the implications immediately. Switching on the computer in the main cabin, he transferred the message and enlarged the writing. The text in English was difficult to translate but slowly and painfully, he was able to make out some of the words and get the gist of the information. The photograph showed a scruffy man with longish blonde hair and the article described the unconventional but very wealthy, Lord Chivington. Boris laughed, what a find?

The article went on to mention Lord Chivington's sense of humour and his eccentricities. So, this wealthy man was playing games was he? He'd decided to venture into new territories - incognito. What an unfortunate mistake for him? A look at the stately home in the photograph told Boris that a very large ransom would be forthcoming should this man ever be kidnapped. Boris began to formulate a plan.

Having no idea that the police would delay the departure of 'The Danube Drifter', he checked the on-line itinerary of the holiday and found that the river cruiser would remain in Budapest only till mid-day, which didn't give him much time. There was an arranged outing for the holidaymakers so if the *target* was included in this, his plan would be scuppered but if the target was at large in the town? He sent Anna a quick text message - '*Were the dogs with the pack or had they been turned loose?*' They were loose! Luck was on his side.

Collecting another member of the entourage, a man who spoke English well and when necessary, could transform himself and present with a very respectable appearance, Boris set out into the town.

There was a large old house, not used any more as a dwelling, which had an excellent and secure cellar. Some time ago Dmitri had negotiated the rental of this for storage and other useful purposes. Boris and his associate headed directly for the house. They took a selection of electrical items in a suitcase; they meant to set up a prison complete with listening devices. Boris congratulated himself. He'd remembered that listening in was always a sure way of getting information. He was positive that he'd covered all contingencies. He checked his supply of chloroform; the man was large and might struggle, this was the only safe way. All he needed now was a lure to get Lord Chivington, into the cellar. He hoped his associate was up to the job; it all rested on his acting ability and the gullibility of the victims.

Pete and Polly had been wandering around Budapest trying to see some of the sights they'd missed the day before. They'd been warned not to return late because as soon as the guests on the delayed morning excursion arrived back, police permitting, the captain was hoping to leave and continue with the planned itinerary, keeping as close to the original timings as possible.

They'd been guided around the day before but were not sure exactly what they'd seen and what they'd missed. A lot of the sights blurred in their memory so they thought that today they would wander at their own pace and then, if they could find it, stop for coffee and cake in 'Ruszwurm', the oldest and most famous of the Budapest cafes, and one of the few to survive the world wars. Buildings were alright but a seven-layer cake, the speciality of the place, sounded great. They had a map and were turning it this way and that to try to locate the street where the cafe was situated. A polite young man, who spoke good English, asked if he could help them and on being asked the location of the said cafe, warned them that it was a very expensive venue and if they had not booked a table, they would not be able to be served there. Before disappointment could set

157

in, he told them that he knew a very good cafe where the food was just as good but for half the price.

'It's where the locals go,' he told them. 'The other place is just for tourists now. It's always very crowded and they take ages to serve you. I'm going past the other cafe, I can show you. There's a short cut. Follow me.'

Pete and Polly followed the man. He led them through back streets and then into a kind of yard.

'This looks like someone's 'ouse. Are you sure this is the way?'

'Of course, we take a short-cut through this low arch. Please bend so as not to hit your head.'

Pete went first, as he bent his head, a hand appeared from the side of the arch and a cloth went over his nose and mouth. He barely had time to struggle before he collapsed in a heap. Before Polly could react, a hand came over her mouth, courtesy of their new friend; this was speedily replaced by a similar cloth. Oblivion followed. They woke up a while later with their hands and feet tied and a gag over their mouths. They were on the floor in some kind of a cellar.

Chapter 16

The Kidnap

On board the river cruiser the captain was looking at his watch; it was approaching midnight. The cruiser needed to turn around for the return journey to Passau. He rang down to the reception area to enquire if the missing guests had returned. The night duty clerk was apologetic.

'Sorry no, Captain. Vicktor is still out looking for them.'

An exasperated captain drummed his fingers on the wheel and cursed under his breath. He was getting more and more stressed. Finally cleared to leave by the police, now he had guests missing. If he was any later setting off, he could lose his berth at Bratislava. Floating about in the middle of the Danube with no-where to dock, would not be a pleasant state of affairs.

Melissa was also very worried, she'd had guests get lost before but with one of her guests dying suddenly, to lose two more so soon after, was beyond belief. Vicktor had called back once and on not finding the pair returned, had gone out again to search. Soon she would have to involve the police – again! Where could the missing couple be? Then there was the other business; she still had to try and sort that out but with all this chaos, it was impossible. There were only a few more days left on the boat to fulfil her quest; without any peace, she would never do it. Why had she ever agreed to this? The stress was too much.

....

When Pete and Polly regained consciousness, they stared up from the floor with some trepidation. The giant of a man in front of them was quite intimidating. Never in a million years had they envisaged a situation like this.

159

Boris, wearing a padded suit with blocks under his shoes, both hidden under a sweeping buttoned-up cloak which fell to the floor, gave the impression of a much bigger man. He wore a balaclava and a mask so that face recognition wouldn't be possible. Anyone describing him would mention a tall large man. In reality, he was short and slender although his muscles were honed and his physique showed nothing to cause derision. It was a clever ruse and it had worked well before.

Disguising his voice, he told Pete and Polly that they were being held to ransom and soon they must make a recording, to send to their families, asking for a great deal of money. Their gags were removed but they were warned not to yell and scream.

'No-one can hear you in this place,' Boris informed, 'but we don't like to hear screeching noises. My friend next door hits people over the head if they're noisy.'

They were given a drink of water. Pete shook his head to clear it, manoeuvred his stiff jaw back and forth, licked his dry sore lips then, in a puzzled tone, started to speak.

'We don't 'ave no family. My old man be dead years and my old mum she were gone a year back.' Turning to look at Polly, he continued, 'She don't have none either.'

Polly closed her lips. Pete had succeeded in deliberately bumping his elbow against her; she knew it was a kind of signal, he was in charge.

Telling them that *he* knew better and recommending that they get themselves ready to ask for a ransom, Boris left the room. Pete nudged Polly again and inclined his head up high to the left, he'd spotted a tiny microphone. Polly understood when he shook his head, he was telling her to leave the talking to him. She remained silent.

'Don't know what they wants us for. What's all that talk about Mums and Dads, eh? I've never been important in me life and we don't have no money, no money at all. We don't even own our 'ouse, so what is they a doing of kidnapping us? You got any ideas Pol?' In response to a shaken head, she replied, 'Nah.'

Boris was listening in. He was surprised. He'd been sure that they would have said something to give themselves away after he'd left the room. Their way of speaking English seemed odd too. Perhaps all the nobility spoke like that? He listened some more –nothing! He decided to leave them to worry for another day. Boris felt smug; he was using his initiative.

....

In the evening after dinner, the two elderly ladies Minnie and Lavinia were in the bar; they cheerfully told everyone that they enjoyed a nightly brandy or two, it helped them sleep and at their age, the health of their liver was of no consequence.

Bob, resting an elbow on the tiny counter, was deep in thought, he was feeling slightly disappointed. He'd enjoyed his wines but he felt that the range on offer was not as extensive as he'd been led to believe. He was a little bored with the trip.

Diane was enjoying herself, she had no complaints and was happily chatting to Minnie and Lavinia. They were talking about the war years; both elderly ladies had served at a young age and Minnie, a nurse from the beginning of the war had carried on working in the same capacity for the next forty years.

David was sitting just a few feet away. He was feeling indignant and annoyed because Elaine had confessed that her boss had contacted her. She'd told a half-truth - she owned up only to being asked to keep her eyes open. Elaine bit her lip and tried the ploy she'd invented.

'Actually, David, you might be interested, it seems that an infamous wanted felon might be active in the vicinity.'
Somewhat acidly David replied,

161

'I've told you that this is supposed to be a work-free holiday and I don't care who it is. I'm *not* interested.' He ended the sentence with a scowl. Slightly hesitant, Elaine continued with,

'Well, it seems that this chap called Ronaldo Marconi could be operating in the area and......'

'Who did you say?'

Bob cut in, awoken from his reverie by the name he heard.

'Sorry, I didn't mean to butt into your conversation but if I heard you correctly, I have a particular interest in the person you mentioned.'

David's facial expression changed. He joined in the conversation, his pique forgotten.

'That's not the *international criminal* you were telling me about?'

'It most certainly is,' Bob continued, all grumbles about wines forgotten. 'I've been after a scoop about that chap for years. He's known as *'The Second Pimpernel'*. He's wanted in so many countries but somehow he covers his tracks brilliantly. David forgot all about not wanting to know and joined in the conversation.

'So this person may be in the vicinity?'

So much for confidentiality, Elaine thought. She now found herself side-lined and was not sorry. Bob and David began an intense conversation about criminality generally and of course, this elusive Ronaldo Marconi.

Diane, overhearing, decided that she might as well join in the conversation. Excusing herself to the old ladies, she asked what this chap was supposed to have done. Throwing caution to the winds, Elaine answered,

'Just about everything but essentially, he's a smuggler of anything illegal. He's a ruthless operator who lets no-one get in his way. There's a sophisticated operation smuggling diamonds in and out of Amsterdam. They arrive there to be cut and then go out again to various countries in the world. We believe an operation of this size is most likely run by him.'

162

The two old ladies had heard every word and they raised their eyebrows in surprise and looked alarmed. Elaine catching sight of this calmed them.

'Oh there's no danger to us,' she reassured them, 'but just the same I'd be grateful if you didn't pass on this conversation, careless talk - you know?' Then looking at the other three present in the group, she added, 'That goes for all of you as well, if you don't mind,'

Elaine might as well have saved her breath. Mary, one of the group of four ladies, had come out of the nearby toilets and passed behind the group just as the name was mentioned and she couldn't fail to hear what this character was supposed to be doing. A good bit of gossip was always welcome so she just *had* to pass it on to her three friends.

Antonio, doing his social duty, greeted the ladies as he passed and was in time to hear the gossip. Beads of perspiration appeared on his forehead, he'd no idea if he was working for this man or for anyone in opposition. He just knew that the sooner he could get away from all this the better.

The captain of the cruiser had no choice, having liaised with his employers, he'd been able to renegotiate his next berth and wait in the present one until midnight, allowing for one more evening to be spent in Budapest, but after twelve he had to move on. He told the staff that when the missing persons were found, they would have to be delivered by car to the next stop on the itinerary. He could not jeopardise the whole trip for two silly people. Consequently, the cruiser left its berth and returned along the previous route, ready to dock at Bratislava for a shortened visit. Guests were not pleased to have their itinerary altered; except of course, for Felicity, who had been sure that the whole thing was fate!

The next morning, as the guests rested on deck and enjoyed the splendid river scenery, Felicity spent much of her time

163

looking back to see if the Prince's cruiser had followed them and was disappointed not to see anything that might possibly resemble it. Having heard that the prince had a fabulous river cruiser, she'd been so sure that an invitation would come for her to visit the said vessel. Her previous good humour faded and once again she became peevish and difficult.

Sebastian was at the end of his tether and managed to slip away to have a quiet coffee in the company of Lillian who was always pleased to see him and grateful for his company. She'd been interviewed at length by the Hungarian police, an experience she didn't wish to repeat, and afterwards she'd found herself drinking far more alcohol than she'd ever imbibed in her life.

The boat eventually berthed at Bratislava. Dinner had been put back an hour to allow the guests time to take part in a short tour; they would be able to wander around the area with a guide. The cruiser would depart from Bratislava later in the evening.

It was a pretty town complete with cobbled streets, little squares, interesting architecture and lots of charisma; most people, with a few notable exceptions, enjoyed the visit very much. Sebastian, still waiting for retribution for absenting himself that morning, was too despondent to enjoy the excursion, Elaine was troubled, David and Bob were on constant watch and Melissa was distracted because Polly and Pete were still missing and there was only one day left before the end of the holiday. If they were not found by the end of the next day, there would be huge problems for her and the company; she hoped that they wouldn't detain all the guests. Problems with *three people* - one dead and two missing on one trip was just too much. In addition, she had to make a big decision by tomorrow and she was not looking forward to it.

Then there was the police. She hadn't informed the guests yet but she knew that it would only be a short time before the results of the post mortem were known and if the cause of Priscilla's death was not immediately identified as *natural causes*, it would most likely be construed as *suspicious* and in that case, with no obvious motive, it would be unlikely to be attributed to strangers. All the people on the cruise would be suspects and the police could detain everybody for questioning.

Lastly, there was poor Vicktor; he'd spent a long time searching for the missing guests and now he was looking strained and tired; he appeared to have lost some of his enthusiasm. He was obviously concerned with all that was going on, after all, it *was* his first job. Melissa felt responsible for him; such a pleasant and willing lad, she should have been a better mentor. My head hurts, she thought. I'm going to give all this up; it's just not worth it.

In her cabin, Melissa was still struggling with files and papers. It was no good, she decided, she would have to make the call but she'd prefer the missing pair to be found first. The looming problems were horrific; a girl could only take so much.

Viktor was puzzled. He'd searched all over the town for Pete and Polly, what could have happened to them? He'd had to come back without them. The police had been informed; he knew that would not be a popular decision.

Felicity was seething, her previous good humour had dissipated; she'd been *abandoned!* Her companion had disappeared - again! *She* was being neglected. Well no-one did that to her. She would go into the lounge, make an entrance and soon there would be people flocking to her side. She would speak severely to Sebastian later, she didn't know where he was but if she saw him, she was going to pointedly ignore him.

Delicately ambulating along the corridor in her soft silver shoes, she made not a sound and so was in the reception area before anyone knew she was there. The desk was empty but a voice came from the office beyond, it was Melissa and Felicity could not fail to overhear her words. Intrigued she stood there a moment and listened; her resolve and anger were soon forgotten in the sheer delicious knowledge that she'd heard something that she wasn't meant to hear. I wonder what I should do with this information, she pondered as she resumed her affected ambulation and entered the lounge.

When Melissa finally made an entrance, she caught sight of Felicity who appeared to look at her strangely and then seemed to be almost preening; she had a sort of satisfied and smug look on her face. Now, what could that be all about? Melissa thought. Christine spotted it too and drew her friends' attention to it.

'What do you think the prima donna is up to? Keep your eyes open girls, I think some fun is looming on the horizon.'

....

Prince Dmitri Romanovsky was deep in thought. His cruiser had now moved to a new berth and was docked not too far away from the Danube Drifter at Bratislava. He was perturbed that there was still this unexplained situation of the old actress who was spying for someone. He just couldn't see it. What was the old *has been* expecting to find out? Should he invite her to his cruiser?

'Keep your friends close but your enemies closer', he reminded himself. It was probably better to stay in control of the situation by getting her on board his boat and plying her with alcohol to loosen her tongue - but then there was the companion, could he be a problem? Dmitri felt irritated and on more than one count. Boris had absented himself; where on earth was he?

....

Sitting in the lounge, Felicity found herself reflecting on Sebastian's defection; she was feeling just a trifle deflated. More often than not, Sebastian seemed to be somewhere else and to cap it all, she had noticed a definite *falling off* of her circle of admirers plus, most upsetting of all, the expected invitation from the Prince had not materialised. She took out her mirror from her handbag and scrutinised her face. Drat! Her mascara had smudged. She needed her glasses to see well enough to repair the damage but there was no way she would allow anyone to see her wearing spectacles; vanity prohibited such an undesirable demonstration. She would return to her cabin and then, just maybe, Sebastian would deign to show up to keep her company. She was going to have something to say to him at the first private opportunity. She would never make a fuss in public, though, that would be lowering her standards and might also allow her to be the object of ridicule. She gracefully rose from the chair and made her way towards her cabin. As she passed the reception area, she was hailed.

'Pardon, madam,' called the young girl from behind the desk, 'this communication has just been delivered for you.'

Collecting the handwritten envelope, Felicity continued to her cabin. There, using her spectacles, she was able to repair her make-up and read the message.

Felicity was elated. It was a delicately worded invitation for her and a companion. Would she care to come over to the Prince's cruiser for cocktails? Would she? Of course, she would. In anticipation of her agreeing, the prince would send a car to collect her in half an hour. Now, where was that useless Sebastian? She must find him immediately because she couldn't possibly go alone - that would not only be flouting correct etiquette but appearing without an escort would reduce her standing with the Prince. Quickly repairing the mascara, she checked everything else was perfect and then hurried out in search of Sebastian.

She was fortunate enough to encounter him crossing the hall, he told her that he'd been taking the air on deck. She looked in horror at his casual clothes.

'Go and change immediately. We are invited to visit the Prince's cruiser for cocktails and you cannot wear that!' Sebastian was despatched to change his clothes while Felicity made her way to the lounge to wait, where she sat, observed by all, smirking like the cat who'd found the cream.

A couple of hours later there were several very bored people on the luxury river cruiser. Sebastian was disinterested and longing to return to the 'Danube Drifter', the substitute bodyguard was nervous, this would normally have been Boris' job; the guard didn't like strangers on board. Dmitri, however, was merely wary and tried to use his charm to loosen her tongue. Felicity was having a wonderful time; there was only one disappointment, Dmitri, though charming, flatly refused to have his photograph taken with her.

Dmitri had begun to suspect that this woman couldn't possibly be a spy because she asked no questions of him; in fact, she spent most of the time talking about herself. If anything, *he* was questioning *her*. Felicity recognised this as the fascination she projected to all things male and revelled in her anecdotes of years gone by.

After she'd bored everybody for at least another half hour, Sebastian tried to bring the visit to a close, citing that they must not outstay their welcome. Felicity was not having that; this might be the only chance she'd ever get to have a real-live Prince to herself so she was going to make the most of it. In desperation to break the monotony, Dmitri asked her if she would like to see the rest of the cruiser. Felicity beamed, Sebastian groaned and the *muscle* looked even more concerned.

In a small chain, they trailed around the boat with Dmitri leading, Felicity following but stopping every few minutes to look or comment on something while Sebastian and *the muscle* trailed behind.

Dmitri, desperate for something else to display, opened various doors including one to the large rope store on deck, he ad-libbed for a few moments in answer to some ridiculous questions and then, trying to change the subject, explained that only the sailors were knowledgeable about this area of the cruiser. Felicity made suitable inane comments followed by an artificial titter and told him that she was interested in *anything* that he had to show her.

The muscle, thoroughly bored, dragged his heels and lagged behind so much that he missed the fact that Sebastian, also trailing behind but further ahead than him, had opened the wrong door to look in and was stunned to see a room full of weapons. These were usually well-hidden but had been extracted from their hiding place for cleaning and checking. No-one had expected anyone to look in there at that time. His wits jerking to his aid, he closed the door quickly before the man following caught up and before Felicity turned back to find him. Sebastian was seriously alarmed. This didn't make sense. A Prince might have armed bodyguards but this was an armoury! Who was this chap? In a moment of revelation, it occurred to Sebastian that they knew absolutely nothing about Dmitri. They'd just taken everything at face value.

Extremely worried, Sebastian suddenly became forceful and to Felicity's annoyance, he caught up with her and told her that they must depart now because their boat was shortly due to leave. He'd no idea if this was really the case but he knew it was the only way he would get Felicity off the cruiser.

Peeved but unable to argue, she sweetly thanked the Prince then told him with a simpering smile and a great fluttering of eyelashes, that she sincerely hoped that they would meet again. He really must come to see her in her new film. Had she told

169

him that she had a leading role as *a spy in a thriller blockbuster*?

Dmitri blinked rapidly, realised what she had just said and then, everything fell into place. He'd been wasting his time with this silly old woman but at least now his mind would be at rest. He smilingly escorted her from the deck and told her that he was sure they would meet again.

Very relieved to have got away safely, Sebastian wondered if he should tell anyone about the weapons he'd seen. Think before acting, he decided. I'll sleep on it.

Chapter 17

The Meeting

It was the last full day of the week-long holiday. The 'Danube Drifter' had gradually made its way towards Durnstein where it had docked mid-morning. The warming sun was now cascading golden light through the windows, lighting up the lounge; it promised to be a wonderful day for exploring.

From one side of the cruiser, the castle could be seen standing proudly on the top of an enormous hill. Susan and Christine had been very keen to explore the famous stronghold where Richard the Lionheart was reputed to have been held captive and where his faithful minstrel, Blondel, was supposed to have found him. The story told was that Blondel travelled for months, visiting all the likely castles in a wide area. At each castle, he'd sung a song out loud which only Richard would respond to.

Today, however, it seemed that only Susan would be going to the castle because her friend had succumbed to a stomach upset. They'd asked beforehand, if anyone else would be joining them on the visit but all had declined because the castle was at the top of an extremely steep hill which had put everybody else off. It seemed that he others would be content with just visiting the picturesque village below.

Melissa was almost frantic to hear that a guest had a stomach upset. She was concerned that the food on board might be blamed. Even worse was the prospect of a contagious stomach bug raising its ugly head. How many more calamities could there be on a one week cruise? However, she needn't have worried, it seemed that it was only Christine who'd succumbed.

The other guests milled about waiting to disembark and the conversation was all about the recent disasters; it was shocking, wasn't it? Firstly, a suspicious death which hadn't yet been resolved and then two missing passengers who hadn't been found. Christine's illness, trouble number three, was hardly commented on.

Guests carefully walked down the railed gangplank and left the cruiser. They broke up into little groups and pairs as they wandered into the fascinating village. However, there was a slight air of nervousness about everyone and guests were not quite as carefree as they had been. No-one wanted to stray too far from the main party in case more people disappeared. However, the shops proved to be interesting and full of souvenirs, bottles of wine and preserves so the visitors soon forgot their fears in the pleasures of shopping.

Minnie and Lavinia had joined the throng. Equipped with their sturdy walking sticks, they carefully made their way along the slightly cobbled main street and wearing straw bonnets, made a cheerful picture as they carefully navigated the many obstacles and people who were spilling out into the street from the many shops.

Bob, as usual, was checking out the wines on offer but as expected, found only local beverages and nothing of interest. He sampled one and nearly gagged at the sweetness; he decided that a *dessert* wine was *too kind* a description. Minnie and Lavinia also tried a little sip, pronounced it lovely and both bought a bottle. Diane also tried a sip, looked around to see if Bob was watching and then quickly bought a bottle too. She wasn't averse to a little sweet sherry at times and this would make a pleasant substitute – as long as Bob didn't find out.

Felicity was still in a euphoric state, so much so that she refused to take notice of Sebastian or his warnings about not knowing much about the Prince. He'd decided to say nothing

172

about the weapons. Any report could only have come from either Felicity or himself and he didn't want either of them to be in any danger. Only one more day, he told himself, then we'll be away from all this and then I don't care what happens.

Felicity had blithely assumed that he was just being churlish, even jealous. She was never more pleased than when men were fighting over her and of late, there'd been a distinct lack of that.

She thrived on attention and being in the limelight; she was always looking for ways in which she might command it. Her thoughts kept returning to the office telephone conversation that she'd overheard; something wrong was happening and it involved that tour guide, Melissa. *Felicity - the heroine - exposes plot;* that would do nicely. She'd known from the start that the woman had something to hide. Women's intuition, she told herself, pure experience of life. I know a bad person when I see one. I was always a perfect judge of character; no-one can fool me. I shall know what to do.

They were running out of time. Wherever they went, Bob and David were now hopefully scrutinising all the men. On the trail of a good story, they'd suddenly developed a heightened sense of awareness of everything around them. Each male passer-by or person sitting in a cafe or bar was examined carefully despite the fact that neither man had the slightest notion as to the exact appearance of the said criminal. David, unused to the *cloak and dagger* side of things, nearly received a punch on the nose for peering too closely at one particular person. In vain had Elaine explained that it was more likely to be Budapest where this person might be found and they had left that town behind. Elaine was not happy, the phone call to her superior had been made and this was all adding to her considerable stress. She was *not* looking forward to their arrival at the UK border.

Melissa was also awaiting trouble but when it came, it was not as expected, it took on quite a different form. Events were now building up and were likely to lead to a variety of situations that any self-respecting tour guide would never want to be a part of.

....

Boris had suffered a setback. On finally returning to the cruiser and divulging the details of his initiative, instead of congratulations, Dmitri had exploded,

'You've done – what?'

Slightly deflated and a little confused by the response, Boris hurriedly explained that he'd had a tip-off that a wealthy English Lord was travelling incognito and was on a river cruiser that one of the *girlfriends* worked on. He'd checked and it was true, the guy owned a British stately house or whatever they called those things; his photo was in a magazine. He'd seen the article and photograph with his own eyes. The guy was loaded and would fetch a good ransom so he'd kidnapped him and the lady he was with and hidden them in the Budapest cellar that Dmitri rented. Boris beamed and waited for the congratulations; they didn't come.

'You imbecile! Where are your brains? The last thing I need at the moment is more police presence. Do you think that they'll ignore a missing *Lord*? No ransom is worth the possibility of the authorities checking up on us. He'll have friends in high places, government links. The police will *have* to find him. They'll search everywhere and if they find him, the trail will lead back to me. What did I do to deserve such incompetence?' Dmitri paced up and down. 'Are you positive this man is a Lord?'

Boris had lost his confident air.

'Well yes, no, not exactly, I did fix a microphone in the cellar so that we could hear their conversation.'

174

'And?'

'Well, er - nothing yet boss.'

'We'll go to the cellar and I'll listen.'

They hurried into a car and as inconspicuously as possible, returned to Budapest. Dmitri walked into the room above the cellar where the listening device was situated. He fixed the earphones to his head. At first, he could hear nothing then Pete's dulcet country tones could be heard. Pete had heard a tiny crackle and had guessed that someone was listening in. He knew that he had to convince them that they had made a mistake.

'Strange this here thing? What be their reason for taking *us*? We is only simple folk. I could have showed 'em me passport to prove it. I got both of ours 'ere in me travel belt round me waist.'

Dmitri took off the earphones.

'Go and relieve them of their passports. The man says he has them in a belt around his waist.'

Boris, dressed in his disguise, entered the room. The two people were still tied but they'd been allowed to eat a little, drink and use a toilet so they were not too uncomfortable apart from the stiffness caused by remaining fixed in the same position for a long time. Boris lunged at Pete and holding him down with one hand and a knee, he retrieved the passports from the belt. The pair were once again left in isolation.

A few moments later Boris was scratching his head in perplexity. The passports were both in the name of 'Smith'; the name 'Chivington', was nowhere to be seen nor was any form of aristocratic title.

'Perhaps they're forgeries,' Boris offered hopefully, but Dmitri was examining them closely and shaking his head.

'I don't think so but just in case, I'll get them checked. Stay close and do nothing. I'll be back early tomorrow.' He turned on his heel and walked briskly away.

Very early the next morning, having been unable to sleep, Pete and Polly were becoming increasingly tired and uncomfortable in the cellar and both were very hungry. They'd been given some food the day before but it was not enough; Pete was dreaming of eggs and bacon.

The passports had been returned from the expert and pronounced genuine. Boris was puzzled. He sent a text to Anna and took the risk of asking her to resend the photograph with the whole article on her phone. Dmitry studied it on his laptop and at once spotted the relevant passage,

'It says here that it's a good thing that Lord Chivington has a sense of humour because when walking in his grounds, he's more than once been mistaken for his gardener who resembles him a little. That's it! You cretin. To collect a ransom, you've kidnapped a pair of penniless individuals; the man's a gardener! It probably took them a couple of years to save up for the holiday. Fortunately for you, there won't be the fuss over a missing labourer that there would have been for a Lord.'

'What shall we do with them?'

'Oh, I am feeling magnanimous today. The poor devils are harmless. Give them back their passports, tie just their hands and blindfold them, bundle them into a vehicle and dump them well away from here. Don't forget to leave the blindfolds on. The less they see the better.'

An hour later a local police car stopped to investigate the strange sight of two people with blindfolds on and hands tied behind their backs, walking precariously along the edge of the road.

....

Despite the burning sun and the extreme temperature, after a leisurely lunch, Susan set out to visit the castle. She wasn't at all worried about straying from the crowd. She packed her

176

camera and a water bottle in a backpack, covered herself in sunscreen and donned sunglasses. She wore shorts with a vest top, placed a baseball cap on her head and a pair of sturdy trainers on her feet. On her wrist was a watch, held in place by a distinctive red woven strap.

The climb was indeed hard work and she stopped to rest from time to time. Poor Christine, she felt bad about that but she absolutely had to make this visit alone, there was no choice. The concoction added to Christine's tea would not do her any real harm and she would soon recover.

Susan reached the top. The old castle stood in crumbling grandeur, it was well worth the climb. She immediately located the small room where Richard was supposed to have been kept prisoner; the authorities had kindly labelled this for visitors in several languages, including English.

She wandered around the site, there didn't seem to be another living soul up there until she turned a corner and suddenly came up close behind a dark-haired man who was looking out at the view. The crunch of her shoes on the dry sandy terrain made him turn around; the shock was electric and mutual. Susan could not decide which emotion was foremost because she felt them all in rapid succession – amazement, bewilderment, anger and then a heart leap that was so painful.

'Susan!' he mouthed after a stupefied moment and she replied,

'Angelo?'

Susan was the first to speak. Her emotions, previously jumbled, now formed up in order; anger was first.

'Well, here's a surprise. You are the last person I expected to see. Oh I know,' the sarcasm was patent, 'you knew I was here and so you came up to find me so that you could explain, even apologise! Well, come on then, out with it.'

There was a pause while Angelo struggled with words.

'You are correct,' he began slowly, 'I must be the last person you expected to meet up here but – for me, it is not an unwelcome meeting. I never wanted to leave without a farewell but – events overtook me – I, I had no choice, I had to leave.'

'And?'

'And?'

'The reason?' There was another pause.

'I can't tell you but please believe it was with regret. There were things that you couldn't imagine. It was better to leave before.......' His voice faltered and he looked genuinely upset; Susan began to calm down.

'You could have told me *something*. At least said goodbye. I might have understood. No, you're right,' she conceded, 'I wouldn't have.'

She looked down at the ground, thinking of what might have been. The relationship had seemed so special until their break-up. His sudden leaving without a word had been a devastating blow - if only. She came back to reality with a jolt. She mustn't forget her reason for coming up here. Looking around her, she could see no-one else; he couldn't have arrived yet. She would have to shake off Angelo. Just my luck, she thought, I meet him again and now I have to leave. What the hell is he doing up here anyway? Is he on holiday too? It's a strange place for a chance meeting. She looked up to see that Angelo was surreptitiously glancing around him; was he meeting someone too? He looked at his watch. Susan's eyes followed the movement.

'I'm so sorry but I must .... leave. I have to meet someone very soon. Maybe we could.......,' his faltering words came to a halt as he saw the expression on Susan's face.

'*You* have a meeting. *I* have a meeting. There's nobody else here. There was no-one on the track and,' she took a backward look, 'the trail leading to the castle is empty. We both have a meeting here this afternoon, don't we? A meeting, it would appear, with *each other*.' She pointed to the red watch strap on her wrist and then looked down at his watch strap, it was red, the agreed identification method.

Angelo sat down on a boulder and stared at her. Events had moved too fast and he was genuinely bereft of speech. Susan went off into peals of laughter.

'As you know, Angelo, my name, is Susan Butler but when I came to England, my surname was Columbo, I had my name changed by deed poll. I'm here today, on behalf of my father, to meet *you*, his Italian contact. You must work for Ronaldo.'

Still giggling at the absurdity of it all, Susan, sat down next to him on the boulder but quietened when he began to speak.

'*You* are the daughter of the boss of an American *syndicate*? If only I'd known. I didn't think you would want to get mixed up with me if you knew more about me. Our time together was a lovely interlude but I regretted so much, that it had to end. Now I find, perhaps, that you are not so very different from me? Tell me, how did this come about? You told me that you'd come to England to get away from your controlling father but you didn't say that he was one of the *Dons*.'

'In my place, would you have owned up to it? In any case, I was sure that, if he'd found me, my father would have sent someone to get me back home, so I told no-one about my home life. As my mother is English, I managed to acquire a British passport and then I changed my name by deed poll as fast as I could, lastly I re-applied for a passport in my new name.'

'But now you *work* for your father?'

'Sort of. It came about in a peculiar way. Some time ago, I felt a bit bad about breaking off all contact with my parents so I sent a letter giving a PO box as an address and my mother wrote back saying that my father wanted to talk to me and was no longer angry. I didn't trust him at first and so being extra cautious, I travelled up to a coastal town, stayed in a hotel for a night and put in a call to the USA. Dad and I had a long talk. He told me that he'd realised that I was so like him and that maybe it hadn't been a good idea to try to marry me off which

179

had been his original intention and the reason I left home. He wanted to make us a family again. Then came the real reason; the cousin from Italy, Giovani had turned out to be useless, a total disaster. If I'd married him, Dad would have been stuck with him. As it was, he'd sent him packing back to Italy. My sister's husband Mario, had turned out well and was now *heir apparent*. Then Dad told me about a new link he'd made in Europe. He'd initially sent Mario for the original negotiations but Mario was now needed at home so as my father cannot travel safely to Europe himself, he asked *me* to represent the family. It was a huge step for my father to accept a daughter as part of the business side of things so I was greatly honoured.

When I discovered the meeting was to be in Austria, I knew it was fate as I had already booked this trip on the Danube. My holiday became the perfect cover. I was told secrecy was vital so when I sent the text suggesting a place for our meeting, I had to ensure that it was unlikely that anyone I knew would be here at the same time; I even had to *nobble* my friend. I had to hope that my contact was fit enough to make the climb - and you were!

Well, that's *my* story. Dad and I now get on fine. I have his total confidence, so let's talk business.'

The negotiations were swiftly concluded and arrangements were made to the mutual benefit of both parties. Angelo told her that he was wanted by the authorities; therefore, he too had to be very careful. Should she recognise him in public she must not, under any circumstances, acknowledge him or let anyone think that they'd already met.

An hour and a half later, Susan set out on the descent. She would be meeting Angelo again. She wasn't going to let him off the hook too easily, she had her pride but she couldn't stop the little satisfied smile that kept appearing on her face. The old attraction was back but she needed to keep a cool head. It had to be business first.

Susan found the downhill climb a lot easier and made good time. With a light heart, she stopped several times to just breathe in the view; it was magnificent. The vista stretched for mile after mile displaying a verdant plain with sunlight dancing on the ripples of the gently flowing river winding through it. Undulating hills, clear and mist free, loomed in the background. Susan felt *so alive*. She was far happier than she'd been for a long time. Everything was going so wonderfully well.

Chapter 18

Starting Back

It was early morning when the 'Danube Drifter' slowly entered her reserved docking place at Passau. Melissa had endured a sleepless night. After tossing and turning, she'd left her bed and walked up and down in the tiny cabin. She'd had to make the telephone call yesterday and was now awaiting events. If that wasn't bad enough, the missing couple hadn't been heard of and the guest who'd died was still an unexplained death. She would never forget this cruise.

Elaine too hadn't slept. She was so sure that she was on to something. The difficulty was that she'd been instructed to try to keep the foreign police out of things. The British police wanted the action to take place under UK jurisdiction - *after* the French customs had been negotiated. They hoped to be in total control. However, following her instructions meant that David had only been given limited information concerning her role. Because of this, should she discover anything, he would be *gung ho* about wanting her to immediately inform the local police authorities. He didn't know about the confidential line of communication which she'd already used or the fact that she was awaiting events.

Bob was also making sure that he was kept in the loop. If anything occurred, he would prefer a British operation but the journalist in him would forgo any of that as long as he was in on any action and he got a story. Retired or not, the satisfaction of a brilliant scoop, which he could sell to whoever he liked in the newspaper world, was keeping him in a state of extra vigilance. The name Ronaldo was banded about a little too much for Elaine's liking and '*walls had ears*'.

It was a dilemma. If any of the staff *were* involved in this, she really shouldn't leave the exposure until the coach reached the border because they, of course, would remain with the boat and could just disappear. What should she do?

Felicity made a decision. It was her duty. She'd heard that Melissa woman and it was quite clear that she was engaged in some nefarious activity. Always careful if she travelled abroad, Felicity had made Sebastian place all the emergency numbers on her phone. In the privacy of her cabin, she made a call to the local German police, asking for assistance in English and in careful, distinctly enunciated English, she gave the details of the overheard conversation.

Most people on board had packed their belongings the night before but there were still the last minute things to add to hand luggage and because of this, breakfast was attended early by the majority of the guests. The suitcases had already been removed from cabins and were waiting outside for the coach to arrive and for Paul to load them into its luggage compartment.

Thus it was that most were enjoying their breakfast when a police car arrived noisily on the wharf. Two severe-looking officers from the local police walked on board. As no-one was entirely sure of the business they were concerned with, it brought out a lot of fevered emotions.

Melissa breathed a sigh of relief, she assumed that their presence meant that her ordeal was nearly over. Susan watched in alarm, Antonio observed in a total panic, Bob and David were on the alert and Elaine was puzzled. The other guests craned their necks to see what was happening. Felicity, wanting a grandstand view and a starring role, had hurried out into the reception area, all ready to gain publicity by adding her accusations out loud as no-doubt, the criminal, was to be carried off by the police. All suppositions were wrong.

183

Before anything more could be said, there was a further disturbance. Two grubby and quite dishevelled figures walked up the gangway to the amazement of the open-mouthed observers.

'I'm starving. Is breakfast still on? I could eat an 'orse.' From beneath his battered hat, the weary face of Pete could be seen. Polly, next to him, was too exhausted to speak. Polly and Pete had been found.

Most people were decent and caring and were truly pleased that the couple had been found safe and unhurt but the smiling camaraderie began to change when the police made it clear that the departure could not go ahead as planned until everyone had been questioned. Paul arriving with the coach, intending to load the cases, walked straight into the police and before he could back away, was hauled onto the boat and told to remain.

The local police, the Landespolizei, was there to return the missing couple but also to try to get some answers concerning the kidnap. At first, it seemed as if they were *pointing the finger* at the holiday company for losing two of their guests but then the suggestions became more threatening. Paul paled. All ready to load the innocuous suitcase, suddenly it seemed that belongings might be searched again. If guests were told to reclaim their luggage for checking, *the* case would stand out like a sore thumb. He could see the case, it was in full view with a made-up address on the bright label. Antonio, even whiter than Paul, had always been the possessor of a strong bladder, today he was not so sure.

Polly, and the usually garrulous but now subdued Pete, were allowed some breakfast and then sent to have a shower, change their clothes and collect their belongings. At first, the police had wanted to keep the couple's clothing for possible DNA evidence but thankfully, it was decided that this would not result in any useful information. Pete, recovering quickly due to his stomach being filled, had given this information to the other guests as he ate. Most tried not to think that in his case, the wearing of police overalls might have been an improvement on his usual mode of dress. Polly, showing signs of tiredness, had little to say but Pete, feeling refreshed, could not resist. Just one last time he had to mention,

'Three meals a day? Not bad is it?'

In view of his ordeal, there was no reply or adverse reaction but this was because the guests had themselves under tight control. One death per voyage was enough.

Susan had managed to slip back to her cabin unnoticed. A quick text to a local number mentioned that *some farmyard animals were scavenging and might be dangerous*. The message was received and understood. Anna too had seen the danger, a second message similarly vague but with a definite warning, was sent to Boris.

Once again Felicity was ignored. Furious that her moment had been taken from her, she tried to talk to the police, insisting that it was her who'd called them and shouldn't they be taking her statement? As this was all said in English with dramatic overtones and the two police were just local officers and not able to converse in English, they took little notice of Felicity's outburst. However, others did and it caused some alarm. The net of intrigue was becoming ever more tangled and was likely to cause some unexpected developments. Still wrapped up in her own difficulties, Melissa had no idea of what had happened and so she was still patiently awaiting events.

If the stupid police were not going to act on her tip-off, Felicity decided, someone else must be made aware. She looked around for someone to confide in and spotted Elaine. Despite Elaine's best efforts to keep her employment information private, the fact that that she was a   police detective, had leaked out all over the cruiser and Felicity saw her as the obvious recipient for information.

Plonking herself in front of Elaine, she gave her no chance to disappear before unburdening herself. She began in a loud voice, one that was used to being heard in a large theatre and today was no exception; everybody heard it.

'My dear,' she began in her usual dramatic manner, 'I simply must inform you of the information I have about the criminality at present on board this river cruiser.' All ears pricked up, including those with something to hide and those who were just plain interested in gossip.

'I know you are a representative of her Majesty's police force and therefore the best person to inform.' Elaine began to reply,

'Actually, I'm on holiday and.....' She was not allowed to finish her sentence.

'I think all police forces must be the same, don't you? You all share a common bond, or whatever it is. Anyway, you would be the best person to deal with the German police about this. I have tried to make myself understood but the cret.....' she stopped; it was not a felicitous comment to make to one police officer about another. 'Those young men do not seem to understand that I have *information*. They would listen to you, being a colleague.' I doubt it, thought Elaine, especially if they knew what I was up to.

Using as much tact as she could muster, Elaine politely declined to become involved reiterating that she was on holiday and wouldn't be able to help. Felicity was incredulous and frustrated, she was unused to refusals. Very well, she decided in a huff, I shall find another way to speak to the authorities. Abandoning the quest never entered her head. She reminded herself that it would enable villains to be brought to justice - it was her duty as a citizen. She also concluded that it might bring her a little publicity which could be quite advantageous and *that* should never be dismissed as unimportant.

Antonio was thinking frantically. He was now aware that Paul was the person who would remove the suitcase and so must be the next link in the chain but was Paul part of the plot or just a driver who loaded all the cases? Paul, in turn, had no idea who'd put the case there. If Paul *was* part of the team, Antonio calculated, it was likely that if Antonio tried to remove the case, thinking Antonio was just an employee, Paul would assume that he needed to protect the contents and so might try to prevent him. Antonio didn't want to draw attention to himself or admit to anyone that he was part of the plot. How could he effect the removal of the piece of luggage without suspicion? I've got it! He congratulated himself on his brainpower. I'll wait till everyone is about to collect their luggage then I'll tell the two elderly ladies not to worry as I will get their cases for them. They won't know that I haven't offered to do this for anyone else so I can put the bogus case under my arm and carry their two cases inside. I should be able to slip away down the corridor with the remaining case. Antonio hovered and watched, never letting his eyes stray from the special suitcase.

Paul was doing the same thing. Having immediately identified the case by its bright label, he racked his brains as to how he could remove the case without being noticed. He came up with a similar idea to Antonio. He surmised, if I start to bring the cases back from outside into the reception area in a random manner, I'll be able to leave that one till last and then in the confusion of everybody looking for their cases, I should be able to slip that one into the luggage compartment and push it to the back out of sight. The police won't search the coach because they'll think they have all the luggage here. All I need to do is open the luggage compartment first and invite the police to look, then I'll leave it open. It was a plan that could go wrong but Paul felt that he had too much to lose not to try. All he needed was an opening, a way to start things off without drawing attention to himself.

The staff on the cruiser were very annoyed, they couldn't clean the cabins or clear up from breakfast because the police stopped all activity. Everyone had to go back and remain in the dining room because the police were waiting for an official interpreter. In the meantime, Vicktor and Melissa were used as unofficial interpreters to inform the guests of the police instructions. Poor Melissa found that not only was her ordeal not over, in some ways it had just begun.

Outraged guests, who could not argue with the police, took it out on the holiday reps.

'How much more of this?' they asked. They told her that it was a bit much to have their belongings searched for a second time. What on earth were the police looking for? Melissa was at a loss, she had no idea. Events were now running out of control. She was relieved that the missing two had turned up but when she heard their story she was mystified along with everyone else. Who on earth would see Pete and Polly as kidnap victims? Many decided that a holiday in this part of Europe was not such a good idea after all; next year it would be back to good old sunny Spain.

The questioning had to wait for the moment but each guest was instructed that when the police interpreter arrived, they must collect their luggage and return to the cabin they'd been staying in. Guests and staff alike saw this as a thundering nuisance. The cleaners were furious – no cleaning, no money and certainly no tips from the departing people who no doubt would eventually scramble off in a rush and forget all about tipping.

Antonio, with self-preservation firmly in mind, found some courage from somewhere and blithely announced that if it would speed up matters, the staff and able-bodied guests,

188

could start to bring everybody's luggage into the reception area. The police conceded that this was a good idea so groups of people headed for the luggage. Paul relieved saw his salvation. Telling Vicktor to ask the police to come and check the coach luggage compartment, he hurried out to the coach followed by one of the officers. The luggage compartment was opened and the officer peered in, noted that it was empty, except for Paul's case, and nodded to signal satisfaction. He indicated that Paul should remove this case and after watching to ensure that he did so, the officer returned to the cruiser.

Paul left the compartment open and confidently walked towards *the* suitcase; it was gone! Wildly looking around, he was just in time to see that it was tucked under the arm of one of the helpful staff, the Hotel Manager. Calamity! That meant that he had somehow to get hold of it from inside.

Due to the throng of people as guests came to claim their luggage, Paul found himself unable to keep his eye on the suitcase. When he reached the Reception area, he could not see it. Someone had removed it. He felt sick.

Antonio had managed to follow his plan, the case was on the floor, he'd kicked it under the curtained reception partition; he should be able to remove it later.

After thirty minutes had elapsed, another police car arrived bringing a senior officer accompanied by a civilian interpreter. It had been obvious to all that the local police were not used to asking questions in this kind of situation. The officer, however, being newly promoted, was keen to show what he *could* do but he was not sure what he *should* do. As it was the Hungarian local police who'd stumbled onto Polly and Pete, they'd passed them on to their German equivalent, the Landespolizei, who'd been tasked to return the couple to their holiday group and to delay the onward journey. The new officer, however, felt that he had to have some justification for being there so he'd instructed his men to take a detective's role. They were now in the throes of *grilling* various likely persons – they would show that the local police had just as much ability to solve crimes as the specialist groups.

Consequently, Felicity, who felt that she had some important information, Elaine who was on to some real leads and guilty Antonio and Paul, were not really bothered with but for some reason, possibly his beard and spectacles, they thought Bob cut a suspicious figure, and similarly Polly and Pete (despite being the victims), because they did not conform to the usual holiday type, were repeatedly questioned. Finally, gathering an audience, the Kommissar began to issue some instructions to the passengers in general.

The Prince's cruiser had arrived at Durnstein. Boris had received a warning from Anna, about increased police presence in the area and although there was no real reason for the Prince and his entourage to have any concerns, precautions were taken – just in case. The armoury was replaced into its hidden position. The back wall of the tiny room was reversed, padded and firmly secured in place so that to any observer or anyone suspiciously tapping the walls for a hollow sound, the room appeared as merely a store. A few items were scattered in there to create the illusion. Dmitri ensured that no business meetings were taking place in the near future and the sim card in his phone was removed and replaced with an alternative that was full of bland calls, mostly to young women. Boris was also instructed to change his phone. Dmitri arranged for some *bimbos* to be on his yacht for a day or two. It was vital that he continued to be seen as a useless playboy.

The other thing that was really *bugging* Dmitri was the fact that he was no nearer to discovering his rival. He was positive that there was a rival and he'd begun to suspect that there was a link to the Danube Drifter but he couldn't get any more information. It didn't help that there were constantly different people on board but he was not devoid of brains, there were constants – the staff and the coach drivers. However, his priority had to be self-preservation and the safety of his men. He couldn't see his way clearly for the moment so preventing discovery was paramount. He would keep an eye on the 'Danube Drifter' and cruise into Passau as if he hadn't a care in the world. Mind you, if that awful woman saw him, he might find that he did have a few more cares. To think he'd thought she was a spy. He must be losing his senses. It didn't do, though, to treat everyone who seemed harmless as stupid. The man who came with Felicity didn't say much but it had occurred to Dmitri afterwards, that he was quite observant in a *laid-back sort of way*. I don't think it did any harm, he surmised, but in hindsight, I think a tour of my cruiser might not have been such a good idea.

Chapter 19

Chaos

Gerhart Kaufer, new Kommissar of the Landespolizei, was enjoying himself. He felt quite important. He was issuing instructions. Instead of the usual mundane local matters, he was dealing with a kidnap; that was more like it, he thought If he could find evidence of some criminal activity connected with this cruiser, then he might be onto the people who'd tried to kidnap two of the guests. A little prestige would go a long way. He convinced himself that he could assist in solving this crime. However, his grandiose daydreams were soon to be shattered.

A black BMW slid quietly into the parking area on the dock and four men, all with sinister expressions and wearing dark suits, stepped out of the car and made their way up the gangplank and into the reception area of the 'Danube Drifter'. They were from the Federal Criminal Police Office, the Bundeskriminalamt, known as the BKA. A visit from these people was never a good thing; even if you were innocent of any crime, you found yourself quaking a little. They were the type of police that you instinctively called 'Sir'. The reception staff understood the crisp German demand and immediately sent for Captain Van Beeke who arrived promptly. He was in no doubt that you did not keep the BKA waiting.

The grouped staff and holidaymakers, aware of another disturbance, glanced up to see the new action. They could not understand the conversation but it was clear that this visit appeared to be nothing to celebrate. The kommissar, who had his back to the reception area, became aware that the guests and staff were not paying attention to the interpreter translating his instructions and, to his intense annoyance, neither were his men. Showing obvious irritation, he turned, spotted the arrivals and was about to mouth an indiscretion about people who interrupted the police, when suddenly he realised who the visitors must be. The comment died on his lips.

Within a moment, in a fairly tactless manner that immediately set up his back, the BKA instructed Kaufer to come to the main reception area. He fumed inwardly, he *was* an officer and so deserved respect in front of his men.

For these officers of the BKA, who were used to dealing with both the highest and lowest levels of humanity, low ranking officers of the Landespolizei meant nothing to them. The local police were looked on as simply a body of people who relieved the BKA of the less important aspects of police work. The crime *they* dealt with was *real* crime. This unit was interested in international criminality and they had been given a *tip-off*. They were irritated to find that the local police had arrived first on the scene.

'We're taking over,' the newly promoted officer was informed without tact or ceremony. 'You can leave now.'

Polizeikommissar Gerhardt Kaufer puffed out his chest and replied stiffly,

'I regret that I am unable to comply with your request.

My instructions clearly state that I must.....' He was cut short.

'We don't require local police for these special duties and don't understand why you should be here. Your men will get in our way.'

'I insist! My superior will require me to return with questions answered. I have been instructed to detain all persons on this boat until my superiors give permission for guests to leave and the cruiser to move.'

'In a case such as this, BKA takes over.'

'With respect,' the kommissar replied, 'in a case such as what?'

Noticing that there was an interested spectator behind the reception desk, the plain-clothed policeman guided the kommissar into the nearby office, nodded at the girl in there to leave and then he shut the door.

'Why are you here?' the BKA officer asked with narrowed eyes.

'The kidnap.'

'What kidnap is this?' The BKA officer screwed up his eyes in a puzzled frown.

'We have just returned two kidnapped victims to this boat and need to question the guests. These people were abducted in Budapest and have been handed over to us by the Hungarian rendőrség.'

'Where are all these people from?'

'The United Kingdom.'

'You question guests who live in the *United Kingdom* for a crime of kidnap that happened in Hungary? Who exactly was kidnapped?'

'Two of the guests.'

'And these guests are important people?'

'Well, er no. Actually, they're gardeners, well the man is.'

'They have been found alive and well?'

A nod followed.

'Then why is it so important to spend so much time and effort on questioning people here? We have a far more important task. You must not get in our way.'

'But,' said the kommissar miserably, 'I was instructed to...'

'Oh very well, but do not cause problems for us.'

With that, he marched back into the reception area and informed his colleagues that the local police would be questioning some people but they would have the first call on seeing anyone they wished to.

Antonio came the closest he'd ever been to having a heart attack. These were the elite police, you didn't fool with them. They would go through any points of interest with a toothcomb and they would hone in on any suspects and think nothing of grilling them for hours on end until they got the required information. Antonio was a coward, he knew it; if they interviewed him and suspected anything - he'd be finished. The sweat began to run down his brow. Where could he hide the case now and, more to the point, how could he even get hold of it? It would only be a matter of time before someone found it.

To his relief, the BKA asked for Melissa first. Two officers went into an office with her and the remaining two walked off into the staff quarters. Antonio hovered but the reception was never empty. Then he was called away by the captain; he had to go, he had no choice. Fate was there like the sword of Damocles – would it fall on him?

Lavinia was very observant. She had seen Antonio push the case under the flap.

'You know, dear,' she remarked to Minnie with a wry grin, 'I think that naughty Antonio, the Hotel Manager, has been doing something he shouldn't. I think he has something in that case that he is trying to hide.'

'Naughty, naughty boy,' Minnie responded chuckling. 'Shall we help him?'

Bold as brass, while Lavinia distracted the receptionist, Minnie walked past the counter and when she reached the small curtained partition, she hooked out the small case with her upturned stick. Then picking it up, she wobbled with it along the corridor to the cabin she had been using. No-one took any notice of an old lady.

Antonio rushed back as soon as he was able, touched the bottom of the curtain with his toe but met no resistance. Pretending to tie his shoelace he peeped underneath - it had

195

gone! Swearing by all the saints that he would live a life so pure and good if only he could have just one more miracle to get him out of this mess, Antonio returned to his duties.

Melissa was completely bewildered. She *had* made a telephone call but it was not her communication that had called these people, it was the one Felicity had made along with another call. As Dmitri had come to suspect that the 'Danube Drifter' could actually be the base for his rival, using a public phone, he'd anonymously tipped off the police that an international crime syndicate had dealings on this boat. He surmised that if they had a good enough reason, the police would do a thorough search and if they found anything, it would put his rival out of action. As long as the call could not be traced back to him, he couldn't lose. If nothing was found on this boat, then he would have to start looking at other river users but somehow, whenever an arrangement was made by his contacts, it seemed to coincide with this cruiser being in the vicinity. Dmitri didn't believe in coincidences.

The first telephone call to the police had specifically named Melissa and so she was being given the third degree. Shocked at the turn of events, she tried to explain but was being bombarded with questions in a language that was not her own. She could speak German but when questioned she needed to mentally translate what was being asked, into English, answer in her head in English and then translate it back into German; it was a slow process and one the German police could not understand. They assumed she was using delaying tactics and so became quite aggressive. What had she been doing? What did the overheard conversation mean?

Meanwhile, Kommissar Kaufer was trying to get some sort of sense from guests who were upset, incredulous that they were being questioned and furious about the ruination of their holiday. Even Pete and Polly said that there was no harm done, they were OK and could they all just go home? Kaufer could not agree, this was his moment of glory and he would *not* have it brushed aside. With a renewed zeal he set about asking even more questions. While playing the part of a detective, he became so puffed up in his own conceit that he forgot the relevant fact that the victims had already been found and none of the questions he asked were designed to discover *why* they had been kidnapped in the first place?

Melissa was becoming distressed. She had no idea what was happening. Why were these officers so aggressive towards her? Finally, realisation dawned. Someone must have overheard her on the phone to her contact.

Elaine was also doing her best to stay on top of events. It was like a whirlwind; there seemed to be so much going on at once. With two lots of police from different departments trying to work at the same time, she knew from bitter experience, how difficult it could be. So one lot were trying to throw some light on the kidnap but what were the others after? Glancing around the room while she waited her turn to be questioned, she caught sight of Felicity. Sitting bolt upright on a chair with an expectant air, she was like an actress waiting in the wings for her finest role. Elaine knew at once. What has that daft woman done? It must be her.

Lavinia walked slowly back into the dining room and looked around for Melissa. She wished to deliver a message that Minnie was a little indisposed but Melissa was not there. One of the officers pointed to a chair and indicated that she should sit. All the guests were being escorted in pairs to their cabins for interrogation by the local police and it soon became Lavinia's turn. She tried to explain to the policeman but he brushed her aside and indicated that she should go to her cabin.

197

She tried again but he wouldn't listen so she gave up. He marched in and began to open drawers and wardrobes that had already been emptied. He was about to sort through the suitcases when he sensed that someone was in the shower room, he flung open the door and there was Minnie, sitting on the toilet complete with long silk drawers about her ankles but hiding her modesty with a voluminous skirt. She immediately shrieked and a red-faced policeman apologised and hurriedly shut the door. After a cursory look through the suitcases with Lavinia wringing her hands and saying over and over, 'I tried to tell you,' he quickly left. Minnie, now with drawers pulled up, sat on the bed with Lavinia and laughed. The small suitcase was still balanced on the toilet seat.

Melissa, still in the room with the BKA and trying to explain herself, stopped in mid-sentence when she heard a further commotion in the reception area. It seemed two other gentlemen had arrived. They were told they had to wait.

One of the two was a very important man, wealthy and influential and he did not take kindly to being bluntly told that he was not to be seen immediately.

'Nonsense,' he retorted. 'Do you know who I am? I own this river cruiser; I own the cruise line!' His protest fell on deaf ears.

Felicity was called for and asked to repeat the conversation she had overheard. She took a deep breath, posed herself suitably for the deliverance of the coup-de-grace and using it as a useful rehearsal for her coming role, began in a slow and dramatic tone. Being urged in clipped tones by a sharp voice, with a strong German accent, to *please hurry up*, she somewhat sulkily abandoned the theatrics and stated baldly that she had overheard what she believed to be evidence of criminal activity. At this moment the door burst open.

'Why have I been kept waiting and why are my staff being interrogated?' The portly, grey-haired and very angry man filled the doorway. His exquisite well-cut suit proclaimed the patrician and his wonderful moustache confirmed his nobility. 'I am Wolfgang Franz Von Liebenstein and this is my cruiser. Fraulein Phipps is a special auditor and she works directly for me.'

Kommissar Kaufer was beginning to feel just a little disheartened. He'd not found out a single thing. He'd questioned so many people and could see that with most of them, it was a complete waste of time. He'd narrowed it down to a few people who seemed suspicious and these he had left till last. He was embarrassed to be told that one of his men had harassed an old lady of over eighty years old whilst she was sitting on the toilet and it was lamentable in his eyes that the two victims, seemed to want him to give up. Well no-one would be able to say that he hadn't done his duty. He'd question the remaining people. He had a sneaking feeling that, apart from Pete and Polly, who were a noticeable exception, many of the guests were a lot more intelligent than he was.

He called Bob and Diane. Bob looked a likely criminal and the officer became even more suspicious when Bob started noting things. On discovering that he was a retired journalist, Kaufer was seriously alarmed, these sneaky people had a way of twisting the truth by omitting the parts that did not make a good story and sensationalising the rest. Kaufer did not want to end up in any tabloids. They were quickly dismissed.

He was down to the last two. The man looked slick and smart, like a confidence trickster and had one of those English *'Public School'* accents – a sure sign of criminality. The wife was somehow different, still feminine but business-like, and had an authority about her that in his view, women shouldn't have. Well, she and he would soon find out who they were dealing with; he had the authority of the *law* behind him.

After staring into the quiet but steady blue eyes of the man, Kaufer began to feel just a little disquiet. He felt worse when on being asked his employment, David replied with emphasis – my *profession* is that of a barrister-at-law. Thrown off-balance, Kaufer tried to concentrate. He asked his next question but found his attention straying. He quickly regained his focus. To his last question, David was replying,

'No I don't know the kidnapped pair other than having met them on this holiday. I have no idea why they were kidnapped and who might have done it. We saw nothing, we were in the company of most of the other guests at the time.'

Kaufer grimaced inwardly. Before starting questioning everybody, he hadn't known that most of the guests had all been together for nearly all of that particular day. It would have saved a lot of time in questioning had he been informed of this earlier. Still, he was a German police kommissar, he could not admit a fault in front of these foreigners and definitely not in front of the BKA. However, on trying to salve his pride by attempting to intimidate Elaine, his ego was squashed flat when she produced her warrant card and told him that she was a senior English police detective (her equivalent German rank being far senior to him) and that although she couldn't help him with any information, she had been interestedly observing German police methods.

When the lack of success, on behalf of the local police, reached the BKA, one of the officers could not resist some sarcastic remarks about incompetence. However, soon it was the BKA's turn to be a little embarrassed as it became clear that Felicity, in the best tradition of overheard gossip, had heard only part of the conversation and misconstrued the rest.

Melissa had been talking on the telephone. She'd confirmed that her audit of the books had shown some irregularities. There were items listed that couldn't have been purchased, alcoholic drinks bought at a more expensive price than they should be and a lot of stock had been repurchased due to supposed loss or damage. Money was being leeched out somewhere and not paid into the company accounts. She'd found the ledgers and managed to make copies of them and then compared them with bank statements and the receipts. It appeared at first view that probably, two things were happening. Small regular amounts were being stolen by *paper fraud* and large amounts of alcohol were being stolen and sold on.

Just before Felicity had walked by the office, Melissa had been saying,

'I have the evidence now. Quite a lot of pilfering must have been happening and it seems *very* organised.' Her telephone contact had asked her what she thought; should they put a stop to it now or wait to be sure to catch all the thieves? It was at this point that Felicity overheard,

'I think the petty pilfering could continue for a time, we don't need to worry too much about it at this stage but we need to sort out this large-scale sale of alcohol quickly in case someone suspects me.'

Krauss, the BMK officer took a sharp breath and gathering his dignity, apologised to the visitor saying,

'My department regrets that there seems to have been a misunderstanding here. Clearly, the other call we had was malicious. We will leave you to interrogate your staff and if you decide that criminal activity has taken place, please call us and we will return.'

He glared at Felicity who for once, was looking somewhat crushed, and by opening the door, gestured that she should leave. Her finest hour had turned into her most embarrassing moment. She crept out onto the deck, as far away from everybody else as she could.

A few moments later the senior man could not hold back his fury any longer.

'This – this, is what we've been called out for? We were given to understand that there was large-scale international smuggling associated with this cruiser. Now we find that the barman has just been stealing some tips! Is this a matter for our department?'

Having had a fruitless mission, both groups of police left the boat. They had no alternative but to give permission for the journey home to begin. Relieved of one care now, Antonio began to panic again. Where could the suitcase have gone? A voice whispered in his ear.

'You naughty boy. What *have* you been up to?' There before him, stood Lavinia and Minnie and *the* suitcase. Antonio opened and shut his mouth. There were words, there were always words, smooth, soothing, charming, consoling, any kind of words needed but today there were none.

'Now,' whispered Minnie,' we aren't going to ask you any questions but you must be more careful in the future. Is it worth it for a few cigarettes and some alcohol?'

No it jolly well isn't, thought Antonio. Thank the almighty that the old ladies are so out of touch. No-one really needs to smuggle small quantities of *those* commodities these days but worth it for something else? Unhappily, I'm afraid that it is.

Chapter 20

On the Way Home

The whole performance had to be re-enacted. All the cases were brought out again and left for the driver to load. Paul had been extremely worried; he would have loved a drink in the bar to steady his nerves but being the driver, it was the last thing he could do.

At one point it had looked as though the guests would be required to stay another night in their cabins, thus ruining the holiday of the next group and the finances of the boat owner, not to mention the chaos to the holiday itinerary. However, as the usual time to leave was well after breakfast with two generous stops later on, Paul calculated that if they only stopped for a few moments, they should still be able to get to the next destination in time for a late dinner and their overnight hotel stay; that is if the police didn't take *too* long and the traffic wasn't *too* heavy. If they were very late all they would get at the hotel would be sandwiches and coffee and that would not go down well at all - no doubt he would get all the complaints aimed at him. He sighed. If it was at all possible, he would have to do it anyway, really there was no choice. He would phone ahead. He hoped that no-one would want to check his tachograph.

Then there was this huge problem of the missing suitcase; what on earth was he to do about that? Somewhat despondently, Paul started to collect the cases and then found himself staring at *the* case. He swiftly looked around, where on earth had it come from? Ask no questions, prayers answered, he told himself, and he quickly put it into the luggage compartment.

A slightly subdued Polly and Pete climbed aboard the coach, they had resisted all attempts by the police to make them take the matter further, No, they had told the officers, it was all over and done with and they just wanted to go home.

Clutching his special wine bag full of bottles, Bob came next. He refused Paul's offer to place his wine in the luggage hold. He looked at Paul as if he was suggesting committing sacrilege, clutched the wine carrier tighter and took it on board. Diane joined him.

Elaine boarded the bus still furious with herself She'd suspected Melissa but that was now proved to be wrong but there *had* to be more, she was sure of it. There was definitely something going on connected with that boat. She cursed her lack of police authority; it helped when you needed answers because without it you could get very little information. She sat in her seat feeling tired and deflated. David sat next to her; he couldn't decide whether he was still cross about the work on their holiday or not.

The group of four ladies boarded the coach. Three were very chatty and full of the previous events, one was not.

'Something wrong Susan?' Christine asked.

'No I'm fine, just tired,' lied Susan. Angelo hadn't got back in touch and he'd promised that he would. Oh well, she sighed inwardly, I suppose yesterday was just business after all. She closed her eyes and pretended to doze off. She didn't feel like talking.

Lillian was looking lost. It had suddenly dawned on her that Priscilla was never coming back. If she was honest, at first it was a relief but now reality had set in; she was not too sure of the sort of life she would be going back to. She had often been lonely and however difficult Priscilla might have been, at least she had represented another person in her life.

Sebastian had arranged car parking with a local garage company. While he and Felicity waited for their car to be delivered, he noticed that some of the BKA officers were waiting near the gangplank; the senior officer had not returned yet from speaking to the captain. Here was his chance. He walked over and in his best schoolboy German, told them what he'd seen on the Prince's cruiser. They listened intently and one made notes then asked Sebastian to describe the weapons he'd seen. It was legal to have registered guns for protection in Germany but certain types of weapons were prohibited for the civilian population. Sebastian described weapons that looked like pistols and assault rifles and the officers were most interested. When their chief came back and was told this information, he was at first annoyed that his men had allowed the informant to leave. However, on the whole, he was delighted to receive the information though he wondered why Sebastian had not told them before. Sebastian had guessed that this question might be asked and had already provided the answer. He told them that he'd wondered if there might be an informant on board the 'Danube Drifter' so he didn't want to be seen giving information to the police. Krauss could understand that.

'I don't think we've finished with this boat.' The BKA officer suggested. 'I'm positive we'll be back.'

On the 'Danube Drifter', all hell was breaking loose. Wolfgang Von Liebenstein demanded to see Captain Van Beeke, Antonio, the two holiday tour guides and other senior staff. With the exception of Melissa, they were all in fear of losing their jobs but all protested their innocence. For once Antonio was on the winning side because he'd had nothing to do with the ordering of stock for the bar and could prove that it was left to the head barperson, however, it seemed that the captain *was* under threat and was at a loss to know why he was being blamed.

Von Leibenstein was not given to being tactful or understanding and rather like a bull at a gate he bellowed,

'Because this is your ship! A captain of any kind of boat or ship has the ultimate responsibility.' Captain Van Beeke politely disagreed with this statement.

'This is not just a river cruiser, it is a floating hotel,' he retorted. 'I can only be held responsible for safety, the departure or arrival timings and the efficient operation of a transport vehicle. My men are honest, they have worked for me for a long time; they have no access to drinks from the bar or supplies other than engine parts. I think Herr Von Leibenstein, you must look elsewhere for blame.'

Melissa tried to intervene,

'Herr Von Leibenstein. If I could just say something.'

'Later,' he snapped then demanded to see the head barperson and the housekeeper. Without warning both were sacked having been told that it was in their areas of responsibility that theft had taken place. This still did not account for the larger orders going astray. Melissa tried again,

'If I could just explain?'

Von Leibenstein had made himself out of breath and began to cough. Melissa saw her opening.

'I wanted to inform you that on further study I have found that there is more to this than was at first understood. I don't think that the discrepancies were initiated by the staff here. I think it is a brilliant ploy to throw the guilt onto them should anything be discovered. The guilty person is the book-keeper or cashier; in other words someone in the accounts office of your company. The account details from head-office do not agree with the accounts kept here because someone has altered the books and pocketed the difference. I think the accounts here are correct, it's the bank deposits that are wrong. It's been cleverly done so that no large sums go missing at one time but as you know, at the end of the year, the losses add up. This is probably happening on the sister cruiser as well.'

Von Leibenstein stared and swallowed twice, he was flabbergasted. His anger deflated and then flared up again.

'I shall be returning to my office immediately and if this proves to be true, heads will roll!'

After such an exhausting day, the senior staff members were having a very short break. The next group had been due that afternoon but because of the possibility of the police delaying things, they were going to be staying at a hotel in Germany, for another night. They would lose part of their cruise but it couldn't be helped. All the staff were discussing the events of the day when the receptionist appeared.

'Please, oh please! Not more trouble?' Melissa groaned.

The girl paused, she had a note in her hand but seemed unsure who to give it to; it was from the local Police. Wearily Melissa took it and on reading it, sighed with relief.

'The 'Danube Drifter' now has permission to leave its moorings.'

....

Sebastian's information had triggered another raid on a riverboat but this time a far grander one. Prince Romanovsky was to receive a visit from the BKA.

The most senior officer at HQ was unsure. This was a new line of enquiry that must be treated with extreme tact. How sure of the informant were they?

The Prince was a very well-known figure. He had contacts at the highest levels and friends in government. He was known to be fabulously wealthy and it was inconceivable that he should be involved in crime. Were they sure that it was not simply an overstatement? The prince had security guards who were armed and licensed to be so. A man of his position was entitled to be careful. Were they sure that the man had not simply seen pistols and the ammunition for them? Perhaps they had mistaken sporting guns for assault rifles. Yes, that must be it. Still, he could not ignore a direct report of a firearms cache. He would have to send his deputy to take charge; he could not risk an overenthusiastic junior officer doing the wrong thing.

Dmitri was expecting a visit and was well prepared. Anna had seen Sebastian talking to the BKA and as instructed, had reported the interesting fact by coded text. Dmitri had surmised that it could only mean one thing, Felicity's companion must have spotted something. He was disappointed that nothing had been discovered by the police on the pleasure cruiser but now he had to ensure that nothing was found out about him. He smiled to himself; he rather enjoyed these cat and mouse games. Lately, he'd been getting a little bored and events like these brightened his day considerably. Not so Boris who was nervously twitching and constantly checking the armoury cupboard where a securely locked gun case, holding two licensed sporting guns, was in full view.

A group of police, from another section of the BMK, arrived in a marked vehicle and swarmed onto the Prince's vessel. Dmitri had deliberately said nothing to the ordinary crew members; he wanted them to look and be surprised. No hint of a warning must be suspected. The officers, having been given strict instructions, were polite but searched as thoroughly as it was possible to do. The haughty aristocrat who greeted them was suitably outraged but compliant so the search went ahead without difficulty. The false wall held up well and nothing, apart from a shotgun and a rifle, which were all properly documented, was found. Prince Romanovsky had been at great pains to show that his bodyguards had licences for firearms and he had a couple of sporting guns, correctly licensed and locked in a secure cabinet. On hearing that someone had reported seeing an arms cache on his cruiser he looked shocked and

208

professed himself to be at a loss to understand. He suddenly added,

'Unless my man was cleaning the guns? I hope he didn't leave them unattended? That must be it. I do apologise. My man will receive a severe reprimanded.'

With nothing else to go on and no evidence of any prohibited firearms, the unit left feeling that they'd wasted their time and they cursed the English fool who'd jumped to conclusions. Dmitri breathed a sigh of relief. He had, in fact, already reprimanded someone. The idiot, who'd left the false wall open for Sebastian to see, had received a large dose of his bad temper.

....

It was mid-evening when the coach pulled into the parking place adjacent to the hotel in Boppard where they were to spend the night. The guests were tired and several masked a yawn as they climbed down the coach steps clutching their overnight cases. One or two people had no overnight bag so they had to access their main luggage in the hold. Paul usually cursed any such individuals, it made more work for him, but this time he was grateful, it made accessing the *special* case less noticeable.

He wasn't used to this method of exchanging goods, it was an emergency measure, triggered because a while ago, there'd been a problem in the chain of communication and he suspected that goods urgently needed paying for. He wasn't sure how he was to pass this suitcase on but he knew the contact would be made at this hotel.

On finally checking in, he soon discovered. An envelope addressed to him was lying on the reception counter. All the guests had gone to their rooms and he was the only one left. He looked around but no-one except the receptionist was there.

'Is this for me?' he asked. 'It has my name on it.' The hotel employee looked confused but agreed that it must be for him. Paul took the letter quickly and read it in his room. He was instructed to leave the case in a secluded place a short distance from the back of the building; there was no mention of where and how to collect the goods for the return journey. This was unusual but no doubt he would soon be contacted. This whole trip had been fraught with problems and changes to the normal routine. It hadn't helped for that woman to have had a heart attack and drop dead. That was all he'd needed. He'd spent all his time carefully avoiding the notice of police and then an event like that had to happen. He wouldn't be sorry when this trip was over; the responsibility was getting to him. He pulled himself together. Just remember the rewards, he told himself. I get very well paid so - I'll cope.

Susan and Christine checked into their room. Susan headed for the shower and while she was in there she heard a knock on the outside door and Christine's voice speaking. Shower finished she dried herself, dressed and wandered out into the cabin to be met by a huge bouquet of flowers. The card with them read *'Happy Birthday Susan from A'* - he'd remembered her after all. She looked at the card, some more words caught her eye.

'I'll be seeing you.....'

Christine interrupted.

'You didn't say it was your birthday! Who are the flowers from?'

'Er - someone from home.'

Susan snapped off the card and quickly tucked it into her pocket. The words echoed in her brain. So the flowers were a polite goodbye. 'I'll be seeing you' – that was a casual way of saying it, wasn't it? She felt angry and hurt and wanted to burst into tears. Christine entered the shower room and shut the door; just as well, Susan thought, she wanted no witness to her initial despair. She just needed a few moments to pull herself together, she wasn't going to cry, she was tough, she was her father's daughter.

She sat on the bed and let her thoughts wander, what might have been her future if her father had known Angelo first and proposed him instead of Giovani? Would she have submitted and married or would she still have wanted her independence?

Minnie and Lavinia were exhausted. No-one had offered to help them so they'd struggled with their overnight case in one hand and their walking sticks in the other. They found their room and both sat down heavily on a bed.

'Do you know Lavinia, I think perhaps I'm getting too old for all this. This was by far the most difficult time we've had when away on one of our little journeys. Don't you think?'

'Well yes dear, it has been a little fraught but we always said that we would never let advancing years spoil our fun and despite all the upsets, we *have* had some fun.'

'Oh yes! Oh, that Antonio! What a joke with his case. He didn't know what to say to us, did he?' Minnie chuckled.

'And there was that sort of battle between Felicity and Priscilla.'

Lavinia sighed as she looked out of the window. Somebody out there in the grounds caught her eye and she screwed up her eyes to get a better view.

'I suppose we shouldn't really laugh now that the lady is dead.' Minnie felt a little ashamed. 'After all, death makes one instantly respectable.'

'It wasn't her respectability that was the problem, was it?'

'No, of course not but what a sad and envious woman. She made Lillian's life a misery; I could see that. At least that poor woman made a friend. Odd though, that it should be the friend of Priscilla's adversary?'

'Even odder was the sudden heart attack. You know, Priscilla didn't walk up that hill to the restaurant. I heard her telling Lillian that a car had been sent for her. Who sent the car? No-one asked about that. If there was no extraordinary exertion, why should she have had a heart-attack there when

211

she seemed fine all the time she was on the cruiser? There couldn't have been any sudden stressful activity.'

'I believe I heard that she suffered a paroxysm of coughing, brought about by eating very hot and spicy food.'

'Well it seems odd to me but it's not our place to question the efficiency of the authorities. Now we'd better get ready for dinner or we won't get any.'

Elaine was tired but her brain was racing. She'd been thinking in a similar vein to Minnie and Lavinia There was something that seemed plain wrong with Priscilla's sudden death. This was not really what she was supposed to be concentrating on but she'd begun to wonder if there could be a connection. She tried *this* possibility and then *that* one. She kept going over and over the little she knew; there had to be a link, a clue, something she'd overlooked. She mentally reviewed all the guests. No-one stood out, it must be the staff. Well, she'd missed her chance now, she wouldn't get to meet the staff again.

When Susan took off her jacket, the screwed up card fell out of her pocket. She bent to pick it up to toss it into the bin. As she held it, the bitter message caught her eye. She stared at it for a moment, unable to stop herself from thinking of what might have been.

'I'll be seeing you in.....' She stopped in her tracks - **in**? She looked closely at the card then turned it over - there was more writing on the back, she'd missed it; her eyes had watered and blurred her vision. She'd made an assumption, jumped to a conclusion. Susan looked carefully at the card and saw the rest of the words - *'in all the old familiar places.'* It was a message. She knew the familiar places, they were back in the UK.

212

Chapter 21

Staying and Going

In his office at Budapest police headquarters, Rendőr Bence Fodor was looking at the report in front of him. There *had* been a murder, he was now sure of this. The occurrence of an elderly overweight and out of breath tourist, choking on hot spicy food and bringing on a heart attack, was nothing remarkable and had nearly slipped through the system. It was lucky for the victim's family and for justice, that the new head of forensics, being extra keen to prove himself, had ordered an incredibly thorough toxicological examination of the body. The test that had discovered the substance was not usually performed. The evidence could so easily have been missed.

Asszony Pilkington (or Mrs, as the English called her) had certainly died of heart failure but *'succinylcholine'* had been discovered in her body and because of this, *'succinylcholine induced hyperkalaemia'* was the cause of her cardiac arrest. She couldn't have acquired this substance naturally, she'd definitely been murdered.

On minute examination of the body, a tiny puncture mark had been found in her neck; the use of a hypodermic syringe was clearly how the substance was administered and it would have taken no more than two or three minutes to work. The difficulty was, finding out who had administered it and why?

This was no random murder, this woman had been targeted. What was the reason for her being *removed* by a *hitman*? Oh yes, he was sure this was a professional job, it was far too sophisticated for an amateur. This type of assassination bore all the hallmarks of organised crime but as far as he could see, this lady had a spotless reputation; what link could *she* possibly have had with the criminal underworld? She was as respectable as anyone was capable of being. She'd been holidaying on a cruiser; he needed to speak to the people she was on holiday with and - he needed to discover why a respectable lady was dining alone at night, in the middle of town.

In the meantime, Fodor had also received some inside information about the smuggling operations that he knew were regularly operating through Budapest and once again the suspicion had fallen on the river as a means of passing the goods. He'd checked on several of the regular users of the Danube. He suspected that both the Rhine and the main Rhine canal featured in the operations too but he couldn't investigate those stretches of water; they were not in his jurisdiction.

The normal traffic was mostly commercial and divided into two types; goods being transported and holiday companies cruising. There were also a *few* private vessels. He'd get one of his officers to make a detailed report of all the regular river users and then he'd see if he might be able to identify anything suspicious. Fodor needed to take this *higher up* because it was a problem affecting all the countries those major waterways flowed through. He did have a useful contact in the German police, perhaps, off the record, he could have a quiet word and see if they could pool information.

If no other reason could be found for the English woman's death then maybe, in some way, there was a link between her, the river cruiser and smuggling. It seemed a remote possibility but he'd learned throughout his long career that often it was the smallest of clues that helped to discover the bigger ones. He wouldn't dismiss a possible link.

Realising that the foreign guests would now be in Germany, Rendőr Fodor acknowledged that he would be unable to re-interview them. He would need to apply for the assistance of the German authorities but by the time the correct permissions had been obtained, the holiday group would have probably left Germany and would be in either Belgium or

France. Had an arrest warrant been in place, international agreements would have allowed them to be intercepted immediately but as it was, diplomacy was needed and arrangements couldn't be effected in time.

After consultation with his senior officer, it was decided to let the guests return home without hindrance and if any were needed for further interrogation, Budapest would rely on the assistance of the British police. To expedite matters, they decided to begin the process immediately by formally requesting the co-operation of the British authorities in the matter of the murder of a British national in Hungary.

However, the staff and crew on the cruiser were a different matter; they could be intercepted before the boat left its present berth. The German authorities would provide swift action if smuggling through their territory was suspected. Fodor would ensure that they were immediately informed.

....

Herman Krauss, a senior officer in the BMK, put down the phone. A telephone call from the Hungarian police had set him furiously thinking. It's that boat again! So let's see, he pondered. First, an anonymous call to say there was smuggling going on, then that woman overheard the nonsense about petty pilfering and now there might be a link to murder as well. Could there possibly be that amount of coincidence? If the Hungarian police want us to investigate that boat, then there must be very good grounds for suspicion. We do have the ability to stop and search on suspicion – but we've already done this and found nothing. He banged the desk with his open hand. We've missed something so maybe a link to murder will be grounds enough for us to check everything once again.

....

Early the next morning, the message arrived at the cruiser. It was delivered by an officer of the German State Police. Melissa and Vicktor, who were crossing the reception area at the time, were two of the first people to hear it. Spoken in German with a strong local accent, Melissa could not easily translate what was being said but seeing the facial expressions of the reception staff and the grim countenance of the policeman, she put two and two together.

'Oh no!' Melissa muttered to Vicktor, 'What is this? Not more trouble?'

The captain was called for and instructed that he must halt his journey; they could not travel that day because the staff had to be questioned again. The captain was not given the full details but was informed that there had been an unexpected development in the case of Priscilla Pilkington's sudden death. Toxicological test results from the autopsy had indicated the presence of an unnatural substance in her blood and this was almost certainly the cause of the heart attack which killed her. The case of 'suspicious death' was now being treated as murder.

Captain Van Beeke was at the end of his tether. He'd been told to expect the new batch of holidaymakers that afternoon and after the various delays, he was late getting everything ready for the next cruise. On being told that all the staff would need to assemble again so that a senior officer could speak to them, he felt like resigning on the spot.

Melissa was having similar thoughts. In order to be ready to welcome the new guests, she was trying to re-affix her happy holiday smile but somehow it just wouldn't come.

Antonio groaned. His domestic staff had managed to clean most of the cabins yesterday but they still had to equip each one and finish the rest of the cleaning. The chef needed to collect supplies and the kitchen staff needed to get on with preparations for the first meal. Never had the staff had to deal with a set of circumstances like these. Coupled with this,

216

Antonio was still in a state of nervous anxiety about the suitcase. Although relieved that it had left his guardianship, he was still worried that the case might be discovered and traced back to him. Hearing the shocking news that the latest development concerned a possible murder and not smuggling, actually came as a huge relief.

....

In the meantime, the previous guests of the 'Danube Drifter', having undergone a reasonably untroubled night at their hotel in Boppard, were boarding the coach for their journey home. They were blissfully unaware of the latest revelation and the renewal of police activity. The group prepared for an early start.

Sebastian began loading the car; as before, he would drive behind the coach. Felicity took little notice, she was in a world of her own - other little annoyances such as a death and a police raid had been brushed aside. She was happy to leave all the petty arrangements to Sebastian. She was far more interested in contemplating and mentioning her new starring role and her glittering future.

'I shall be a star again,' she told her long-suffering companion. 'The whole world will remember me and wonder why I haven't been seen for such a long time. Those producers who've neglected me will be very sorry. I shall be in demand everywhere. Oh, I expect after this it will be back to Paris and Rome. You won't mind will you Sebastian darling?'

'Of course not. Don't give it a thought,' he replied, thinking, no, he didn't mind at all because he had no intention of still being with her. Sebastian had had enough.

....

Elaine was feeling a little trepidation. She'd *primed* the office of her suspicions about the driver and it had been agreed that the UK 'Border Agency' would take over as the port would be the best place to search the coach and its occupants. Everyone would have all their belongings with them and no-one would suspect trouble; this would prevent anyone hiding or disposing of contraband. They couldn't exclude any of the passengers, they told her; there might be accomplices. The search had to be impartial. David had been telling her how glad he would be to get back home and how he was looking forward to a trouble-free onward journey. She began to squirm as Bob and Diane joined in the conversation, each repeating the same wish - to be home with no more upsets or delays.

The coach pulled out of the parking space and began its homeward journey. The guests were now very tired and a little bored after all the excitement. The countryside drifted by and unlike the outward journey, when everyone was excited and bubbly, this time, three-quarters of the passengers fell asleep. The rolling hills, farms and plains were like a soothing balm and even those who never slept on such journeys found themselves gently dozing, encouraged by the smooth motion of the coach.

Paul, however, was wide awake, he had to be. Sheer adrenalin had kept him alert for days and he was afraid to let go now. Apart from the necessity of needing all his attention for the road, he was aware that his brain was whirring with constant activity. Nothing about this trip had been straightforward and so much had been different and stressful. He could not help but worry.

He'd been expecting instructions concerning the *collection* of goods but nothing had come. He knew that a journey this long would not be wasted by his *other* employer. If *he* hadn't been given the goods, where were they? He could only

218

conclude that they'd been hidden in the coach somewhere. This must mean that there was another contact, one that he was not aware of, who was travelling on the coach. Were they experienced? Sometimes the customs could be very thorough; it had taken Paul a long time to work out his method of concealing things and as the coach driver, he was usually treated differently anyway. He'd rather not be part of any coach load where a passenger was found to be smuggling. Even if *he* was not arrested, his face would remain known and his *nice little earner* would be over for good. Would his employers blame him? They might, he guessed, they were probably ruthless. This supposition was the reason he'd never crossed them or let them down. A horrible thought occurred. Suppose there *had* been a message and he'd somehow missed it. He felt sick. They would not be too pleased with him if he'd missed a collection through stupidity.

He felt himself going hot and then cold; it was fear. For the first time, he began to comprehend just what he'd become embroiled in. If he was caught, it would be a long prison sentence and if it was in Eastern Europe, they'd throw away the key. If he *had* lost a shipment, what would *they* do to him? He was mad, it wasn't worth it. He pictured his family. I did it for them, he thought. Would a judge say, 'Oh that's alright then?' Of course, he wouldn't.

Paul continued to berate himself until he was jerked out of his daydream by a car sharply braking in front of him and by pure reflex, he found himself braking too. The inevitable jolt woke some of his passengers. Becoming aware that he'd allowed himself to lose focus on the road, Paul forced himself to concentrate. He acknowledged that there was absolutely nothing he could do until he reached home so he would just have to stay alert, keep calm and await events.

The coach pulled into the waiting area at the French border where the passengers were requested to step down holding their passports. While everyone filed past the French staff, Paul, having shown his documents first, drove the coach ahead and waited. When his passengers had all returned to the vehicle, he was directed to proceed to the second checkpoint, the UK 'Border Force'.

Three things were usually uppermost in the minds of the British border authority; illegal immigrants and terrorists, drug smuggling and the carriage of dangerous goods such as arms and explosives. The usual procedure was very straightforward. Taking their passports but leaving their luggage on board, passengers were required to alight and pass through immigration where their documents were scrutinised. Travellers were not prevented from taking their handbags, light document bags and cameras with them; on holiday coaches, these were not usually even inspected. Any non-EU visitors were questioned and as well as being required to show their passports, they had to produce any necessary visas to prove that they had permission to be in the country. While all this was happening, officers with *sniffer* dogs normally checked the vehicles and in the case of holiday coaches, the dogs, with their superb sense of smell, would sniff all the seats, floor areas and the luggage compartments. It was a fast and efficient method and no doubt adequate for the average holiday travel coach. Paul relied on this happening. Today it didn't. As soon as the passengers had left the coach for the second time and before he'd become aware that something was different, the coach was being directed into another area where a team of operatives was waiting.

On being asked to alight a second time, the group had acquiesced without any more than the usual grumbles and though a few eyebrows were raised at what seemed to be an unusual procedure for passing through customs and immigration, outrage only occurred when everyone saw that a team of men had unloaded all the luggage and brought it inside;

every suitcase was to be searched - again! The passengers were told that they must identify and unlock their cases.

Very soon everyone was watching their personal items, underwear and unmentionables, being thrown around for all to see and the ladies were horrified as cold-faced individuals ploughed carelessly through their belongings. Elaine gulped as she saw her own suitcase go through the same procedure and she cringed as she saw her pretty and expensive lace underwear being roughly handled and screwed up. However, this was nothing to the general embarrassment when the ladies discovered that their dirty washing was receiving a minute inspection.

Next, all passengers were going to be individually searched with a *sniffer dog* nearby; most looked nervously at the dog. If Fido sat down they would definitely get a very unpleasant additional search experience in a private room. Any belongings or bags on their person or items in their pockets plus coats, bags, shoes, boots, phones, tablets and cameras were to be subjected to an X-ray machine. It was intimidating and intrusive but although the customs personnel were polite, there was a menacing element to the whole thing. The coach itself was almost taken apart.

There was an air of perplexity and astonishment mixed with fury amongst the passengers; most of them vowed never to cross the channel ever again. All was confusion as they fell into an untidy line to place their belongings on the conveyor belt. It was obvious that no provision had been made for age or infirmity. Lavinia, a little ahead of her sister, was struggling. She managed to put her walking stick and purse through the X-ray machine but having stood in line for some time, she began to look quite ill and seem to sway and be very unsteady on her feet. On being made aware of the lady's age, the customs officials, not wanting a sudden death on their hands, did relent a little and a chair was found to enable her to rest for a few moments. Her belongings had passed through the security scanner so she asked if she might have them returned to her. She particularly needed her walking stick because she found it difficult to walk without it. A helpful and slightly embarrassed official obliged. Minnie arrived next and greeted her sister, she was directed to follow the same procedure as Lavinia.

Both ladies were then escorted to a private area where they were subjected to, in their case, a fairly cursory and sensitively conducted body search by a female officer. When their ordeal was over, they were relieved to again be offered seats while they waited for everyone else. As usual, the two ladies smiled sweetly and thanked the officers, unlike the rest of the group who after initial protests, were forced to suffer many indignities in grim and tight-lipped silence.

Elaine was overcome with guilt when her husband complained bitterly about this unusual and *over the top* procedure. Having been identified by her passport, she'd received far less intrusive treatment. When later, he'd asked her what she thought of it all, she could find no ready answer and just wearily shook her head.

Chapter 22

Questions to answer

Paul was in shock. What could have gone wrong? Never had this happened before. He was so relieved that this time he was *not* carrying anything illegal. He was, for once, totally innocent and it should have calmed him but he had to admit that it didn't. He understood what it meant, the authorities were on to them. Yes them, not him. He'd been treated no differently to everybody else - or had he? He *had* detected a slightly more aggressive approach than he'd encountered before but if they were checking everyone and everything, it could only mean a suspicion and not any actual proof.

He wondered how long they would have to wait. The coach was undergoing a really thorough search so they must have had some information. Was there an informer? Could it be one of the guests? That seemed a crazy idea, these people were on holiday; they were only away for ten days and on the cruiser for seven. How could that be enough time for anyone to discover anything? He'd heard some gossip from one of the passengers, that there *was* a police lady travelling but it seemed that her husband was quite fierce about all work being left at home. When that stupid actress woman in the car had tried to implicate the tour guide in some misdemeanour or other, he'd been heard to say that they were on holiday and not to be bothered; no it was unlikely to be her. Mind you, he remembered, there was also that strange death in Budapest; could there be a connection? The woman who died, by all accounts, *was* a troublemaker but she didn't seem the type. Spies kept a low profile, didn't they? He understood that she'd been one to push herself forward into the limelight, all the time. Paul racked his brains but could find no logical answer. Who the hell could it be?

They were using the dogs all the time; that usually meant they were looking for people smuggling or could it be drugs? Well, he was sure, wasn't he, that the organisation he worked for were not into the latter? He would never have become involved with drug smuggling of any kind. He was actually rather offended, though of course, he could hardly protest that he was a decent kind of smuggler. Perhaps they were unsure as to what they were looking for and so they were taking no chances?

A few minutes later Paul was invited into a separate room and he underwent a *grilling*. His very ordinary background came to his aid.

'Who me? Do what? I'm just a simple driver, that's all I do.'

On being threatened with detention while they checked his bank accounts he was more than willing for them to do so because he knew that the money he'd made had been received in cash and much of it had immediately been spent by his wife and family; there was little to show for a life of crime in his records. His *savings* for his old age were not in any bank. His ordinary and modest house and standard of living had nothing to do with wealth and success and the very fact that he drove all those miles regularly did not reflect a rich or affluent lifestyle. He was clean. Nothing could be found on him or in his belongings and strangely, nothing at all was found in the coach or in any of the other passengers' bags, cases or on anyone's person. Paul was genuinely puzzled and very worried. Although it had meant no incarceration by the authorities it could also mean that he'd missed the collection and that would entail placating far more dangerous people. He was in a *no-win* situation.

The holidaymakers, with their tempers and dignity bruised and battered and their belongings crushed carelessly back into their cases, were eager to continue their journey. Looking a little less tidy but ready for the re-loading of luggage, the coach was given permission to be driven aboard the next ferry. Sebastian, driving the hired car, was also ready to board. On dutifully driving behind the coach, he'd found that the car he was driving was included in the search, consequently, they too had been obliged to undergo the undignified experience. Felicity had been outraged and now had lapsed into high sulks. Sebastian was quietly resolute; he'd no idea what this was all about but could surmise that the authorities were acting on a tip-off. Remembering the arms cache he'd spotted on the Prince's cruiser, he wondered what they might have become embroiled in. Thank goodness they were now on their way. He couldn't wait to get home.

Gradually, Felicity began to return to her optimistic mood. Still positive that she was returning to instant stardom, the lure of fame provided balm to her wounded dignity; she bored Sebastian all the rest of the way by discussing her imminent success.

Elaine was totally perplexed and very dismayed. What had happened? She was so sure that Paul was smuggling and that something *had* to be found on him or if not on *him*, in the coach. She'd stirred up a hornet's nest but they'd found absolutely nothing! That Priscilla woman's demise was unexplained too. OK, it *was* possibly a natural death, she was overweight and no youngster but they'd ascertained that she'd taken a taxi to her dinner date so she couldn't have been over-energetic which might have produced a raised heart rate. Why should that simple excursion have set off a heart attack? The answer just *had* to be on the cruiser, everything seemed to lead back to there. Perhaps the local police should check the cruiser again? They needed to search as thoroughly as the 'Border Agency' did on the coach. There were just too many loose ends and she'd only had seven days to investigate together with the fact that she was supposed to have been on holiday. There simply had not been enough time to complete her task. Never-the-less she was going to be highly embarrassed on her return to work.

The channel crossing took place without incident and soon all the ferry passengers were filing back into their coaches and cars. Bob and David sat together so that their wives could chat but it was the men who really wanted to talk together. Now that the annoyance was over, both being highly intelligent, they wanted to discuss things. They were intrigued about all that had happened and Bob commented that considering all the drama, it was a shame that old Ronaldo Marconi had failed to put in an appearance to make it all worthwhile. David wondered if there could have been a connection with him and the intensive search they'd all been subjected to at the border. Elaine, overhearing parts of their conversation winced and tried to look as if she was listening to Diane talking about fashion.

The group of four ladies sat across from each other in two's and chatted together across the aisle. The experience at the border had been daunting, they agreed, but the ferry crossing, with its bracing sea breeze, had re-energised them. They conceded that overall, they had enjoyed their trip. On being asked if she would organise another holiday for them during the next summer, Susan was not too sure. She thought that perhaps by then, she might prefer another kind of travel. She might be making a trip to the USA.

Pete and Polly were keeping quiet, they even dozed a little. Their adventures were catching up on them. Polly looked rather pale and tired and Pete didn't seem quite his usual self. On being asked by one of the other passengers, if they would be glad to get home they looked at each other and wearily nodded in unison.

Minnie and Lavinia had thankfully taken their seats: they were exhausted. Ladies of their age could enjoy a gentle holiday but the ordeal at the border was unexpected and very tiring. Still, true to form, neither complained. They closed their eyes and rested. Paul was glad to see a taxi waiting for them at the first *drop off* point. He watched them walk steadily down the coach aisle, navigate the steps and with the careful use of their walking sticks, finally walk towards the taxi. Paul identified the ladies' cases by the labels and the taxi driver loaded them into the boot of his vehicle before helping each lady into his cab. Game old dears, Paul thought, but they certainly went through it this time, didn't they?

At the next drop-off, he noticed a rather *up-market* vehicle waiting for the coach. He was puzzled. Who'd joined the group here? He was stunned to see Pete and Polly walking down the coach aisle. It surely couldn't be for them, could it? Mind you, I suppose this was a *one-off* holiday for the couple so perhaps they'd treated themselves to a bit of luxury. They liked a bit of show; well you only had to look at their dress sense, didn't you? No, he thought, it was far more likely that the daft twit had booked a car and they'd caught him for an expensive one. He watched them leave, thanked them for the gratuity envelope and was fascinated by the contrast as the gaudily dressed pair climbed into the classy mode of transport.

On delivering passengers to their various *drop off points*, it was customary for Paul to receive gratuities; the convenient basket, placed at the front of the coach, served as a receptacle for such things. Some people deposited cash in it whilst others placed money in an envelope. Paul thanked each person as they left, he would not be sorry when the last person had departed. He apologised to each one for the upsets but skilfully managed to make his passengers aware that *he* had been mightily inconvenienced too; this was to ally himself with them and not allow himself to be seen as part of the opposition. The holiday company was likely to receive some stiff letters of complaint. After the last passenger had left, he gathered up the offerings and placed them in his pocket.

Greatly relieved that his ordeal was over, he returned the empty coach and promised his concerned employers that he would soon send them a full report but first he needed a rest. Later that evening he remembered his gratuities and emptied his pocket. On opening one envelope, he was amazed to see a few very large banknotes together with a missive. The letter informed him that his *other activities* were now ceasing. Don't worry, it stated, you didn't miss anything, you did well and your money will come through as usual with a bonus but this will be the last run. Paul was not sorry and if his wife didn't like it, she could lump it. He needed to think up a story about being demoted or maybe it would just be easier to leave and say he'd been made redundant. Somehow the novelty of driving thousands of miles abroad had lost its appeal.

....

On returning home, there was disappointment all round. Detective Inspector Elaine Forest was requested to make a full report and this she did but she was aware that in her superior's eyes, she'd failed. It wasn't fair, it *was* her holiday after all and she'd had no authority to investigate. She was about to send in the report when the phone rang and she was once again requested to visit the office where the whole thing had started. Elaine sighed and muttered under her breath,
'Now what? It seems this isn't my year.'
The appointment was not, as she'd feared, for criticism but to inform her of some new information. Priscilla had not just suffered a fatal heart attack, it was confirmed that she'd definitely been *murdered*. So Elaine had been right to be

suspicious. Her eyes widened as she read an extract from the translated report, sent by the Hungarian authorities, suggesting that this was a professional hit.

'Priscilla Pilkington died of a heart attack induced by the administration of succinylcholine, a strong muscle relaxant which paralyses the respiratory muscles. A high dose was administered and the victim suffocated. A tiny mark left by a hypodermic syringe, high up in her neck and obscured by the hairline, was at first overlooked in the initial post mortem.'

Remembering the rather obnoxious woman, Elaine could see that many people would have enjoyed throttling her but she could see nothing that would involve Priscilla with serious crime; the woman had been the epitome of respectability, the daughter of a vicar! Was it because of the information she'd tried to tell me? Could it have been *that* important? Well, thanks to David, I'll never know. If it was the case, obviously someone had stopped the woman from talking.

The likely possibilities were discussed for some time. Finally, Elaine took the files back to her office for further study. It seemed that her failure concerning the smuggling had been put on hold and her remit had widened now to include this murder. There were some leads she would pursue; it should be easier now that she was able to work freely and was not obliged to resort to subterfuge. She had a list of the holidaymakers who'd been on the cruiser and coach and she mustn't forget Felicity and Sebastian who'd chosen to travel by car instead. Elaine was grateful that only one coach party had been cruising during that week.

All the documents had been translated into English so Elaine began to read. It seemed that the Hungarian authorities were formally requesting the assistance of the British police in

229

the case of a murder of a British citizen in Budapest. Elaine read through steadily, really they had very little to go on. She was rather alarmed by the turn of events and felt frustrated at the limitations of her previous observations. She'd been told to observe the staff but now she was supposed to know all about the guests as well. This murder had drastically opened up the investigation.

Melissa had started out as being her chief suspect but suspicions about her had come to nothing. Then there was Paul, in her view, the obvious criminal candidate, but he'd been interrogated to no avail and both he and his coach had been searched and nothing had been found. The rest of the crew seemed not to stand out in any way. She considered the captain; she had seen little of him and from the notes, he seemed just an ordinary man doing a good job. The nautical crew came from a variety of backgrounds and countries but all had worked for the captain for some time. Then there was the hotel manager, the *ladies' man*; he seemed *too soft* to be involved in crime but you never knew. She considered the cabin staff and waiters, cooks and receptionists – any one of them could have been involved and finally, Vicktor, the young and good-looking enthusiastic tour rep. This is madness, she thought, I have absolutely nothing to go on.

And now, I have to consider the guests too! It's very unlikely that these holidaymakers are involved, really it's up to the Hungarians to follow this, not us. Are they suggesting that Priscilla Pilkington is a criminal mastermind or a gang boss? What could she possibly know that was so serious that it meant she had to be put out of the way? At best, she might have overheard a bit of gossip I suppose. The memory surfaced again. That woman was about to tell me something, wasn't she? David stopped it and I never saw the woman again. So if the woman did have some important information, what on earth could it have been to make someone kill her? Furthermore, it had to be someone in the lounge who'd heard her tell me that she wished to divulge something to the police. Who was in the lounge and near enough to hear? She came to the unwelcome conclusion that apart from David, the only persons present were Bob and Diane. No, impossible, she told herself, there must have been others but who? A picture came into her mind of a conversation.

'What do you do?' she was asked and ....got it, it was Susan from the group of ladies, I told her the nature of my work and hearing me tell her had prompted Priscilla to come over. Could Susan have heard Priscilla? But then Priscilla had a booming voice, probably half the guests had heard her; it only took one with a special interest to pass on that information.

Elaine returned to the file on Priscilla, she skated over the preliminaries and moved onto the day of her murder. Aha! A receptionist had confirmed that Priscilla had received a phone call that had seemed to please her. So that must have been the murderer arranging a dinner date with her.

According to the notes, Priscilla arrived at the venue but her escort didn't turn up She ordered and was served soup and then a main meal. Next, she began to choke. She ate – oh hot goulash. OK, that makes sense, so she does what? She takes a drink then appears to eat some more goulash and chokes again then leans back with her hand over her mouth still coughing.

Elaine continued to read the witness statements before her. It now seemed very confused. Who came over first? It stated-someone with more water, who? Then more coughing, next, she appeared to pass out and slide off her chair onto the floor. A few seconds later, several 'waiting' staff came over, a doctor appeared, but by this time she was completely senseless and lying on the floor. So who got to her first?

She looked through all the papers, several waiters were interrogated including the man who'd served her the goulash, which he insisted she'd particularly asked for. It was not clear which member of staff reached her first. There was obviously some confusion but a lady at the next table had stated categorically that a single waiter arrived by her side first to offer her water, several moments before the others and he was nowhere to be seen after that.

So it was *him*! That first waiter was the assassin; but who the blazes was he? What did Priscilla know that was important enough for her to be silenced? The Hungarian police would need to re-interview all the staff at the hotel. Surely they didn't expect *her* to go out there again?

The fact that a hypodermic needle had been used with such precision and stealth told its own story. The substance used wouldn't have been detected had it not been for the forensic expert who was unusually thorough. There was no such thing as co-incidences. All of this had to be linked with international crime and the poor old *so and so* had somehow got herself caught up in it. So going back to my original brief, who is the head of the smuggling group and is it this infamous Ronaldo Marconi?

Elaine continued to hypothesise, why would this smuggling ring suddenly have such a high profile? Surely the intelligence suggested that they'd been operating for some time. The essence of this type of crime was secrecy and yet, somehow things were coming out into the open. It didn't make sense – unless? That was it, there was a rival! It fitted now - two rivals for the same trade; that would *make waves* and could easily be a precursor to violence.

Pleased with her new line of enquiry, Elaine started to make notes. We *could* re-interview the guests, she considered, but I think the answer will probably lie back on the 'Danube Drifter'.

About to pack up the papers in front of her, she was suddenly aware of what she'd just thought – '*the answer lies back on the 'Danube Drifter'*'- the river cruiser. Why weren't they investigating other Danube users? She'd seen many industrial barges and pleasure boats, cruisers both commercial and private; some for weekly jaunts, some for day trips. Who else used the river? Oh yes, there was that Prince somebody? He was up and down the Danube and other waterways, mind you, if he was as fabulously rich as he was supposed to be, why would he be involved? Still, she'd do a little digging and see what she could find out about him.

Chapter 23

Revelations

Susan had been back in England for a month but hadn't yet been in contact with Angelo. She'd puzzled over the message – *'I'll be seeing you – in all the old familiar places.'* What did it mean? It was weird but more to the point, how much did she really know about *him*. Well, for a start, he was as crooked as her father, well in fact, as crooked as she now was. He couldn't contact her at home because she hadn't given him her new address. They'd said goodbye quickly and she'd confidently expected to see him again before she left Germany, but he hadn't shown up – just the flowers and the card. She'd gone through all the possibilities in her mind, over and over again. He might have been delayed and missed her – no, he'd sent flowers so he knew he wasn't coming, she tried again, he'd been arrested – no she would have heard by now or at least her father would have heard from his sources. So what could she expect to happen? It was back to the message and the faint hope it brought. Which meant precisely - what?

It meant that here she was again, sitting in this pub garden that overlooked the river near Hampton Court. This was the time and the place where they'd sat and talked and, as she'd thought at the time, fallen for each other. They'd been to lots of other locations but this place was special; she hoped he'd thought so too and this was where he meant. She'd been here twice before on a Saturday evening and it was becoming difficult. An attractive woman sitting on her own inevitably brought the odd predatory male over to annoy her and it was difficult to get rid of them. In normal circumstances, she could walk away but she needed to stay here. Oh no, she winced, as she saw the same man who'd annoyed her the week before.

'Well, well,' he began, 'you came back to see me, did you?'

'Go away. I'm meeting someone.'

'Yes darling, me.' The obnoxious moron sat himself down. 'Let me get you a drink.'

'No, thank you. Please leave.'

'Now, I'm one who is famous for my charm. Don't tell me you haven't noticed.'

Susan glared at the intoxicated man.

'Get your drunken ass off this bench and sod off.' Her American accent had suddenly intensified and coupled with an authoritarian and slightly menacing look, a direct inheritance from her father, it unnerved the drunk who got up muttering about *stuck up cows*.

A man who'd been sitting at another table, walked over. 'Oh no! Not another one,' she muttered under her breath. Screwing up her face to deliver a stinging comment, she was prevented by a familiar voice saying,

'I hope you're not going to tell me where to go.'

'Angelo?' she mouthed in an astonished whisper. He looked completely different, his hair was blonde, he wore spectacles, he was taller and he appeared to have put on weight.

'I'm too recognisable, I have to disguise myself,' he whispered and then in a louder voice with his hand extended, 'Miss Butler, I presume? I'm Steven Price, the representative of Gladstone and Mayhew. May I show you to our offices?' Slightly dazed but ecstatic, she concurred,

'Of course Mr er Price. Please show me the way.'

They walked for some distance before speaking. Susan had opened her mouth to begin to say something but he'd put a hasty finger to his lips and slightly shaken his head. Mystified, Susan remained silent.

They walked on until they reached a parking area where Angelo showed her into a waiting car. They drove off and at last, he spoke.

'I'm so sorry you had all this to deal with. I was hoping you'd think of this place. I have to be so careful in England, the authorities here would love to find me. I'm on their wanted list. I had to have a new identity to come here so at the moment I'm Steven Price, nationality English and a representative for a company selling components for agricultural machinery but if I was investigated thoroughly, my identity wouldn't hold up for long.'

'What happened back in Germany?'

'There was suddenly a lot of police activity so I had to lie low but don't worry I wasn't compromised.'

'So you can pass for English? You hide your Italian accent well.'

'As you're able to hide your American accent.' He laughed, 'We make a good pair. By the way, your father and I have concluded our business to our mutual satisfaction.'

'How long will you stay in England?'

'Not long, it's too risky but will you come to me if I send for you.'

'I might. It depends on where you plan to be.'

'I have some business to conclude first so I'm not exactly sure where I'll be but by the time I contact you again, things will be sorted out and you needn't worry. I promise you, you won't regret it. Just make sure your passport is up-to-date.'

Oh, what the heck, she thought, why not?

'OK, I'll be there but make sure you don't keep me waiting too long this time.'

....

The oil painting hung in pride of place in the large wainscoted drawing-room. It depicted a gentleman sporting

236

an elegant pencil-line moustache, who stared sightlessly down on the two persons lounging at their ease on either side of the great fireplace.

One of the two individuals raised his glass and toasted the picture.

'Here's to you, grandfather.'

The female occupant of the other chair looked up at the painting.

'After all this, I'm not so sure that I want to toast grandfather,' she said sarcastically. 'I still haven't recovered from yesterday's journey and the debacle at the port, not the mention the worst part of the week.'

'Oh come on Pauline, or should I say, *Polly*? It all came out alright in the end, didn't it?'

'No thanks to grandfather.'

The young man began to laugh.

'You know the old saying – *If I knew then what I know now.*' They both dissolved into laughter.

'You have to hand it to the old man though, Pauline, back in the day, he saved the situation. We would have all gone down the road to penury without him; you and I wouldn't have had our comfortable existence.'

'So remind me how it started. I don't think I ever quite understood.'

'It was during the last world war. Grandfather was a colonel in the army and when the war was ending, he headed a unit designated to sort out some of the mess the Nazis had left when they were all running, trying to save their necks. He came across some diamonds that had been *liberated* from Holland. He was sure that they'd never be returned to their rightful owner as the poor devil would have died in a concentration camp with all his family. He knew that they'd just end up lining the pockets of somebody higher up so he decided that if the owners definitely couldn't be traced, he would make better use of them. You see his being in the armed services meant that he couldn't work on trying to save the family estate which was on the brink of bankruptcy, so he simply forgot to mention them and brought them home. Somehow he found a means of *fencing* them. At that time, the whole of Europe was a mess, it wouldn't have been difficult and many others were keeping things they'd found. It sounds awful now but it probably didn't seem so bad then but anyway, it did save the estate. Having established such a profitable way of making money, he found a way to smuggle some more; it became *the* family business.'

'So it just it carried on?'

'Well yes. You see, when grandfather died, father quickly discovered that financially, we wouldn't survive unless the *business* continued. He did try to find other ways of earning money but none worked as well as this. Somehow open days and festivals in the grounds didn't nearly cover the expenses so the books were cooked to show that these other activities were very profitable – but they were all subsidised by diamonds!

It couldn't go on indefinitely, of course, the authorities were getting closer and closer. When father's health began to fail, I was taken into his confidence and told that eventually I'd have to take over the family *business* and then I'd need to make some difficult decisions because things were starting to get out of hand. Father should have done something before but he became increasingly unwell and let matters slide. I knew, when the time came, that I'd have to see for myself exactly what was happening but I'd have to do this in a way that made me above suspicion. It would be down to *me* to ensure the continued respectability of the family name as well as finding a way to fill the family coffers.

When father passed away suddenly a year ago, I was at a loss to know what to do and then I thought of dear old Pete. When I'd worn a long blonde wig for the fancy dress ball on a New Year's Eve, everyone had joked about my likeness to

238

Pete the gardener; I saw salvation. That was when I started to dress very sloppily, became a sort of Bohemian in my free time, and I let my hair grow. Then it was easy to change places with him and use his passport.'

'Didn't he mind? I thought you must have bought a forgery.' Lord Chivington laughed,

'He didn't know.'

Pauline Dorrington-Smith, sister to Lord Chivington, looked at him with amazement.

'How did you arrange that?'

'Several years ago, I thought I might need to take Pete with me to choose some plants for the tropical greenhouse which would have meant travelling abroad. At the time I helped him to apply for a passport which, of course, I paid for. He was happy for me to keep it in case he lost it; he's probably forgotten I have it as we never actually went abroad together. Mind you, with these new passports that are machine read and store exact facial measurements, you probably wouldn't be able to fool anyone. I think I just got the old type in time.

I'm so glad I took you into my confidence, Pauline; you had to know sometime but father would never tell you. With your husband being abroad and you willing to help by posing as my wife on a river cruise, it was so easy. It wasn't even difficult for you to be called Polly, the same as his wife. If you say your name quickly, it almost sounds like 'Polly'. I was hoping nobody would notice your passport surname but then, luckily, half of it was 'Smith' anyway and married women often retain their maiden name by linking it to their new married one. Besides, who was to know if Polly and |Pete were even legally married? No-one ever asked. Sorry about having to share a cabin with me though; at least we had twin beds.'

'Goodness, we did take a chance though, didn't we? When you said that in the pursuit of family salvation, we were going to have a laugh and fool everybody, I didn't mind acting a part because it was funny and I enjoyed it and *I* wasn't doing anything illegal - but I didn't expect to be kidnapped. That was not in the deal!'

'No, sorry, that wasn't ever part of the plan, I had no idea it could happen. I thought a gardener would be of no interest to anyone. You can see how dangerous it was all becoming.

I'm so glad that I've closed down the smuggling route now. My conscience had been troubling me since I became aware of, and certainly didn't give permission for, some of the things that have happened. The local *agoni was exceeding* father's orders and he used rather cruel and drastic methods of recruitment; other mistakes were being made too. That lady, for example, she shouldn't have died. I've never condoned killing and I cannot conceive how that was allowed to happen or even if it was to do with my operation. I've no idea who killed her or why? However, I did discover that there is a rival syndicate operating the same smuggling route as we use and rivalry in crime does spread violence. Fortunately, they won't know my identity.

To protect us, the family idea was always to keep a high level of secrecy so that very few people knew who was running the operation. People were always contacted anonymously so as not to give away identities. I suppose there'll be a few angry responses now at the loss of income and maybe some will try to set up on their own but it's up to them if they want to court trouble with the rivals.

I'm really sorry though, that *you* went through some unpleasant things but I have to say what a fantastic actress you are; I couldn't have done it alone so, here's to you sis, or should I say *Polly?*'

'And you're a good actor too. It was hard to keep a straight face sometimes. You did look so like Pete but I'm glad you've had your hair cut now and you've smartened up a bit.' There was a pause, broken by Pauline saying, 'So after all our adventures, this last journey was just a dummy run then? What a relief! After that nightmare at the port, thank goodness nothing could be found.'

Lord Chivington smiled as he sipped his wine.

'Who said it was a dummy run? Actually, we did rather well and we should all be well *set up* for some time.'

Pauline stared at him,

'You mean there *were* diamonds on that coach! Suppose they'd been found? Where on earth were they?'

....

Minnie and Lavinia were glad to be home.

'Shall I put the kettle on dear?' Minnie asked.

'Oh, that would be lovely, just what I could do with. I'm rather tired. You know I hate to admit it but I think I'm getting too old for this.'

'Well, we can't complain, we've had some wonderful adventures over the years, haven't we?'

A few minutes later, the two ladies sat down with a tray between them which held two elegant bone china teacups complete with saucers, a teapot, milk, sugar and two silver spoons. Minnie poured the tea.

'This is most enjoyable,' Lavinia purred, sipping her tea, 'so English.'

'Well, we haven't always been able to be so elegant, have we? Gosh, remember the war years, when I was an army nurse in France, I was lucky to get tea in a tin cup.'

'And I never got tea at all, just coffee because I was supposed to be French and the locals didn't drink expensive tea. Sometimes the resistance didn't even get coffee.'

'They were dangerous days, weren't they? We needed some spirit then.'

'Good job we never lost it,' Lavinia stated with a little chuckle. 'We *were* young and pretty in those days and we had our share of romance too, didn't we? You met that handsome doctor. So sad he was killed just as the war seemed to be over.'

'And of course, you were sweet on dear Alfred Chivington.'

Lavinia sighed, a mental picture of a dashing officer who had liaised with her resistance group entered her consciousness. He'd been a slightly older man but she'd fallen head over heels in love with him. She would have done anything for him because he'd saved her life, rescued her from probable execution and torture by the Nazis. The problem, however, was that he was married so all she could do was to help him when he needed it – and she did. She'd always helped him and then later, his family too but maybe now, at her age, it was time to call it a day. This last run had been so fraught and had she not had her wits about her, might have gone terribly wrong.

Lavinia leaned over rather awkwardly and picked up her walking stick, it was a beautifully carved object with interesting lines of wood grain showing in an irregular pattern on the surface of the natural wood; it was identical to the one Minnie used except that a small silver collar, which could easily be removed, allowed the sisters to differentiate between the walking sticks. A hard tap on the floor in conjunction with two precise twists of her wrist, followed by pressing down, produced a faint *click*. The edges of the pattern separated in one place and the top portion came off to reveal a hollow inside carefully coated with a fine layer of rolled lead; it had been constructed by a master.

However, Lavinia had always worried that somehow this might not be fool-proof and that despite the lead lining, if it was ever x-rayed, it might show something - these machines were becoming ever more sophisticated. When she'd arrived at the port and seen that the normal procedure had changed - a most unusual occurrence, she'd decided that they must try

242

to perform their rehearsed *plan B* to avoid the stick travelling through any security measures.

Lavinia had gone ahead, passed the normal silver-trimmed walking stick through the machine and then feigned a near-fainting fit so that she would need a seat before she went any further. When her stick was returned to her, unnoticed, she managed to undo the clip for the silver trim, hold it under the cardigan she'd placed on her lap and then stand the stick upright by her chair. Minnie, having deliberately delayed well behind, appeared and when talking to her sister, rested her stick against the chair. Picking up the safe stick (which now resembled her own), she left her stick in its place. With a swift *sleight of hand*, the silver collar was quickly clicked in place. The same innocent stick passed through the machine twice though it looked like a different walking stick. It was a dangerous plan and she'd only had a few moments to wonder if it might work. She'd decided to use her age as an excuse and *be confused* if she'd been caught swapping sticks and then they would have had to pray that the clever mechanism and the lead coating did its work. There was no doubt that the whole thing had been exhausting but, as she told Minnie, it would take a lot more than a border authority to make her drop dead on the spot.

She shook out the tight packing of sawdust, so important to make the wood seem solid, together with the small cylindrical-shaped cloth bag holding the diamonds. Lavinia pulled open the drawstring and scattered the collection of gemstones on to the nearby table; they sparkled and glittered, displaying a myriad of prismatic colours as they caught the light from the lamp.

....

Elaine reported her suspicions to her superiors. She felt certain that answers would only be found in and around the Danube but never-the-less, in an attempt to try to tie up some loose ends, she arranged for a few of the guests to be interviewed again. Some she summarily dismissed, these included Pete and Polly; their intelligence level was so low that they couldn't possibly be involved in international crime. Just to be on the safe side, however, she'd asked someone to investigate them; their identity had checked out, no criminal records, they were nothing but uneducated simple-minded gardeners who must have saved up for a special holiday.

She informed her superiors that the likelihood was that the murder and the smuggling were both connected to the 'Danube Drifter' but as her only leads had become dead ends, she feared that she couldn't throw any more light on matters; certainly not from England. Through lack of evidence, the murder enquiry began to slip down the ranks in importance.

The Hungarian and German authorities were having similar problems. They were reluctant to share files because old rivalries die hard. The Hungarian police paid lip service to solving the murder but both were far more concerned with the damage to their economy that smuggling might bring; the murder of an insignificant elderly foreign lady stayed on file.

It became a muddled triangle. The British police were automatically offering help because the victim was English but apart from re-interviewing the holidaymakers, they could not do a lot from England. The Hungarian police wished for no foreign interference so no application for British Police to travel to Budapest was requested. The German authorities were reluctant to spend money on the case if the kudos was going to either the British or more likely the Hungarians. Consequently, Hungary, Germany and England did not agree on a united plan of action. Whilst the smuggling was of great concern, it looked as if the murder was not going to be a priority for anyone.

Elaine sighed and gritted her teeth with frustration, she hated unsolved crimes. If only she'd heard the message from the deceased woman. There were times when she could cheerfully *brain* her dear husband. Mind you, it could have been nothing; those types of women often saw trouble where there was none. Look at Felicity Fanshawe. Look at *me*, she thought, I suspected Melissa too and look where that ended up. Had Priscilla just been nosy and jumped to an incorrect conclusion, it was easily done - a mountain out of a molehill? Her foolish utterings may have caused a misunderstanding that could have led to her death

Elaine came to a conclusion - there is no doubt in my mind that organised crime is operating there and possibly our friend Ronaldo Marconi is behind it or at least involved in it somewhere but unless they send me or a British team to Budapest and the other countries of the Danube, which means that someone has to find the money for the investigation, there is little I can do. Maybe Interpol will take over but in any case, as far as we're concerned, that's another case on file! Elaine bundled everything together and returned it to the office.

....

Back in Germany, Antonio teetered on the edge of a nervous breakdown when, once again, he was handed an envelope by the receptionist.

'Another letter for you, Antonio?' She sweetly smiled at him as she handed over the post. Accepting it with the same enthusiasm as being handed a live grenade, Antonio felt his hand shaking. Oh no, he thought, suppose this had arrived when the police were here? Suppose they'd asked me to open it? He pulled himself together. You've got this far, he told himself, you can do it, just take some deep breaths.

He hurried to his cabin and tore open the envelope. His eyes stood out on stalks as he gasped,

'Thank God, oh thank God.'

He crossed himself and collapsed onto the bed in sheer relief. The letter contained a simple message:

You will be glad to know that your services are no longer required. Your employment is terminated and you will not hear from us again.

Chapter 24

Eventually

About the time Susan was meeting Angelo, Bob was sitting in his lounge at home reading a tabloid newspaper. He was just about to complain to Diane about the standard of journalism when an article caught his eye and he called out to her.

'There's a mention here about the death of that Priscilla woman in Budapest. It states that it's been recorded as *'murder by a person or persons unknown'*. They haven't a clue! The story has only been deemed worthy of a tiny section on one of the inside pages.'

'Did the British police ever speak to you again? They contacted me while I was doing my voluntary work.'

'Yes, I told you, some chap from the Met came round but he didn't stay long. Just going through the motions. I didn't know anything anyway. I asked him if there was any news of Ronaldo Marconi but he looked so blankly at me that I don't think it was an act. They're not connecting the two things at all.'

'So your theory that this Ronaldo had something to do with it was wrong.'

'Not necessarily but no-one seems to *want* to link the two. I'm pretty sure that chap was up to something in the region but until someone can identify the man, he remains a modern *'Scarlet Pimpernel'*.

David and Elaine were discussing the same topic.

'I can't say that I'm sorry,' Elaine concluded, 'I'd rather not get embroiled in this investigation anymore. It's the sort of case that can ruin a career. When you're dealing with a foreign country, your hands are tied and you can't operate as you wish but *you* end up looking the fool. I'm not in charge so I'm going

247

to distance myself from it now. Let Interpol handle it, really they are the only ones who can operate with any speed and authority but until someone agrees that there *is* a link between the death of an elderly English middle-class lady of impeccable background and an international smuggling ring, it won't happen.'

'So what does happen in the meantime? Do they bury the woman?'

'Her body will be returned to England, her travel insurance will likely pay for that, and unless there is an objection, she'll be interred or cremated as her family wishes. I think her cousin, the one who was on the cruise, is her next of kin.'

....

Sebastian was sitting in a comfortable armchair; he was being waited on hand and foot and he loved it. He had no regrets, he wished he could have lived like this years ago. Lillian felt the same, never had she been so happy. She was used to fussing over somebody and it had always kept her busy but now she was appreciated and thanked, instead of being criticised, for everything she did. He was a lovely man.

Sebastian knew he'd done the right thing. He knew that before, he'd been in the wrong. He'd pursued Felicity, not because he loved her but because she was wealthy and was *somebody,* however *thin* the last part had become in recent years. He'd been a person who thought that he needed a bit of limelight, even if it was reflected from someone else. He'd been so wrong. There was no limelight with Lillian and no great wealth but he'd never been happier.

Lillian felt rather guilty. Priscilla had been her cousin but she hadn't liked her very much; she'd become a kind of habit, a burden that could never be lifted and it was Priscilla's death that had been the catalyst for her present happiness. Disturbingly, she'd been the recipient of Priscilla's estate;

everything had been left to her. How unexpected it had been and how kind of Priscilla to think of her. She would have been less elated and certainly would have felt less guilty, had she known Priscilla's thoughts at the time of making the will.

I'll leave it to Lillian. She is very poor so it will appear as if I'm giving to charity. Poor little mouse. Of course, she won't get it because I have no intention of leaving this earth before her but it will make me look admirable in the eyes of the eventual executors and the rest of the family. I really intend it to go to a new 'Priscilla Pilkington' village hall which will remind everyone of me and show them how important and charitable I was.

On a nearby shelf stood a framed photograph of the two of them and Lillian glanced at it and then studied it closely.

'Well I never,' she exclaimed. 'I was much better looking than her, wasn't I? It was being told so many times that I was plain and dowdy that made me believe it.'

Twitching her new smart skirt with matching top, she almost bounced back into the living room to sit with her new fiancé.

....

Felicity was enjoying surprising success. Staggered at first by Sebastian's defection, it had been subtly suggested to her, by the astute Mrs O'Shea, her housekeeper, that her fame of being known as a great actor was more important and would last longer than being merely beautiful. She shocked and surprised everybody by throwing herself into the part and delivering a fantastic performance which resulted in a BAFTA nomination. Her career kick-started and once again she was surrounded by admirers and sycophants. Felicity was in her element; she was *somebody* again. Mrs O'Shea negotiated a generous pay-rise.

....

Melissa was working in an office on dry land. She never wanted to see another cruiser of any kind - ever. She was surrounded by sheets of figures and a computer full of data and she was in her element. She'd received a bonus and a large pay rise and planned to take a proper holiday this year- in a hotel and nowhere near boats or rivers. She smiled to herself in satisfaction as she tucked into a large jam doughnut.

....

Susan was glad to be home in the good old US of A. She was surprised to discover just how much she'd missed it. So many years away, a whole lifetime of experiences in another country and now she was back and not in disgrace but back in her father's good books. She'd done the very thing he'd always wanted, she'd arranged to strengthen the family by marriage. Her father had been flabbergasted when she'd introduced Angelo as her new husband-to-be, and then explained that he was her father's contact in Europe but that reaction was nothing to the sensation caused just afterwards when Mario entered the room. He shook hands with Angelo, greeted him as an old friend and on being told that this was Susan's fiancé, burst into a torrent of congratulatory Italian and then said to his father-in-law in English,

'So Ronaldo Marconi himself is to unite with the family.'
Susan looked thunderstruck and mouthed at Angelo,
'Are you Ronaldo Marconi?' A rueful nod was her answer. Before she could display her well-known temper and take him to task for the deception, her father intervened. Smiling broadly, he'd suddenly remembered his paternal duties and *tongue-in-cheek* enquired if this prospective husband could guarantee the future status of his daughter and maintain her in the style to which she was accustomed. At this, her annoyance

evaporated and Susan giggled. She remembered her life since she'd left the States; she might be accustomed, but she didn't ever want to live in that style again. However, the shocks were not over. The recipient of this question assured Don Columbo that he was well able to support his new partner's daughter in as grand a style as might be required, and as for status, he need have no fear. When they were married, Susan would be known as Princess Susan Romanovsky.

....

Boris was in charge and throwing his weight around. The rest of the crew were sulky. Dmitri had left him to run things for the time being but warned him that there would be some changes coming. Boris didn't like the sound of that so he was plotting to take over; he had no intention of waiting for Dmitri to return.

Anna was furious, it seemed that she had just been used. It had leaked out that she was merely one of many informants known as girlfriends and she was in no way special to Boris; he was now ignoring her. Power had gone to his head. She had big plans for herself and they didn't include being discarded and dumped. She began to plot with some of the other crew members. A rival organisation was being formed and an assassination planned.

Two Years Later

Sian and Vicky were sneaking a five-minute coffee break. The old folk in 'Sunny View Residential Home for Gentlefolk', had been particularly trying that day and they were both worn out.

'Glad to get the weight off my feet for a few moments,' Sian began, looking at her watch, 'but we've still got another three hours of our shift to do.' She gave a great sigh.

'It's not that bad really, is it?' Vicky suggested. 'Sometimes it's a laugh. Like - some of the things the old folk say, they do crack me up.'

'Oh me too, especially Lavinia. You would have loved her story today.'

'It's nice to see her cheer up again, she was really upset when her sister died. Was it more of her adventures during the war?' A nod was the answer as Sian stuffed a biscuit into her mouth, chewed and swallowed.

'Today was a real *humdinger*. I haven't heard it before.'

'Well come on then, share.'

'It was her usual story at first, you know, the French resistance, the blowing up of railways, hiding in barns from the Germans and all that stuff. Then she went onto the handsome officer bit; we had all the dreamy stuff as she remembered him kissing her, bless her. I had a job keeping a straight face but I couldn't upset the sweet old dear.'

'Where do you think she gets these stories from?'

'I reckon she's read a lot of books in her time and she sort of gets them muddled up with real life. They do that you know - when they get old.'

'But you said she had a new story?'

'Oh yes, get this. In her resistance cell in 1944, they had a young man who'd escaped from Hungary when the Germans invaded, and he'd managed to make his way across Europe until finally, he'd joined up with her resistance group in France.

Now for the best bit - this guy was a deadly assassin who'd learned to kill silently in a variety of ways; he could appear like a *ghost* to kill his quarry. She said he was fiercely loyal but was inclined to act on his own initiative and the group worried that he'd become a bit of a liability - although when you met him, he seemed harmless and pleasant, like butter wouldn't melt in his mouth. She heard that this ability to kill was not due to military training, it was passed down the generations, like a family apprenticeship sort of thing.'

'Nice apprenticeship,' Vicky chuckled.

'Well, the old dear told me that when she was on a river cruise a while ago, she came across someone who looked just like him. When there was a mysterious death, she knew immediately who the murderer was.'

'Oh come on! What a story! If that was true, she would have said something at the time, wouldn't she?'

'Well, according to Lavinia, she didn't like the victim very much and she had no actual proof but - get this - telling someone would have en-dan-gered someone else that she *did* care about.'

'Oh dear! These wicked foreigners! Fancy meeting a deadly assassin on holiday? There you are, having a lovely restful time, watching the world go by when all the time wicked murder is being planned. Do you think we should all be worried when we go on holiday?' The pair couldn't stop giggling.

'You know what this means? Somewhere, a poor innocent person is being mistaken for a bloodthirsty killer.' They both sat back again and roared with laughter.

....

The 'Senior Tour Manager' on the 'Danube Drifter', was listening to the endless complaints from the troublesome guest. Appointed when Melissa had left, he'd been very happy in the well-paid position. Now, all this was being threatened by one difficult man.

'I'm sorry but this is not good enough,' the guest grumbled; his list of complaints seemed endless. 'I'm going to write to your head office about this. I'm holding you personally responsible.'

The practised and courteous professional expression remained firmly in place. The deliberations, however, were anything but.

I think I might have to find that syringe again, thought Vicktor.

Books by the same author

Deadly Enterprise

It should have been a good idea. An old shopping arcade transformed into a trendy retail and business venue, designed to attract an elite clientele in a classy area of London. No-one would dream that such an innocuous setting could hide a plethora of personal dramas, nor would anyone have suspected the mysteries that would be present inside its walls.

As the story unfolds, a group of diverse characters, who are in the main, complete strangers, find that their lives are intrinsically interwoven. A truly horrific crime brings the attendance of an *old hand,* Detective Sergeant Baker plus his egotistical and newly promoted senior officer, Detective Inspector Desmond Royce.

How could so much drama occur in one place and what did it all have to do with events in history that were long past but not forgotten?

Readers' reviews: *An excellent read, skilfully enticing the reader into a deep web of deceit beneath a shallow veneer of respectability. I believe that she continues to deliver with ever more intriguing plot lines, all the time developing her craft as a master   storyteller. Superb literature - eagerly awaiting her next novel.*

An intriguing back story for a number of characters of different generations, leads to an unfortunate incident with the interesting twist which characterises Ms Bradley's books. I was gripped by this one and enjoyed the whole experience.

ISBN: 978-0-244-44978-0

Death on a Yacht

The year is 1998. Sir George Arlington, a despicable and ruthless businessman, who has spent most of his life plotting and scheming against others, is now the target for retribution. He has no idea of the web of intrigue growing around him. An Italian Contessa, a retired Captain of the Royal Navy, gangsters from the East End of London and those with dark secrets, brought together with four young friends from very different backgrounds, who each have their own agenda, find themselves cruising with Sir George, on a luxury yacht in the Mediterranean.

Plots and schemes abound, a death occurs and more confusion is added by a pompous Spanish police officer who resents the inevitable intervention of the British authorities.

When the plots unravel, who are the winners and who are the losers?

Review – Indie Authors

I was hooked from the intriguing opening of "Death on a Yacht" by Carolyn R. Bradley and my interest never faded for a moment! Bradley brings a fresh attitude and literary style and makes it all her own. Recommend for anyone (adults) who enjoy a well-written, action packed, true-to-life suspenseful international thriller with plenty of unexpected twists and memorable characters. (5 stars) Anabella Johnson— Goodreads; Barnes & Noble; Indie Book Reviewers

ISBN 978-0-244-33075-0

The Ski Lodge
Written as Carolyn Bradley

Larger than life Texans, outrageous cockneys,
haughty aristocrats, crooks, villains and those
who are not what they seem to be; thrown together
in a ski lodge with inept Police, in a romping,
keep you guessing,
'Who Done It'?

Readers Reviews:

*I ordered the book after meeting the author. I am six chapters in
and am finding I can't wait to go back to pick the book up to
continue. I will look for further books by Carolyn Bradley.
(Amazon reader)*

Brilliant book perfect who done it!!! (Miss A Whitbread)

*First class who-dun-it that keeps you guessing right to the end. A
good light read. (Amazon reader)*

*A colourful set of characters with comprehensive back stories that
give clues to the events that unfold. However the outcome cannot
easily be guessed as it contains a clever and surprising twist.
(T. Pemberton)*

ISBN978-1-326-71978-4

*All titles available as a paperback and E reader from on-line
bookshops: Lulu, Amazon, Barnes and Noble, Ingram and many
others. Available world-wide including UK, USA, Canada,
Australia and Spain.*
Facebook Authors: Carolyn R. Bradley

Made in the USA
Columbia, SC
04 November 2020

23968452R00141